Forsaken

Sloane Kennedy

Copyright © 2016 by Sloane Kennedy

Published in the United States by Sloane Kennedy

Cover Images: ©www.periodimages.com, © iko

Cover Design: © Jay Aheer, Simply Defined Art

**ISBN-13:
978-1535578691**

**ISBN-10:
1535578696**

Trigger Warning

Note that reading this warning may cause spoilers so if you don't want to know, please continue on to the next page*

This book contains references to the sexual assault of a minor.

Table of Contents

Table of Contents..4

Trademark Acknowledgements 6

Acknowledgements 7

forsaken 8

Prologue...9

Chapter One...15

Chapter Two...33

Chapter Three 41

Chapter Four 52

Chapter Five 64

Chapter Six 75

Chapter Seven..88

Chapter Eight 98

Chapter Nine 108

Chapter Ten 132

Chapter Eleven..146

Chapter Twelve 157

Chapter Thirteen...166

Chapter Fourteen..183

Chapter Fifteen 198

Chapter Sixteen...206

Chapter Seventeen 212

Chapter Eighteen 221

Chapter Nineteen 234

Chapter Twenty 242

Chapter Twenty-One...252

Chapter Twenty-Two 259

Chapter Twenty-Three..269

Chapter Twenty-Four...282

Chapter Twenty-Five..291

Chapter Twenty-Six..309

Chapter Twenty-Seven..314

Epilogue 328

*** Sneak Peek *** 337

Connect with Sloane Kennedy 344

Thank you for reading Forsaken! 344

Other books by Sloane Kennedy................................346

Trademark Acknowledgements

The author acknowledges the trademarked status and trademark owners of the following wordmarks mentioned in this work of fiction:

Harley Davidson

Thor

Hawkeye

Spiderman

X-Men

Professor Xavier

Google

Acknowledgements

Rita, at the risk of sounding like a broken record, thank you for another amazing beta read. I feel like we've known each other forever with the many times we've chatted and the never-ending support you've shown me from the moment you first reached out to me. I can't believe it hasn't even been an entire year since that day! I am so glad you enjoyed Mav and Eli's tale but am not surprised that they were unable to dethrone Logan and Dom as your faves…I'm kind of glad they didn't because Logan and Dom deserve that title.

Kylee, Claudia and Mari, my soul sisters…beyond just the support and encouragement you shower on me with every new book I release, your friendship has come to mean something to me that I can't even describe. From epic battles to heart felt talks to quick every day chats, I've found something that I didn't realize was missing from my life. And for that I will be forever grateful.

Autumn Reich, thank you for giving Mav the badass Harley that he needed! It was a perfect fit.

To all my readers, this year has been just amazing and you are the reason I get to pursue a dream I didn't even know I had. I took the leap to writing full time because of the support and encouragement you've shown me and I take so much pleasure in knowing that I get to share a little bit of the lives of my little family of men with you.

forsaken

adjective for·sake·n \, fawr-sey-kuh n\

Abandoned or deserted.

Prologue

Mav

I didn't see him at first because unlike so many of the other times he'd been walking down the busy hallway towards the hospital room I was guarding, his head was hung and he didn't speak to any of the various nurses and other staff who greeted him. In fact, he was so distracted that he nearly slammed into me as he turned to enter the room. I managed to grab him by the upper arms just before he walked into me and I didn't miss his startled gasp as he lifted his eyes to meet mine.

The young man was nothing like the men I usually went for. First of all, he was just way too young. He was in his early twenties at best. Second, I liked them a little on the sturdier side. This man was so lean and slight, I'd worry about breaking him if I put all of my weight down on his back while I was fucking him from behind. And third, and most importantly, he was skittish. Exceedingly so. I didn't mind a little shyness here and there, but I wasn't into fucking guys who were terrified of me. And with the way his whole body had seized up when I'd first grabbed his arms, I knew that was exactly what he was.

"Sorry," he whispered, though it was hard to hear him over the din of the people coming and going through the hallway.

"No problem," I responded, though I had yet to let him go. With it being summer, he was wearing a short-sleeved shirt, so my fingers were in contact with his bare skin which was wreaking havoc on my senses. Not to mention his big, luminous dark brown eyes and his slightly parted lips that looked so full that I couldn't help but wonder if he'd just been kissing someone or if they were just naturally that plump and supple looking.

I'd first noticed him a couple of weeks earlier when the young boy I was keeping an eye on, Matty Travers, had been readmitted to the Immunocompromised Services Unit of the children's hospital. I'd only met the little boy about six weeks earlier when my boss, Ronan Grisham, had asked me to keep an eye on one of my colleagues, Hawke, in case he decided to single-handedly pursue the men who'd murdered his wife. Under normal circumstances, Hawke wasn't the kind of guy who needed backup, but when Ronan had learned that the murderers had taken up with a Mexican drug lord, all bets were off and he'd ordered me to stick to Hawke like glue.

Weeks had passed, but Hawke hadn't gone looking for the men as expected and when the man he'd lost his heart to, Tate Travers, and his five-year-old son had shown up to visit him at his ranch in Wyoming, I'd been there to witness the reunion and I'd known then that Hawke had chosen a future with them rather than seeking vengeance for the rape and murder of his wife and unborn child ten years earlier. I'd ended up sticking around town for a couple days so I could explore the mountain ranges surrounding Rocky Point, but on the day I'd finally gotten on my Harley to head to my next assignment, Ronan had frantically called me and told me to get back to Hawke's house because the men he'd given up on hunting had found him instead.

I'd made it back to Hawke's ranch just in time to save him from the bullet one of the drug lord's lackeys had been about to put in his brain, and then he and I had managed to get Tate and Matty to safety. For someone so young, little Matty had been beyond brave as a gun had been held to his head and I'd felt a kinship with him from the start. So when Ronan had asked me if I'd stay in Seattle for a while to keep an eye on the family in case the drug lord made a play for them, I'd readily agreed.

And that was when I'd seen the young man.

He arrived every day like clockwork to spend time with Matty and I'd learned from Hawke who had given me the okay to let the guy past me, that he was someone who had just started volunteering in the pediatric oncology unit. I hadn't missed how beautiful he was with his dark skin tone that hinted at Hispanic heritage and pretty, expressive eyes, but I'd dismissed my intense attraction to him because of the way he'd looked at me that very first day when he'd told me his name as he'd sought entry into Matty's room.

Eli.

I'd let the name roll off my tongue as I'd automatically flirted with him, but when he'd looked at me like I was going to jump him, I'd let him pass without further comment and I'd done my best to ignore him all the other days that he'd stopped by. But it had been an almost impossible task because there was always this inevitable moment when Eli stepped past me, that his eyes would lift to look at me for the briefest of moments and I wouldn't see fear in them…I'd see something different. Something that had my stomach knotting with anticipation and my fingers itching to reach up and stroke over the smoothness of his cheek.

But now as I held on to him, he wasn't only looking terrified, he was practically shaking in my grip, so I quickly released him.

I knew I wasn't the safest looking guy in terms of appearance, especially considering the tattoos that covered my arms, torso and back, my large build, long hair and the leather motorcycle pants I wore, but it wasn't like I'd overtly come on to the guy or done anything that would cause him to be so fearful of me.

I expected Eli to quickly move away from me and rush into the room, but other than taking a step back, he didn't do anything else. His eyes held mine as he tried to get control of his breathing and then he shook his head slightly. "I'm sorry," he said again, a little louder this time, but still very low and quiet.

I had no doubt the second apology had nothing to do with running into me and I desperately wanted to ask him what he was sorry for. But then I saw it.

Longing.

My breath caught in my throat as I realized what the look meant, but before I could question Eli or even respond, he stepped past me and into the room. I heard both Matty and Tate happily greet him and there was no fear or tentativeness as Eli greeted them in return. The idea that Eli might actually be attracted to me was an unexpected distraction and it took everything in my power to keep from looking through the glass walls to see Eli and Matty interacting. My job was to focus on my surroundings and keep the little boy inside that room safe.

It was only about a half an hour later that Eli left the room and I willed myself not to look at him as he walked by, but I failed miserably when I sensed his gaze on me. Our eyes met briefly and I felt my cock harden uncomfortably in my pants. Eli was the one to tear his gaze away first, but I kept my eyes on his slim back as he hurried down the hall towards another room and it wasn't until he disappeared inside of it that I finally managed to snap out of whatever spell I'd fallen under. Irritation flooded my system and I cursed both my own traitorous body, as well as the young man who, with just one look, had fucked with my head for those few seconds.

My shift outside Matty's door lasted only another hour and when Hawke arrived to relieve me, I said my goodbyes to Matty and Tate and hurried towards the parking garage so I could get my Harley between my legs and use the massive bike to work off some of the tension that was still lingering in my system. It took just a few minutes to get to the garage and I automatically bypassed the elevator for the stairs that would lead to the lowest floor of the garage where I'd left my bike. But the second I opened the door, I went on high alert when I heard someone yelling, "Stay the fuck away from him, do you hear me?"

The sound of flesh striking flesh had me moving and when I heard someone let out a small cry, I leaned over the stair railing and yelled, "Hey! What's going on down there?"

There was another distressed cry and then a door was opening and closing. I knew the assailant would be long gone by the time I reached the bottom landing, but I took the stairs as fast as I could anyway so I could make sure whoever had been struck was okay.

I saw the young man immediately before I even reached the last step. He was sitting on the concrete floor, his back to the wall and his arms over his head. I could hear him crying softly, but the flickering security light affixed to the wall above him made it difficult to see anything else.

"Hey, you okay?" I asked as I knelt on the floor in front of him. He flinched when I carefully tried to pull his arms away from his face. "You're safe now," I murmured as he finally relaxed his muscles enough to drop his arms. And when I put my fingers under his chin to lift his face, the light above us stopped flickering and I held my breath as I realized who it was under the bruise that was already forming along one cheek, the blood trickling from the split lip and the tears streaking down his face.

Eli.

Chapter One

Mav

"Eli," I said as gently as I could despite the rage that was surging through my blood. "It's me," I added. "Mav."

I hadn't actually ever told Eli my name, but he clearly recognized me because he nodded.

"Can you stand?"

Another nod and then Eli used the back of his left hand to wipe at his tears. But when I reached for his right arm to pull him to his feet, he let out a harsh cry and grabbed his wrist with his free hand.

"Okay, okay," I said softly as I watched fresh tears fall. I studied the wrist Eli was protecting and saw that it was already swelling. "Eli, can you move your fingers on this hand?" I asked as I pointed to his injured arm.

Eli hesitated and then carefully tested each finger. Pain was written in every line of his face and harsh breaths were seesawing in and out of him. "Yeah," he finally managed to say. "I think it's just sprained," he added between clenched teeth.

"I'm going to help you stand, okay? We'll take it nice and slow."

Another unsteady nod. I reached out for Eli's uninjured arm and supported his weight as I carefully lifted him to his feet. The younger man leaned back against the wall as he tried to catch his breath and I kept my hand on his elbow to steady him. "Can you make it back up the stairs?"

It took Eli a moment to slow his breathing enough to talk. "My...my car's parked on this level," he said with a nod to the door leading to the parking area.

"Eli, you need to have someone take a look at your injuries." Despite it being a children's hospital, I doubted they'd turn Eli away. At worst, they'd arrange for him to be transported down the block to the general hospital.

"No," Eli murmured and then he pulled himself upright. "I'm okay."

"Eli-"

"Thank you," Eli said as he carefully pulled free of my hold and stepped around me. He used his uninjured hand to open the heavy door and I quickly grabbed it from him. He mumbled another thank you and then began walking towards a darkened corner of the garage. I scanned our surroundings as I easily caught up to Eli and carefully drew him to a stop by putting my hand on his uninjured arm.

"Eli, talk to me. Who did this?"

But Eli just shook his head and tried to step past me.

"Was it an ex or something?" I asked.

Eli didn't seem surprised or annoyed that I was making the assumption that he was gay. "Can you just let me go, please?" he whispered and I could tell he was on the verge of crying again. He tried to tug his arm free of my grip, but I maintained my hold on him. I ignored the zaps of electricity that were firing through the pads of my fingers and up my entire arm.

"At least let me call someone for you," I offered. "Your family. A friend."

I expected him to mull my suggestion over or at least tell me no, but instead his entire countenance fell and then more tears began silently slipping down his face. I felt an unexpected ache in my chest at how lost and broken he looked and I struggled to find the right words to say. But nothing came to me and I knew it was because that kind of bone deep pain couldn't be taken away with a few carefully chosen words. Whatever Eli was going through inside was so much worse than the beating his body had taken.

I felt my skin itch as the overwhelming urge to escape hit me. Give me a gun or a knife and I was an unstoppable force. Hell, even with just my hands, I could take on anything thrown my way. But this...fuck, I wasn't equipped to give the young man in front of me what he needed. I wasn't wired that way...not anymore. But as Eli tried to move past me once again, I tightened my grip on him and drew him forward instead. He was stiff against me at first, but the second I pressed my hand against the small of his back to keep him from moving away, he let out a broken sob and dropped his forehead

17

on my chest and began sobbing in earnest. I was careful not to put any pressure on his injured arm as I pulled him in even closer.

I didn't say anything as his tears soaked my shirt and before I could stop myself, I lowered my head and let my lips skim his temple. I was right about him being slight because even with my loose hold on him, he felt so very breakable. I had a good six inches on him at least and while he wasn't actually bony, my guess was that I outweighed him by at least fifty pounds. I used my free hand to test the softness of his coal-black hair and I marveled at the curls that shifted beneath my fingers.

I had no idea how long we stood there for, but at some point, Eli's free hand had wrapped around my back and I could feel his fingertips pressing into me, their warmth heating my skin through the thin material of my shirt. His sobs had eased, but he was still holding onto me like I was his lifeline. And the only thing that kept me from crushing him against me the way I wanted, was his injured arm which was pressed against my abdomen.

The door leading to the stairwell opening caused Eli to jerk away from me and he let out a gasp as he bumped his injured wrist against me. His wide eyes shot to the doorway where a woman in nurse's scrubs was searching out her keys from her purse. She gave us both a quick once over and then hurried towards the opposite side of the lot. Eli managed to gather himself as he stepped away from me.

"Sorry," he whispered.

"I'm not," I said before I could think better of it.

Eli's eyes lifted to mine in surprise and I took advantage of his distracted state to reach up and wipe away a small dot of fresh blood from his lip. He trembled at the contact and I had trouble hiding my own reaction at the feel of the smooth pink flesh against the rough pad of my finger.

"I should go," Eli managed to say and then he was stepping away from me again. I knew I should just let him go since he clearly didn't want my help, but I followed him to his car anyway. But as he neared an older model sedan that seemed to have more rust on it than paint, he stopped and just stared at the car. I scanned the vehicle for any damage or sign it had been messed with, but didn't see anything.

"What's wrong?" I asked as I came to a stop next to him and angled my body so I could see his face. He looked at me as if just realizing I was still with him.

"It's a stick shift," he finally said and raised his injured arm slightly. His right arm.

"Where are your keys?" I asked. "I'll drive you home."

Eli took a small step away from me and I felt a mix of anger and frustration go through me, but I quickly quelled it. Fine, the guy didn't like me...didn't mean I should be a prick and ditch him like I was half tempted to do, though.

I pulled out my cell phone and held it out to him. "Then call someone...a friend, a cab, whatever."

I couldn't keep the irritation from my voice and Eli flinched at my tone. I tried to remember what the young man had just been through, but his rejection still stung. Which was the epitome of stupid because I'd been rejected my entire life. It certainly wasn't a new feeling for me.

Eli still hadn't moved or responded in any kind of way so I stepped away from him and shook my head. I had already turned to go when he finally spoke, his voice barely a whisper.

"You scare me."

I stilled and then slowly shifted so I was once again facing him. His admission surprised me and I had no idea what to say to that. I finally settled on, "I have that effect on a lot of people." I forced out a small laugh in an attempt to add levity, but Eli didn't react. Instead his eyes scanned my entire body and I felt my dick starting to fill with excitement.

"That's not why you scare me," Eli said quietly. "Not anymore," he added.

I didn't know what to make of that statement, but I didn't get a chance to ask him what he meant because he said, "It's Mav, right?"

I nodded.

"Matty talks about you a lot. He says you and his daddies saved him. He calls you Thor."

I smiled at that. Matty's obsession with superheroes was well known, but I hadn't realized I'd been included in the fold. "He's a good kid," I murmured.

"He is," Eli responded. He turned so he was facing me head on and quietly said, "Mav, I'd be grateful for a ride home."

I loved the way my name fell from his lips…like a subtle caress with the promise of something more. His dark eyes held mine, drawing me in and I moved towards him. "Keys?" I finally managed to ask, my voice sounding thick and husky even to my own ears.

"My pocket," Eli responded. "My right pocket."

I swallowed hard at that. With his injured arm, there was no way he'd be able to reach into his pocket and fish them out. And since he was wearing jeans that hugged his lithe body…

Fuck.

I told myself to make it quick as I reached my fingers into his pocket, but between the subtle increase in Eli's breathing and the feel of his firm flesh beneath my fingers as I pushed into the too small pocket, I was struggling just to keep control of my own raging desire. It took several tries to snag the key ring and when I finally hooked the keys, I swore both Eli and I let out a sigh of relief at the same time.

Eli stepped around me and went to the passenger side. There was no key fob to unlock the door so I had to do it manually and once I had the door opened, I realized the locks weren't power ones so I dropped down into the driver's seat and leaned across the passenger seat and flipped the lock. While the car wasn't comically small, it was a tight fit for me and my head kept brushing the roof even after I slid the driver's seat all the way back. I glanced at Eli who was watching me with a small smile on his face and I felt something shift in my chest at how different he looked. Yes, he was clearly still in pain, but to see that momentary change in his expression made it all worth it. But when his eyes shifted up to mine, he quickly shuttered them and reached for his seat belt. I watched him struggle for a moment before I reached across him and grabbed it and clicked it into place. The move had my arm nearly brushing his chest and my head precariously close to his, and I didn't miss his indrawn breath when I held there, our mouths just inches apart. To say that I was tempted to lean in and take a taste of him was an understatement, but then I remembered his admission about being afraid of me.

I moved back into my own seat and fumbled with the keys. It took several tries to get the car started and when it finally did turn over, I had to give it a little gas to keep the engine going. It took a couple of minutes to work our way through the multiple levels of the parking garage to get up to street level and Eli pointed to his parking pass in the cup holder when we got to the gate. After that, the only words spoken between us were Eli giving me directions to his place.

Based on the shitty car Eli drove, I wasn't expecting much when it came to Eli's house, but it wasn't as bad as I thought. I'd been in Seattle long enough to have a chance to explore the city, so I knew we were within blocks of the University of Washington as I pulled up to a large green house that had clearly been converted into multiple residences. Most of the houses up and down the street also appeared to be geared towards student housing, but since it was the middle of June, there was little activity going on.

The reminder that I was lusting after someone who was likely still in college had me asking, "Are you a student?"

"Um, I start medical school in the fall," Eli said as he unbuckled his seat belt.

A sliver of relief went through me that he wasn't just this side of legal, but I shoved the thought away. It didn't matter how old he was. I might be attracted to him, but that was as far as it went. That was as far as it would ever go. Because I knew without question that Eli wasn't a no strings, quick fuck kind of guy. And if he was, he'd made it clear that just like he wasn't my type, I wasn't his either.

I got out of the car and met Eli around the other side and handed him his keys.

"Thanks," Eli said. "How will you get back?"

"I'll call a cab."

Eli nodded and when he turned to go, I couldn't stop myself from reaching out to stop him. He flinched briefly, but didn't try to escape my hold. "Eli, this guy…if you know who he is, you need to tell the police. Press charges."

Eli held my gaze for a moment and then dropped his eyes. "I'll think about it," he finally said, but I knew it was lie. Frustration coursed through me, but I kept it to myself as I searched out my phone to call a cab. I might not be able to force Eli into seeking help, but I could do a little recon on my own to see if I could identify the bastard who'd hurt him.

"Do…"

I looked up as Eli's voice caught. He was shifting back and forth on his feet, his injured arm still pressed to his chest.

"Do you want to come inside while you wait for your cab?" he asked, his voice shaky.

I could tell he was regretting the question as he waited nervously for my answer. The smart thing to do would have been to call the cab and just wait on the curb. But that invisible pull that always made me look at Eli as he walked past me when he was leaving Matty's hospital room was working overtime now, and I was nodding before I could think better of it. And instead of calling the cab, I tucked my phone back in my pocket and followed Eli up the walkway. He kept glancing over his shoulder at me as we neared the house, but instead of taking the stairs that led up to the porch, he walked around the side of the house. A set of rickety wooden stairs led to a door on the second floor along the side of the house and as I stepped on the first one, I couldn't help but wonder if they would hold my weight. But they were sturdier than they looked. The landing at the top of the stairs was narrow, so I was practically pressed up against Eli's back as he tried to get the key into the lock with his left hand.

"Here, let me," I said as I took the key from him. Eli gasped as my front brushed his back and I actually found myself holding the position once I got the key into the lock. I made sure not to touch him anywhere else for fear of scaring him, but it didn't matter because his breathing steadily increased as I held him that way, caged between my body and the door. It was only when my dick began to pulse painfully behind my pants that I turned the key. As soon as the lock disengaged, Eli used his good arm to push the door open. I sucked in a deep breath to try to get control of my raging libido and followed him inside. The second I stepped over the threshold, a huge Rottweiler appeared and placed himself between me and Eli who was putting his keys on the small kitchen table several feet inside the doorway.

The dog and I studied each other for a few seconds and when the big animal finally approached me, I remained still so he could check me out. I glanced up to see Eli watching us, but his eyes were actually on the dog and I wondered if he was using the animal as a barometer of sorts to figure out if I was trustworthy. I had my answer a moment later when the dog began licking my outstretched hand because Eli expelled a rush of air. His eyes lifted to mine and I saw a flash of shame go through him.

He shook his head and opened his mouth to speak, but I quickly said, "Don't." I slid my hand over the dog's massive head. "If this is what it takes, I'm good with it."

Eli swallowed hard and then nodded. "His name is Baby."

I chuckled and looked down to study the big dog. I could tell he was an older dog because of the considerable silver lining his muzzle, but he was still an impressive animal. "He's beautiful," I murmured as I stroked the big dog's face. He nuzzled me for a few more seconds and then went to seek out Eli.

I watched as Eli dropped down into one of the kitchen chairs and wrapped his free arm around Baby. I moved farther into the apartment and closed the door behind me. Eli's demeanor was so different around his pet that I was momentarily mesmerized and I felt a ridiculous sliver of envy for the big animal. I moved past Eli and went to the refrigerator and pulled open the freezer. I found a couple of packs of frozen vegetables and took them to the kitchen table. Eli watched me, but didn't say anything as I went to the sink and searched out a clean dishtowel and wetted it. I moved the remaining kitchen chair until it was across from Eli and sat down. He didn't protest when I put my fingers under his chin to steady him and began cleaning the small gash on his lip. Once the dried blood was gone, I reached for both bags of frozen vegetables. I carefully placed one over his wrist which he was still holding against his chest and then I shifted forward so I could hold the second one against his cheek. He winced slightly, but didn't move away from my touch.

We sat there in silence as Eli's eyes held mine and even though I wasn't actually touching his skin, I may as well have been, because I felt a surge of electricity go through me. And I could see that Eli wasn't unaffected because his lips parted just a little bit and I could hear his breathing ramping up. But when his tongue came out to moisten his lips, my cock hardened painfully in my pants. Desperate for a momentary reprieve, I managed to growl, "Do you have any ibuprofen?"

It took several long seconds for Eli to answer, but just before he did, his tongue once again slid over his lips and I had to wonder if he had any idea what he was doing to me. If he hadn't been shouting "hands off" with every other part of his body, I would have been certain he was doing the move just to tease me.

"In my bathroom. I'll get it." Eli made a move to get up, but I put my free hand on his thigh and he sucked in a breath.

God, this guy was going to be the fucking death of me.

"I'll get it," I bit out.

Eli managed a nod and said, "You have to go through my bedroom to get to the bathroom. It's in the medicine cabinet."

I nodded and I as removed my hand from the bag that was still pressed against Eli's face, his hand came up to take over holding it in place. His fingers brushed mine and I barely managed to bite back the curse as another flash of heat shot through me. I stood and headed for the hallway that I assumed led to the bedrooms. There was actually only one bedroom and it turned out to be tiny. A full sized bed was pressed up against the long wall. There was no closet but there was a small dresser with books stacked high on it in one corner. I noticed several framed pictures on the dresser as well and I couldn't stop myself from stopping to take a closer look. The biggest picture was of a young woman with two children; a teenage girl and a boy no more than ten years old. Eli probably.

There were a few smaller pictures of various men and women, but it was an overturned picture that caught my attention. It was lying face down on the dresser like it had either fallen down or someone had put it that way. I picked it up and studied the image looking back at me. It was clearly the same woman from the other picture, but this time she was wearing a wedding dress. Next to her was presumably the groom, a good looking guy who looked to be about ten years older than the woman. In front of them was a younger Eli, a big grin on his face. I guessed him to be around fifteen or sixteen in the picture. The man's arm was draped across his shoulder and the woman had her hand on his other shoulder. There were two other men in the picture, one on each side of the happy couple. One appeared to be five to ten years younger than the groom and was bald with a heavy build. The youngest of the three men was beautiful with his thick black hair, pale blue eyes and wide smile.

I studied Eli again for a moment and then put the picture back the way I'd found it. I went to the bathroom and searched out the ibuprofen and then made my way back to the kitchen. I gave the living room a quick glance and noted it looked similar to the bedroom with its sparse furnishings – one small, threadbare brown loveseat facing a 32-inch TV. More framed pictures lined a bookshelf in one corner, but my eyes instantly fell on the single picture frame that was turned over.

Just like in the bedroom.

And just like in the other room, all the other pictures were of several men and women along with kids and dogs.

I itched to look at the picture that was overturned, but forced my attention back on Eli who was sitting as I'd left him. His eyes were on the big dog whose head was draped across his lap. Eli looked up as I made my way back to him, but I bypassed him and went to the refrigerator to search out something to drink. I grabbed one of the only two bottles of water and returned to the chair and sat down. I reached for the frozen bag on his face and carefully removed it and then handed him a couple of pills along with the water.

"Thanks," he said softly as he put the water down on the table.

"How does this feel?" I asked as I lifted the bag on his wrist and examined the swelling that was already starting to go down.

"Better."

I lifted my eyes to Eli, but he wasn't looking at me. His eyes were on the fingers he was running over Baby's head.

I hated his silence. I hated that I couldn't find even one sign of the young boy from the picture in his bedroom. I hated that even now just sitting there across from him, our knees almost touching, that it wasn't enough. I didn't even know what *it* was.

I needed to go. The young man before me didn't want my help. He'd made that crystal clear. And even though his body was reacting to mine, it didn't mean anything. He was as far from me mentally as he could get. But even as my mind told my body to stand up and walk away, I couldn't make my limbs obey. Instead, I found myself reaching out to cup the uninjured side of his face.

I ignored the way my body drew up tight and softly said, "Eli."

It took him a long time to lift his eyes to meet mine.

"Tell me who did this," I urged. "I can help you."

If I'd dropped my gaze even for a second, I would have missed it. The desperate look in his eyes. The one that told me he wanted more than anything to tell me…to accept my offer. But it was gone just like that and Eli dropped his eyes and murmured, "It was a misunderstanding. It won't happen again."

Frustration cut through me, but before I could respond, there was a knock on Eli's door and then it was opening.

"Eli, you here?" came a man's voice and Eli instantly pulled away from me and stood. I looked over to see a young man standing in the open doorway, his eyes shifting between me and Eli. "Oh, sorry, I didn't know you had company," he said awkwardly.

"It's fine," Eli said shakily. "Come on in."

The guy was about the same age as Eli and had a rangy, muscular build. His black hair stood in sharp contrast to his bright green eyes. The gorgeous, clean cut man was exactly the type of guy I typically went for, but every cell in my body was still focused on Eli and I automatically stepped closer to him before I realized what I was doing.

The man stepped farther into the apartment and slid his hand over Baby's head as the dog greeted him, but his eyes remained on Eli. "What happened?" he asked as his eyes registered the damage to Eli's face and I didn't miss the dark look in his gaze as he glanced at me when he strode past me to get to Eli. I had no doubt the guy was wondering if I was the cause of Eli's injuries.

"Nothing," Eli murmured as he let the other guy turn his face to get a better look. I hated the bout of jealousy that filtered through me. "I fell down some stairs when I was leaving the hospital."

The lie caught me off guard and when my eyes connected with Eli's, I saw the silent plea there. The other man looked at me briefly, but I kept my mouth shut.

"Brennan, this is Mav. He helped me out at the hospital and drove me home. Mav, this is Brennan Devereaux."

"It's nice to meet you," Brennan said and then reached out to shake my hand. His grip was firm and steady.

I desperately wanted to ask Eli who the guy was to him, but I forced myself to step back from the pair and said, "I should get going." It felt like acid was burning my insides as I gave Eli one last look and then turned towards the door. I cursed the all too familiar sensation that had no business appearing now. Eli was nothing to me, so to feel the pain of losing something I hadn't actually had was beyond ridiculous. The fact that I still felt it at all after so many years made me angrier than I wanted to admit.

I had my hand on the doorknob when I heard Eli say, "Mav, wait," and then his hand was closing over my forearm. The contact felt like a punch to the gut because it was the first time he was willingly touching me. I both wanted the moment to end and for it to last forever. I turned until our eyes met.

"Thank you," he said with a nod. But it was his eyes that spoke volumes. The acid in my belly settled and was replaced with another equally unwelcome sensation.

I nodded and opened the door, ignoring the feeling of loss as Eli's fingers dropped from my arm. But instead of moving forward, I glanced at him again and whispered, "You know where to find me."

And with that, I left the apartment.

Chapter Two

Eli

My fingertips were still tingling where I'd held on to Mav just before he'd walked out the door. Even worse, his rumbly voice was still stroking over my entire body as I replayed his words in my head.

You know where to find me.

That was the problem. And unless I was willing to give up my nearly daily visits to the ICS unit, it would continue to be a problem.

The first time I'd seen the tall, burly, long-haired man outside room 421, I'd actually stopped in my tracks and debated skipping the room all together. He'd been wearing almost exactly the same thing he wore most days – black leather pants, black boots and a black T-shirt that stretched across his broad chest. Tattoos covered much of his arms and disappeared under the wide leather wrist cuffs he wore and I'd had no doubt they continued to his shoulders and beyond because I'd seen a hint of ink peeking out from beneath the neckline. His long black hair had been tied back with some kind of band or tie, but I'd gotten a good enough look to see that it would fall at least to his shoulders when loose.

I'd only had a profile view at that point, but I'd felt an uncomfortable stirring in my gut as I'd taken in the hard line of his scruff-covered jaw, his wide lips, and straight nose. His darker skin tone had given him an exotic look and I'd cursed the fact that I hadn't been able to tell what color his eyes were from where I'd stood trying to pretend I wasn't watching him.

But none of that was what had truly frightened me. It was the way he'd held himself as he'd stood there outside that door, his eyes scanning each and every person in the crowded hallway.

Assessing.

Unforgiving.

Dangerous.

And then he'd looked at me. And he'd kept looking at me. I'd felt it even after I'd dropped my eyes and pretended to look at the list of patient names in my hand.

I'd wanted to run like the coward I was. But then I'd looked down at the list of kids who were a thousand times stronger and braver than me and I'd forced my feet to move. I'd somehow managed to greet the various nurses and staff as I'd passed by them, but I hadn't managed to lift my eyes even once when I'd reached the door to the room where little Matty Travers was spending the next several weeks undergoing treatment for leukemia.

It had taken several minutes to even get past the big man after he'd asked me my name and I'd used those moments to sneak peeks at him as he, and another man I would later learn was one of

Matty's fathers, spoke to the Director of Volunteer Services to make sure I was who I said I was.

His eyes were green. Not just plain green but deep, dark green like the tall evergreen trees that were predominant throughout the Pacific Northwest.

I hadn't asked why the little boy in room 421 had someone standing guard outside his room, but my whole body had been surging with electricity during my entire first visit with Matty and it had taken everything in me not to keep shifting my gaze to the door to try and get more glimpses of the man.

Mav.

"You sure you don't want to get checked out?"

I jumped at the sound of Brennan's voice because I'd completely forgotten about his presence. My entire body ached and my wrist was throbbing like a son of a bitch, but I shook my head. "No, I'm fine," I murmured as I turned around to face him. "Do me a favor and don't tell Dom, okay?" I said, forcing a lightness I wasn't feeling into my voice. "He'll want to wrap me in bubble wrap or something," I joked.

Brennan chuckled and reached for one of the bags of frozen vegetables on the table and handed it to me. I walked around the loveseat and sat down. Brennan came around the piece of furniture to join me, but when his eyes fell on the bookshelf, he paused and then went over to it and righted the single picture frame that had been lying face down. I felt my stomach tighten as my eyes settled on the photo in the frame, but I quickly tore them away and focused on getting the cold bag back on my wrist.

"I should probably warn you then," Brennan began as he dropped down on the loveseat next to me. "Dom and Logan are planning a welcome home party for you this Saturday. They were going to do it last weekend during family dinner, but since you had other plans…"

I forced myself not to chew on my lower lip as I was prone to do when I was stressed. I'd only been back in Seattle for a couple of weeks and while I'd come back specifically to be around the men and women who'd become my surrogate family, I'd yet to actually see any of them except for Brennan and Dominic Barretti, the man who'd saved my life.

Literally.

I'd been certain that coming home would change things for me, but the second Dom had shown up at my apartment the day after I'd arrived and enfolded me in his arms, I'd started to wonder if I hadn't made a terrible mistake.

Because the guilt of all I'd done had come boiling up to the surface the moment he'd wrapped his arms around me and whispered, "Welcome home, Eli," in my ear. He'd taken the few tears I'd shed as a sign of happiness, but the second he'd left, I'd slid to the floor and let everything go. And when the invites to come visit all the various family members had started rolling in, I'd begun making excuses.

"Do you think you can talk them out of it?" I asked. "I offered to take a shift at the hospital for another volunteer," I lied. I knew my reprieve wouldn't last long, but I just wasn't ready yet. Not to mention the bruise on my face wouldn't be gone by then and while Brennan might have bought my excuse, there was no way in hell Dom would have.

I felt Brennan's eyes on me so I forced my own up. Brennan was close to my own age and while he wasn't as seasoned in picking out lies like Dom was, he was still a smart guy. He studied me for a moment and then nodded his head. "I'll see what I can do."

"Thanks."

"I stopped by to see if you wanted to come look at apartments with me," Brennan said. He looked at my wrist which I still had pressed against my chest. "But seems like you should get some rest."

"Yeah," I mumbled. "You're getting your own place?"

Like me, Brennan had returned to Seattle after graduating from UCLA but unlike me, he had actual family to stay with. His brother Zane and his husband Connor lived in Queen Anne with Zane and Brennan's younger sister, Hannah, as well as their five-year-old son, Leo.

If I hadn't been looking at Brennan at that exact moment, I would have missed his small smile just before he said, "Tristan's transferring to the UW this fall. We're sharing a place."

Even though it had been a while since I'd last seen Logan and Dom's adopted son and Brennan together, Brennan's reaction didn't surprise me. I'd seen early on that Brennan was infatuated with the younger man, but I suspected the feelings went one way because as far as I knew, they'd never been anything more than just friends.

"Are you guys-" I began.

"No," Brennan quickly interjected and a mask of indifference fell over his face. "It just makes sense to get a place together."

I wanted to ask Brennan if that was the best idea considering how deep his feelings appeared to run, but he caught me off guard when he quietly asked, "So how are your parents?"

My stomach rolled, but I swallowed hard and nodded. "My mom is good. She's trying to keep busy with the charity work she does for veterans and their families."

"And your dad? How is he holding up?"

"He's good," I managed to get out and I steeled myself for the inevitable next question.

"And Caleb?"

"He's hanging in there," I murmured non-committedly.

Brennan sat back against the couch cushions and shook his head. "Fuck, poor guy. Finding his own brother like that…"

I could feel bile rising in my throat and I quickly stood and went to the kitchen and snatched the other bag of vegetables off the table, putting both back in the freezer.

"Sorry," I heard Brennan murmur and I closed the freezer door to see him standing a few feet away. "I shouldn't have brought it up," he said.

"No, it's okay," I responded with a sigh. "It's just been a rough few weeks."

Brennan nodded in understanding. "I'll make sure Dom and Logan hold off on the party."

"Thanks," I said and when Brennan leaned in to carefully hug me, I actually felt a moment of relief.

"It's good to have you home, Eli," Brennan said against my shoulder.

Tears stung my eyes as I said, "It's good to be home." Because it was yet another lie in a long line of lies I couldn't seem to escape.

"I'll catch you later," Brennan said as he released me and turned to go. "Go easy on the stairs, man," he added with a chuckle and then he left, giving Baby a quick pat before closing the door behind him.

The second the door clicked into place, the tears fell without warning and I covered my mouth with my uninjured hand to stifle the sobs in case Brennan was still within hearing range. I sank down into one of the kitchen chairs and tried to get control of myself, but when Baby bumped my good arm, I lost it and reached down to wrap my arm around the big dog who'd been the only certainty in my life from the moment Dom had given him to me. By the time all my tears had been spent, I was physically exhausted and every part of my body hurt. I got up and started to go to my bedroom, but stopped when my eyes caught on the picture frame Brennan had righted. I used my arm to wipe away the tears on my face as I went to the bookshelf. I stared at the eyes in the picture that were staring back at me and I wondered how I hadn't seen it. Of all the things I'd seen in the eyes of the men who'd used me when I was a kid, how could I have missed what I so clearly saw now?

I bit back another sob and quickly turned the picture over before heading to my room. I just needed to forget for a little while. Tomorrow would be here soon enough and I'd have to figure out where to go from there. An unbidden image of forest green eyes jumped into my head as I crawled under the covers of my bed.

You know where to find me.

Yes, I did. And that was part of the problem.

Chapter Three

Mav

"Thor would so kick Hawkeye's butt," I declared as I shot the man across from me a challenging smile.

"Nuh-uh," Matty interjected as he sat up in his hospital bed and searched out the Hawkeye doll that he always had close by along with the well-used Spiderman doll. "Hawkeye has a bow and arrows," he said quickly as he pointed to the quiver of arrows on the Hawkeye doll's back. "He could shoot Thor before Thor even knew what hit him," Matty insisted. "Isn't that right, Papa?" Matty asked as he turned his attention on the man sitting on the other side of the bed.

I didn't miss the way Hawke's whole body drew up tight when Matty referred to him that way and I suspected it was a relatively new thing. I also suspected Hawke loved every second of it. "That's right," Hawke managed to get out, though his voice was heavy with emotion.

Matty looked at me triumphantly and I put up my hands. "Okay, you got me Professor X."

I felt my own chest constrict painfully as I took in Matty's small body and bald head. Logically I knew the little boy's treatment

41

was progressing exactly as it should and he was responding well, but for all the good days he had, there were plenty of bad ones too where he was too sick to do anything but lay quietly in bed, sometimes in the arms of one of his fathers as they told him the superhero stories that he so loved.

I felt Hawke's eyes on me as I studied Matty, but I forced myself not to look at him. Taking this job had been the epitome of stupid. Because what had started out as the simple need to protect a little boy from an unseen threat had morphed into something so much more. I had stopped looking at Matty as just a little boy fighting for his life. And the men in his life…the men who'd banded together to become the family he needed…

I shook myself free of the path my brain was going down. Thoughts like that were exactly why I'd told Ronan I needed a break. A week to just get on my Harley and disappear.

I held out my fist and said to Matty, "Professor X, I'll see you next week." Matty smiled and bumped his small fist against mine.

I flashed Hawke a glance as I headed for the door and didn't miss the way he was watching me with a mix of curiosity and pity. Fucker was just too damn perceptive.

"Take care of yourself, Mav," Hawke said.

I ignored the uncomfortable sensation in my chest as I gave him a quick nod and left the room. I hated the anxiety that overcame me as I stopped next to Dante Thorne, the man who would be guarding Matty in my absence. I needed to get the fuck away from this place so I could regroup. But I couldn't make sense of the feeling that I was already exactly where I was supposed to be and that walking away wouldn't solve anything.

"Keep them safe," I murmured to Dante.

I'd never worked with the young man who was leaning casually against the wall next to the door, one leg raised so that his foot was resting flat against the wall. He was a relatively new addition to Ronan's team and while he'd already garnered a reputation for his cocksure attitude, he'd impressed more than a couple members of the team with his ability to sense when things were off. And while he looked like he didn't have a care in the world, I knew he was aware of every single thing that was going on around us.

"Yep," was all he said.

I started to walk past him, but thought better of it and turned to face him. "The volunteer who visits the kids every day…"

"You mean the guy with the tight ass?" Dante drawled.

I ground my teeth together in irritation, but didn't take the bait. Besides being an arrogant son of a bitch, Dante Thorne was also a horny one and he'd fuck anyone and everyone, regardless of whether they had a dick or pussy between their legs. "You seen him today?"

"No. Shame too, 'cause he's the highlight of my day." Dante flashed me a wide smile, but his eyes quickly shifted back to scanning the hallway. I ignored the urge to punch him and made my

43

way towards the hallway that would ultimately get me to the parking garage.

In the week since Eli had been attacked, I'd seen him every day, but he hadn't spoken a word to me, nor I to him. We'd gone back to the roles we'd had before I'd found him that day in the stairwell. It was the fact that he hadn't tried to interact with me even once in the days following the attack that had kept me from calling our tech guy, or girl rather, to get some more information on Eli in the hopes that I could figure out who had assaulted him. Just like with Matty, I'd realized that I'd started to get too caught up in the young man's life. Because instead of going home every night after my shift at the hospital ended, I found myself driving past the young man's apartment. What the hell I expected to see, I had no idea.

That was how I'd known I was getting in way too deep.

Eli Galvez wasn't my problem. Matty Travers wasn't my problem. One was a former distraction, the other was my job.

Simple.

Some badass assassin I was…I couldn't even get my shit together long enough to be honest with myself. A week exploring the Pacific Coast Highway on my Harley would fix that. Hell, if I was really lucky, Ronan would call me up and tell me he had another job for me and I wouldn't have to set foot back in Seattle again.

I was letting the prospect of not having to see Eli again roll through me as I reached the stairwell door that led to the parking garage floors, but the moment I pushed the heavy door open, the shimmer of disappointment that had started to take root somewhere deep inside of me fled.

Because sitting on the very top step was Eli.

He turned the second I entered the stairwell and then he was climbing to his feet. And although his face was still an ugly purple color, I was pleased to see that his lip was healed and from the normal way he was holding his arm, I suspected his wrist was better as well.

"Hi," Eli said nervously.

My body was already reacting to being so physically close to the younger man, but it was my insides that were churning with excitement.

"Hi."

We both stood there in a tangle of awkward silence until I finally said, "Did you need something?"

"Um…yeah, can I talk to you about something?"

Eli was still clearly afraid of me, but since it was the most he'd ever spoken to me, I was very curious to hear what he had to say. "Sure," I said and I began walking down the stairs. Eli fell in step next to me, but he didn't actually speak and I figured he was trying to work up the nerve. It wasn't until I pushed the door open leading to the floor where my Harley was parked that Eli finally opened his mouth.

"I was wondering…do you know how to fight?"

"Fight?" I asked as I approached my Harley. I noticed that Eli's car was parked right next to my bike and I wondered if he'd figured it was mine and parked there intentionally. We were parked in the farthest corner of the garage so there was little foot traffic.

"Yeah...I mean, like do you know self-defense stuff?"

My body tensed up at that and I turned to face him. "Did something happen?" I asked.

Eli began chewing on his lower lip and before I could even think about what I was doing, I reached up with my fingers to free his tender flesh from the hold his teeth had on it. Eli stilled at my touch and then closed his eyes like he was in pain. But I knew it wasn't pain that he was feeling.

Fuck, why couldn't I get a grip around this guy?

I dropped my hand and took a step back so there would be more room between us. Maybe then I wouldn't fucking reach for him again.

"So do you?" Eli asked, ignoring my question.

"Yes," I finally said. "I know some self-defense moves." I knew a lot more than *some*, but I didn't say that.

"Would you teach me?" Eli asked in a rush.

"Eli, if that guy is still bothering you-"

"Please, Mav, can you teach me or not?" Eli interrupted. The desperation coming off of him was palpable. "I...I can pay you."

I studied him long and hard before finally saying, "I don't want your money." If teaching him some moves was the only way to get him to trust me, then I'd do it in a heartbeat. Because he was clearly still in trouble.

I expected my statement about not wanting his money would have relaxed him somewhat, but it just made him more tense. That lasted only for a few seconds before there was such a profound shift in him that I was momentarily speechless. His fear disappeared just like that and his whole body went lax. And then he scanned the garage before reaching for my hand.

I was so caught off guard by him initiating the contact, that I barely noticed as he led me past his car. "Eli-" I managed to say, but then he was maneuvering me behind a foundation column next to his car and he released my hand. There was a light hanging a few feet over, but it wasn't working correctly because it would flicker now and then, but otherwise left the spot we were standing in bathed in shadows.

I was about to ask what the hell was going on when Eli's hand stroked over my groin. I bit back a curse as his fingers brushed over my growing erection and when he gripped me through my pants, I actually did moan and dropped my head back against the pillar behind me. Eli's hand held me for several long seconds before sliding down to search out my balls. His touch was driving me insane with need so when I felt the button on my pants open a moment later, I didn't protest. The zipper sounded obscenely loud in the garage, but my groan as Eli's hand snaked into my pants to play with me had to be a thousand times louder.

"Fuck," I growled when Eli pulled my cock out of my pants and began stroking me. His eyes were on my rigid shaft so I dropped my hand to his head and threaded my fingers through his hair. He let me maneuver his head so that he was looking up at me, but all my desire was snuffed out when I saw his eyes.

Because there was nothing there. Not one goddamn thing. Not desire, not pleasure, not fear…nothing.

What the fuck was going on?

My insides went cold as Eli tugged free of my hold and dropped to his knees. While my cock was still responding to the young man at my feet, the rest of me was still trying to process what was happening. I managed to come to my senses just as Eli leaned forward to take me in his mouth and I bent down and grabbed him by both of his upper arms and pulled him to his feet.

"No," I said firmly. "Not like this."

Eli's dead eyes held mine and it wasn't until I reached up and ran my fingers down his cheek and whispered his name that he finally seemed to snap out of whatever daze he'd been in. Life rushed back into his gaze and he looked down at my cock which was still hanging out of my pants. He let out a startled gasp and took several big steps back from me. I used the time to tuck myself back in, but I was still drawing the zipper up when Eli bolted.

"Eli-" I shouted as I followed him. I reached him just as he was opening his car door and I slammed it closed before he could get in. I pinned his body with mine to keep him from trying to get away.

"I'm sorry!" he cried. "I'm sorry!"

"Eli, it's okay," I said as I reached up to grab his arms. He was wearing a short sleeved shirt so I was able to touch his skin which actually felt cold and clammy. He was shaking like crazy and

48

I could hear sobs rattling deep down in his throat. I sensed he was on the verge of a full blown panic attack so I wrapped my arms around him and dropped my mouth to his ear.

"Shhhh, just take deep breaths, okay?"

My words seemed to have little effect on him and he kept repeating over and over that he was sorry. Something inside of me took over as Eli's distress grew and I began murmuring words that I had learned long ago…before I'd realized that they didn't apply to me.

I kept repeating them over and over until I felt Eli start sucking in deep breaths. We were leaning heavily against his car door, my body holding his in place, surrounding him. His shaking eased as his breathing slowed, but he was still trembling. The sobs had stopped, but I could feel moisture dropping down onto my forearm which was still braced across his upper chest. I let the words trail off, but instead of releasing Eli, I leaned down to brush my lips across the back of his neck. His skin was soft and much warmer than it had been a few minutes earlier and while he was still taking deep breaths, they weren't as agonized as they'd been.

We stood there for several long minutes and as the adrenaline in my system began to wane, I realized how good Eli's body felt pressed up against mine. At some point he'd lifted one of his hands to close over the arm I had around his chest, but he wasn't trying to get free of me…it was more like he was holding on. Like I'd become his anchor. It wasn't something I should have encouraged, but I couldn't force myself to release him.

"I…I need to go," Eli said shakily, though he didn't release his hold on me even when I loosened my grip just a little.

"We need to talk about what just happened," I said, but even before I finished the statement, Eli was shaking his head.

"It was a mistake. I'm sorry."

"Eli-"

"Please, Mav…please just let me go."

I hated how frail and uneven his voice sounded. While he wasn't in a near panic like he'd been before, he was definitely still on the edge. I reluctantly let him go and stepped back. The second I did, he was opening the car door. He whispered yet another apology to me and then he was climbing in his car. It sputtered to life a moment later, but Eli didn't look at me even once as he pulled out of the space and drove off. I wanted to follow him and demand that he tell me what the hell had just happened, but I knew it wouldn't get me anywhere. My plans to leave town forgotten, I pulled out my phone and started to dial the number for Daisy, the young woman Ronan had hired to handle the IT side of the underground vigilante organization he ran and that I'd been working for for nearly five years. But as I was about to hit the button to initiate the call, I felt a rush of impatience go through me and I put my phone away and climbed onto my bike. It would take Daisy hours to get the information I wanted and that was assuming she didn't have any high priority cases she was working on. And it was more than likely that any information she shared with me would be shared with

Ronan as well. Since he knew Eli, he'd want an explanation as to why I was digging into the young man's past.

It was something I wasn't ready to try to explain…not to Ronan and not to myself.

Chapter Four

Eli

I was tempted to not answer the knock on the door, especially since I had a good guess as to who it was. Humiliation blazed through me as I wiped away the tears that I hadn't been able to stem from the moment I'd realized that I'd made a terrible mistake after Mav had told me he didn't want my money.

The way he'd looked at me as I'd finally woken up from the daze I'd been in…

I shook my head and climbed off the loveseat. Baby was already eagerly waiting by the door, his big butt wiggling in anticipation. As I approached the door, I used the hem of my shirt to wipe my face, though I knew the move would do little to hide what I'd been doing for the last couple of hours.

I tried to force myself to relax as I turned the knob, but it was a wasted effort because the second I saw Mav on the other side of the door, I was back in that garage, knees on the dirty, grease covered floor and Mav's stiff cock pulsing in my hand. I opened the door wider to let him in because I knew he would be full of questions and I doubted he would go anywhere until he had the answers he was seeking.

And I had no fucking clue what to tell him. Certainly not the truth.

But instead of coming in, Mav remained outside and studied me intently. Baby was sniffing Mav's hands excitedly, but Mav kept his eyes on me when he said, "Do you still want to learn how to fight?"

The question caught me off guard and it took me several long seconds to nod since my voice had escaped me.

"There's a gym at my hotel. Go change into something loose-fitting and meet me downstairs."

And with that, Mav turned and trotted down the stairs.

"Baby," I murmured and the dog instantly came back into the apartment. I was reeling from the fact that Mav hadn't asked me about the events in the garage, but my desperation was still high so I hurried to my room and changed into a pair of athletic pants. I searched out my sneakers and dragged them on as quickly as I could even as my stomach rolled with anxiety.

I wasn't a particularly athletic guy and never had been, but the events of last week and the terror of what had happened the previous night had me desperate to learn to defend myself. I gave Baby a quick pat before locking the door behind me and hurrying down the stairs. I slowed as I rounded the house and saw Mav leaning against his big motorcycle. I would never get used to how gorgeous he was or the effect he had on me besides just intimidating the hell out of me. It wasn't like I hadn't had my fair share of attention from other men. Between my leaner build and borderline effeminate features, I'd often attracted men from all walks of life and while I'd used my looks to my advantage when I'd been younger, it wasn't something I had ever been particularly proud of. But something in the way Mav looked at me felt different. Yes, the desire was there – I wasn't completely blind after all. But there was something else too. I felt it even now as he watched me approach and although I was nervous about spending time with him, especially considering what I'd done to him a couple of hours ago, I was also kind of looking forward to it too. Though I wasn't really sure why.

But the thought was short-lived when Mav held a motorcycle helmet out to me.

"I can just take my own car," I stuttered as the thought of climbing on the huge bike behind Mav made me both hot and cold at the same time. When he'd held me earlier in the garage as I'd tried to make my escape, I'd been too upset at first to notice how good his body had felt against mine. But then I'd heard his voice in my ear and while I hadn't understood the foreign language he'd been speaking to me at the time, just the sensation of his voice rumbling against my back had been comforting.

"This won't work if you don't trust me, Eli," Mav said quietly as he continued to hold the helmet out.

I swallowed hard. I knew he was right, but he had no idea what he was asking of me. Being able to escape was all I had.

Mav didn't budge as he held my gaze and I automatically began gnawing on my lip before I realized what I was doing. I forced myself to move forward and take the helmet from him. It wasn't a full face helmet so it was easy to put on and I fiddled with the strap as I watched Mav climb onto the bike and start it up. I seriously considered calling the whole thing off, but then I remembered the terror and helplessness that had spiked through me a week ago and again last night and that had me striding up to the bike. I put my hand on Mav's arm to steady myself as I climbed behind him. The raw power I could feel between my legs was intimidating, but it had nothing on the sight of the broad back in front of me. Every time Mav shifted, his muscles rippled beneath his T-shirt. I had no idea what I was supposed to do with my hands, but before I could even find a place to put them to brace myself, Mav turned slightly and grabbed my right hand. He tugged it forward until it was wrapped around his waist. I nearly swallowed my tongue as I felt the hard muscles of his abdomen beneath my palm and to my own surprise, I was eager to wrap my other arm around him as well.

The bike shifted and began to roll forward and as much as I tried to maintain the distance between us, the movement of the bike had me sliding closer to Mav so I could get a better grip on him. The result was every part of my lower body pressed up against him. Thighs, ass, waist…there was no escaping. And I found for the first time in my life, I didn't care. I didn't even question what made me lean into him so that I could rest my chest along his back and my cheek on the back of his shoulder. I just allowed myself to feel something I hadn't felt in years.

Freedom.

* * *

I was sweating long before Mav even began breaking down the elements of the first move he was going to teach me.

Mav had been surprisingly quiet once we'd reached the hotel. He'd escorted me to the gym and instructed me to get warmed up by jumping on the elliptical machine while he went to his room and changed. He'd been back within ten minutes wearing a pair of navy blue long athletic shorts and a white T-shirt and when he'd climbed onto the treadmill next to my machine, it had taken every ounce of concentration to maintain my pace. He'd started running on the machine within a few minutes and I hadn't been able to stop myself from sneaking peeks at his muscled body as it powered forward.

Fifteen minutes passed before he stopped his machine and mine and while he'd barely broken a sweat, I was seriously worried I was going to pass out. Mav tossed me a towel and I followed him to a corner of the gym where there was a clear area. I tried not to let my eyes fall to his ass, but I couldn't help myself and when I finally looked up, I realized there was a wall of mirrors in front of us and Mav could have easily seen me checking him out. But if he'd noticed my perusal, he didn't say anything. In fact, he was all business as he began breaking down the different steps and while that should have comforted me, it didn't.

I was doing pretty well with following Mav's instructions, but when it came time to actually practice the first move from beginning to end, all my fear came back because Mav had to pretend to grab me around the throat so I could break free of him. The second his big hand closed around my neck, I felt pain start to spread throughout my chest and every breath I took fell short.

"Eli," Mav said gently. "Look at me."

I barely heard him over the roaring in my ears, but when he repeated the order, his voice heavier, I opened my eyes which I hadn't even realized I'd closed at some point. Even though Mav was still holding me by the throat, just seeing his face immediately helped ease some of the panic that was trying to consume me.

"Break it down," Mav said firmly.

I managed a nod and concentrated on all the steps I'd just spent the better part of an hour learning. It seemed like every one was in slow motion, but when I finally reached the last step to knock Mav's hand loose, he released his hold on me.

"Good," was all he said and then his hand came up to grab me again. "Again."

I didn't give myself time to think about my fear and managed to get through the moves again, this time just a little bit faster. I knew in a real situation that I wasn't putting enough force behind the steps to actually reach the end result of escaping the grip on my throat, but the more I repeated them, the more empowered I felt. By the twentieth or thirtieth time, a fierce surge of energy was rushing through me and I began to get excited by the prospect of Mav's hand closing around my throat. Over and over I knocked his hand away, not caring if I was throwing too much force behind my blows. When

Mav finally stepped back to indicate we were done, my lungs were burning and my skin was flushed with heat and sweat.

But that wasn't the only thing.

I was crying.

I was fucking crying and I had no idea why.

And it felt amazing.

"I…I…" I started to say to Mav in way of explanation, but shook my head because I had no idea how to explain how good I felt. He probably thought I'd completely lost my mind.

But instead of looking at me like he was wondering what kind of head case he'd hooked up with, Mav stepped forward and brought his hand up to gently cup the bruised side of my face. His thumb stroked through the track of tears that were streaming down my face. And then it was dragging the moisture of my tears down to my mouth. All my excitement and pride settled in my gut and exploded into something bigger…something that had me wishing I could find out what his lips would feel like against mine.

We stood there like that for several long seconds until a door opening somewhere jolted us both and Mav dropped his hand. "Nice work. Let's work on another one."

And with that, whatever moment there'd been between us disappeared and Mav went back to how he'd been when we'd started this whole thing. Distant, clinical…a stranger.

We spent another hour in the gym going through the four moves Mav wanted me to learn and while I hadn't had another cathartic episode, my body was buzzing with excitement. While I wasn't ready to take on someone of Mav's size and strength, at least now maybe I had a fighting chance. I just hoped my instinct to fight would kick in even when my brain sought to escape into the world I'd created so long ago where nothing could touch me.

Mav grabbed us a couple of waters from a small refrigerator on one side of the gym and I watched as he took several long swallows from his. I could feel my body reacting to the sight of the muscles in his neck working and I actually had to turn away from him so he wouldn't see my dick swelling behind the thin material of my pants.

"You mind if I take a quick shower before I take you home?"

"No," I murmured. "I could just call a cab if it's an inconvenience."

"Don't worry about it," was all Mav said as he threw the empty bottle into the recyclable container next to the refrigerator. "Why don't you come on upstairs to my room? You can watch TV or something. And if you want to shower-" Mav's voice dropped off as his eyes fell on me and I realized he must have seen the fear that I couldn't hide.

Shame went through me at the knee jerk reaction. If Mav had wanted to do something to me, he would have done it a long time ago. But I didn't know how to explain to him that it had nothing to do with him.

"You know what, never mind. I'll have the front desk call you a cab."

Mav turned to go and I felt a moment of panic that it would be the last time I'd get to talk to him if I didn't do something. I grabbed his arm and stepped in front of him. "Mav, wait, please."

He stopped, but he didn't look happy about it. I tried to search for the right words to say, but I couldn't figure out how to tell him that the events of my past still shaped everything I did today…that in so many ways, I was still the same fifteen-year-old kid who'd never been kissed but had been fucked more times than he could count and who knew how to suck cock like a pro…because that's what he'd been.

But I couldn't tell him that. Because I didn't want to see the disgust in his eyes that I knew would be there if he knew the truth about me…that or worse, he'd look at me the way all those men had looked at me. Like I was garbage. Theirs to use and throw away when they were done with me.

"Would you like to have dinner with me tonight?" I finally blurted out.

I was as surprised by the offer as Mav seemed to be, but the idea didn't terrify me like it should have. "Um, I could cook for you…at my place. As a thank you for today."

Mav was quiet for so long that I began to shift uncomfortably in place. I was on the verge of telling him to forget it when he said, "I'd love to."

The relief was overwhelming and I couldn't help the smile that spread across my lips. "Okay," I managed to get out.

"Did you want to wait down here or come up to my room?" Mav ventured.

I took a deep breath and said, "I'll come up."

Mav nodded and I followed him from the gym. We didn't speak as we got onto the elevator and while my nerves had started to return, the fear wasn't there like I would have expected. I lost track of what floor we were on because I'd spent most of the elevator ride staring at my shoes, but when the doors slid open, I followed Mav to his room which turned out to be a suite that included a kitchen and living space.

"Make yourself at home," Mav said. "There's food and drinks in the fridge. I'll just be a couple of minutes."

I nodded and watched him head towards the bedroom which was separated from the rest of the living area by a set of double sliding doors. I assumed the bathroom was attached to the bedroom. I was about to turn to try and find the remote for the TV when I saw Mav reach for the hem of his shirt as he neared the bedroom. I actually had to stifle a moan when the shirt came off and revealed a tattoo of two huge snakes, their heads curled over the backs of Mav's shoulder muscles and their winding bodies covering the expanse of his back and disappearing beneath his pants. That tattoo on its own stole my breath, but add in the way Mav's muscles flexed as he moved and I actually had to grab a hold of the kitchen counter to steady myself.

Fuck, the guy was gorgeous.

Instead of watching TV like I planned, I went to the wall of windows and took in the sight before me. Mav's room was high enough that he had a view of the city and the mountains beyond the water. While I'd spent most of my younger years in Seattle along with my mother and older sister, it wasn't this Seattle that I'd grown up in. As an illegal immigrant, my mother hadn't had access to good paying jobs or an education, so most of the places we'd lived had been in run down neighborhoods that were far from the tourist filled city. But as hard as my mother had worked to give my sister Elena and me everything we'd needed, she'd never failed to make us a family first. There'd never been any doubt in her mind that Elena and I would have everything she hadn't had herself…a stable home environment, college, careers. And we'd been on track until the day INS had shown up at our door and taken her away. One minute we'd been eating dinner, the next our mother was gone and my eighteen-year-old sister had been left to find a way to care for both of us. And then Elena was gone too…

"Hey, you okay?"

I turned to see Mav watching me from the doorway to his bedroom. He was wearing a pair of jeans, black boots and a black T-shirt. His damp hair hung just past his shoulders, the ends curling into loose ringlets that should have looked strange on a man but, in fact, looked sexy as hell.

"Yeah," I said, my voice sounding rough. I pushed the thoughts of my mother and sister away. "I was just thinking about what to make for dinner."

I had no doubt Mav could tell I was lying, but fortunately he didn't call me on it.

"Are you ready to go?" I asked as I began walking towards the door.

"In a second," Mav said. "I want to talk to you about something first."

"Okay," I said, my body going on alert at the reserved tone in his voice.

Mav ran his fingers through his hair and lowered his eyes for a moment as if struggling to find the right words to say. When he finally lifted them, I felt my heart clench because I suspected he was finally going to ask me about what had happened in the garage.

So I was completely unprepared when he said, "Eli, the man who assaulted you…was it Dominic Barretti?"

Chapter Five

Mav

"What?" Eli asked, his voice barely a squeak. I felt my stomach drop out as I realized I was right because there was no other explanation for the pain that filled his eyes.

"Eli, it's okay," I said quietly as I began moving towards him. "I can protect you from him."

"Oh my God," Eli gasped and then he shook his head violently. "No," he whispered. "No!" he said more aggressively and then he was coming at me. Tears flooded his eyes as he shoved my chest hard with both his hands. "You have no right!" he screamed and I had to grab his wrists to keep him from lashing out at me again.

"Eli-"

"Dom saved my life, you asshole! He'd never hurt me in a million years! Don't you ever fucking say that about him again, do you hear me?"

Eli's rage was completely unexpected and I knew I'd made a terrible mistake.

"He fucking saved my life!" Eli shouted again and I had to shake him hard to get his attention.

"I hear you, Eli!" I said sharply. "I hear you," I said again when he finally stopped struggling in my grasp. "I'm sorry. I got it wrong."

Eli was breathing hard, but he settled down. I had yet to release him and he wasn't trying to escape me. Just like in the gym, this sight of another side of Eli was messing with my head and I was drawing him forward before I could even consider what I was doing. I released his wrists and slid my hands up his arms until they were resting on his neck. But instead of removing his hands from my chest, Eli opened his fists so that his hands were pressed flat against me. I wanted a taste of him more than I wanted my next breath, but Eli carefully tugged free of my hold before I could act on my need.

"How did you know about Dom?" he asked as he took several steps back, the anger in his voice fading and quickly turning to suspicion. "Did you Google me or something?"

I could have lied and told him yes, but knowing what I now knew about him, I couldn't bring myself to do it.

"I started with the internet," I began. I sat down in the plush living room chair in the hopes Eli would follow suit and sit on the couch that was directly behind him.

He didn't.

"Started?" Eli said quietly. "What does that mean?"

"I have access to a lot of resources," I hedged. "After I saw the story about what happened to you and that young woman-"

65

"Riley," Eli whispered.

"Riley," I said with a nod. "After I read about what Cyrus Hamilton did to you and Riley, I wanted to know more about you...the stuff that wasn't in the papers."

When I'd started my search on Eli this morning, I'd expected to find the basics...credit reports, financial records, family information. What I'd found had left me completely stunned. And that was long before I'd even got into the details.

The second I had typed Eli Galvez into the internet search engine, I'd been swamped with the same story over and over and I'd instantly remembered it from the news eight years earlier. Eli had been a teenager at the time, barely fifteen. He and a young woman named Riley Sinclair had been abducted by a man who'd been the prime suspect in the disappearance of several women, mostly prostitutes. Eli's own sister, Elena, had been among the victims. Her body, along with more than a dozen others, had been found on Cyrus Hamilton's property after Dominic Barretti, his brother and Dom's lover, Logan, had tracked the killer to his remote house in Summer Hill, Washington. They'd arrived just in time to watch as Cyrus's own daughter took his life before he could kill Eli and his friend.

"What...what else did you find?" Eli managed to get out. He still looked like he was ready to bolt.

"I know what happened to you after your mom was deported and your sister disappeared."

All the color drained from Eli's face, but instead of turning to leave, he sank down onto the couch, the water bottle he'd been holding crushed to his chest.

"Dom said he got those records sealed so no one would find out…" Eli whispered before his words trailed off.

"They are sealed, Eli. It would take someone with a lot of skill to get to them."

Eli's gaze shifted from the floor to me. "Someone like you," he murmured. I didn't miss the accusation in his tone and for the first time in a really long time, I wasn't proud of the tech skills I was known for.

After reading about Eli's abduction, I'd been in a full-on rage and I'd actually had to take a break and go down to the gym and vent my fury on the weight bag they had down there. But within minutes of sitting back down in front of my computer, all the emotions I'd managed to tamp down had come roaring back when I'd discovered the arrest records. I'd suspected even before I'd opened them what the charges were, but a part of me had hoped and prayed they'd been for some stupid, immature stunt that teenage kids sometimes pulled.

They hadn't been for a stunt.

They'd been for solicitation.

I'd read the charge three times before I'd finally accepted what my eye were seeing.

Fifteen fucking years old.

I'd struggled to keep doing my research after that because I'd felt violently ill. I'd stuck with it long enough to discover that it was

Dom Barretti who'd gotten Eli off the streets and had brought Eli's mother back to the States and given her a job at his security firm. I'd been hailing the man as a hero in my mind until I'd found a picture of him. And then my rage had come back in full force because I'd seen the man before…he'd been one of the men in the picture in Eli's bedroom. The picture that had been turned over.

So he wouldn't have to look at it. So he wouldn't have to see the face of the man he'd once trusted, but who'd had turned on him for some reason. That had been my thinking up until a few minutes ago. But the passion with which Eli had defended the man…

"Why did you think it was Dom?" Eli asked sullenly.

I hated that all the fire he'd displayed down in the gym was gone and that the fragile trust I'd finally managed to establish with him – enough that he'd even felt comfortable enough to ask me to dinner – was snuffed out just like that.

"The picture in your bedroom…the one you turned over."

Eli looked up at me. "You saw that?"

I nodded. "The man owns one of the most reputable security firms in the country, but instead of going to him for help after you were attacked, you came to me."

Eli dropped his gaze again, but I didn't miss the flash of shame in them. I had no doubt he was remembering the episode in the garage. An episode I finally understood now.

"Eli, look at me," I said softly.

He didn't.

"Please."

Eli shook his head slightly, but finally raised his eyes. Pain shot through my chest at the gamut of emotions I saw there, but I pushed it back and said, "Nothing I found out today changes anything. What happened in the garage doesn't matter. You survived...you're here. That's all I care about."

Eli studied me for a moment and then shifted his gaze so that he was staring out the window. "When you said you didn't want my money, I went right back there, you know?" Eli loosened his hold on the water bottle and began rubbing his thumb back and forth over the label. The self-soothing move tore at my insides.

"I knew what Elena did to get us money after our mom was deported. But I didn't really get it. Elena was always really good at making it seem like she just had a lot of boyfriends who liked to take care of her. I guess I was pretty stupid."

"No, you weren't. Your sister was trying to protect you."

Eli nodded. "When she didn't come home, the food started running out. Then the landlord started coming by every day to collect the rent. I told him Elena would be back with the money soon. After a week, he told me I either had to pay up or get out."

I saw Eli swallow hard and my gut clenched as I realized what was coming.

"I didn't know it was something guys did with other guys...I mean, I knew some women sold themselves for money, but I didn't know guys did it too. The landlord...he told me how Elena paid the rent and he told me I could do the same thing. Since I knew I was gay, I thought maybe it wouldn't be so bad."

I felt the bile rising in my throat and I had to clench my hands together to keep from reaching for the decorative glass bowl on the coffee table in front of me, because all I really wanted to do in that moment was hurl it through the fucking window.

"I hated every second of it and after he was done, part of me wanted to die. But another part of me was just so damned relieved because those few minutes had ensured I'd have a roof over my head for another week. The next guy meant I got to eat for a couple of days. The guy after that made it possible for me to keep the heat on. In a way, it became easy after a while. I mean, I wasn't proud of it or anything…I knew what those men thought of me. Most of them didn't even bother to hide the fact that they thought I was garbage."

Eli looked up at me. "Today in the garage when you said you didn't want money, my head just went to how I could get what I needed. I thought…I thought you wanted me like that."

Fuck, I needed to tread carefully here. "You saw me, Eli. I think it was pretty obvious that I wanted you."

"Then why-"

"Because I want *you*," I said firmly. "Not that guy on his knees in the garage who thinks no one will ever see him as anything other than garbage."

Eli seemed to have trouble holding my gaze, so he dropped his eyes again and stared at the bottle in his hands.

"Eli, this guy who hurt you, did you have a run-in with him again? Is that why you asked me to teach you to fight?"

He was quiet for so long that I was sure he wasn't going to answer me. But he finally took in a deep breath and said, "Last night at my place, Baby jumped out of bed and ran towards the front door. I thought maybe he had to go out or something so I got up to check on him. He was staring at the front door so I figured I was right and went to get his leash. That's when I saw it. The knob…it jiggled just a little."

My insides went cold at Eli's words.

"Then there were these sounds like metal against metal, but real quiet. And then the door unlocked. I just froze. And then it was opening."

I could see Eli was shaking, so I got up and went to sit next to him. I put my hand on his knee in the hopes of soothing him, but he barely seemed to notice.

"Baby started growling at that point and when the door opened just a little, he started barking like crazy. I heard footsteps hurrying down the stairs."

Eli looked at me. "It was probably just a random burglar or something, right?"

My lack of a response was answer enough and Eli dropped his gaze again. "I figured I should know some moves in case Baby wasn't around if it happened again."

I was barely containing my anger and actually had to get up and walk away from Eli so I could get control of myself. The thought of how close he'd come to getting hurt again, or worse, was driving me insane.

"Tell me who this guy is," I finally managed to get out.

Unsurprisingly, I was greeted with complete and utter silence. I wanted to hit something. I wanted to grab Eli and demand he give me some answers. I wanted to never take my eyes off of him again.

I went back to the chair I'd been sitting in and murmured, "At least tell Dom."

Eli still refused to look at me. He seemed like he'd gone off to some unreachable place in his mind because he had the same dead look in his gaze that he'd had in the garage. While I understood his need for the coping mechanism, I hated that he felt the need to use it around me. It was a reminder that I wasn't anything more to him than the men who'd used him when he was a kid.

"Can I use your shower before you take me home?"

I quelled my frustration and murmured, "Sure," and watched Eli carefully set the water bottle down on the coffee table before heading towards the bedroom. The shower came on a couple minutes later and between the anger that was still surging through me and the realization that a very beautifully naked Eli was just feet from me, I was struggling to keep myself in check. I was half tempted to call up Dominic Barretti and tell him what was going on just so I could get on my Harley and take off like I'd been planning a couple short hours ago. But the idea of leaving Eli when he was clearly in danger made my insides burn and when I reached for the room phone on the table next to my chair, it wasn't to call the man who'd saved Eli once before.

"Front desk, how may I help you?" said a pleasant young woman's voice.

"I need to arrange for a rental car."

"Of course, I would be happy to assist you."

It took several minutes to secure the rental and I was assured it would be delivered to the hotel within a couple of hours. By the time I was hanging up with the front desk, Eli was coming out of the bedroom. He didn't speak to me at all; he merely went to the door and waited so I grabbed my phone and wallet from the kitchen counter and followed him from the room. Unlike the ride from Eli's apartment to the hotel, Eli made every effort not to lean against me and his grip on my waist was only the minimum necessary to keep himself from sliding off the bike. I missed the feel of his front pressed to my back, his thighs hugging mine. I'd been so turned on during the ride over, that I'd actually thought about jacking off in my hotel room after I'd left Eli waiting in the gym for me while I'd changed. Now all I felt was a stark disappointment that he was pulling away from me in every way that he could. It was a feeling I should have been immune to by now and the fact that I wasn't around this man just angered me more.

By the time we reached Eli's apartment, he was off the bike before I'd even turned it off. I took the helmet he handed me, but I didn't get off the bike because I knew what he was going to say just from the way he was shifting back and forth on his feet and refusing to make eye contact with me.

"Maybe we can do dinner some other time…I'm pretty tired."

"Sure," I said, though I knew there wouldn't be 'some other time.' I was being kicked to the curb. I ignored the pain in my belly as I watched Eli head around the side of the house. I'd pulled forward enough when I'd parked the bike so that I could see the stairs leading to his apartment and I made sure he was safely inside before I started my bike up again and headed back to the hotel to get the rental car.

Because even though Eli didn't want anything to do with me, I wasn't walking away. I'd do what I did best…I'd make sure he was safe and when the threat was extinguished, I'd be the one to leave…something else I was really good at.

Chapter Six

Eli

"Darn, you win again," I said as I frowned and shook my head dejectedly at the little boy who was grinning from ear to ear.

"I'm really good," he said, his little hand coming to rest on my arm reassuringly. "I've had lots of practice."

I smiled at that and glanced at the man sitting next to the hospital bed. I shifted uncomfortably at his intense blue eyes. It wasn't that the man I only knew as Hawke scared me; it was more like every time he looked at me, he saw things I didn't want him to see. And that reminded me of Mav.

Who I was trying desperately not to think about.

And failing miserably.

"You know what, Matty?" I said as I wrote a big *M* on the piece of paper covered in Tic Tac Toe boards. "I am going to go home and practice and tomorrow I want a rematch, okay?"

"Okay," Matty said and he gave me what I could only perceive as a placating smile. Of all the kids I visited each day, Matty was one that stuck close to my heart, though I wasn't really sure why. Maybe because he had an uncanny ability to empathize with a person; it was unexpected in someone so young. But the first thing he'd asked me the day after I'd left Mav sitting on his bike in front of my apartment three days earlier was why I was so sad. And while sad might not have been the exact right word, the five-year-old boy had come pretty close to nailing what I was feeling.

Lost.

Which made no sense because I'd spent a cumulative total of a couple of hours with Mav and that was it. And what I should have been was angry.

Angry for him prying into my life. Angry that he'd seen the things I'd worked so hard to hide. Angry that he'd let me go when I'd walked away from him.

I started to rise from my chair when Matty held his arms out expectantly. I leaned down and carefully hugged him, mindful of the central line in his chest. I felt tears sting my eyes as I always did when I said my goodbyes to one of the half dozen kids I visited. I'd never known true strength until the day I'd walked through the doors of the ICS unit and seen the smiling faces, little bald heads and frail bodies of the kids who'd been handed the raw deal of being stricken with cancer. And this particular little boy had wormed his way into my heart even further. Maybe because of his compassion or his obsession with superheroes, I wasn't really sure. I knew part of it was the men who'd banded around him to form a family and that reminded me of the family I'd always dreamed of being a real part of…of the men who'd saved me and showed me what family was even when there wasn't a shared drop of blood between you.

"I'll see you tomorrow, okay?" I said to Matty as I released him and stood.

Matty nodded and then did something I wasn't expecting. He lifted his Spiderman doll and said, "Do you want to borrow Spidey?"

"I…um…don't you need him?" I stuttered, completely flustered.

Matty glanced over at Hawke before turning his attention back on me. "He helps people," Matty said as he held the doll out expectantly. "Papa was sad but now he's happy," Matty explained, though I had no idea what he meant.

I lifted my eyes to look at Hawke and he gave me a small nod. I took the doll from Matty and shook my head and then leaned down to give him another hug. "I'll take good care of him," I murmured.

I held Matty for a little longer than necessary, but the little boy didn't seem to mind and when I finally let him go, he was grinning again. I stepped around his bed and started to leave the room when Hawke stood and said, "Are you heading out? I'll walk with you…I left something in my car."

I'd made it a habit of making Matty my last visit of the day because I inevitably ended up spending more time with him than the other kids, so it didn't surprise me that Hawke knew I was heading home after the visit. What did surprise me was that this was the second time in three days the man had "forgotten" something in his car.

"Matty, I'll be back in a few minutes, okay?"

"Okay," Matty responded and I saw him flip open a coloring book that was on the tray in front of him.

Hawke followed me out of the room and spoke to the man standing guard outside. "Dante, you mind sitting with him for a bit?" Hawke asked.

The good looking young man's eyes slid over me for a moment before he nodded and turned to go into the room. I hadn't missed the man checking me out on more than one occasion, but surprisingly, the looks never made me uncomfortable; not like so many of the men who often leered at me. With them I was always propelled back to the past when men used to size me up as they decided if I was worth the money I was charging for them to use my body in any way they wanted. With Dante, it was more like he was appreciating something, though I really didn't know what.

But even though there wasn't that discomfort I'd expected to feel, there wasn't anything else either.

Not like what I felt whenever Mav's eyes raked over my body.

Even the thought of his dark green eyes touching every part of me had my body drawing up tight with excitement. Fuck! How could I miss something I'd never had?

"You're really good with him," Hawke said to me as we made our way towards the parking garage.

"He's an amazing kid," I murmured. "You and your partner must be really proud," I said.

The smile that spread across Hawke's face was distracting because it changed his entire countenance. With the burn scars that marred his cheek and neck, he always had an air of danger about him but now he looked...

He looked like all the men and women in my family after they'd found their other halves.

"That's all on Tate," Hawke said.

I'd met Matty's other father several times, but lately it had been Hawke who was with Matty when I did my rounds.

"Is Matty..." I began, but then hesitated when I realized the man might not like the question I'd been about to ask.

"Is he what?" Hawke asked.

"Nothing," I murmured. "It isn't any of my business."

"Eli, I know how much you care about him. Ask your question. It's fine."

I hesitated, but my concern for Matty was greater than my need to not make this man angry by asking intrusive questions. "Matty, is he in danger?" I asked. "I mean, there's always someone outside his door like Dante or Mav..."

My voice dropped off as I said Mav's name and I hoped to God that Hawke hadn't noticed.

"It's just a precaution. Some guys from mine and Tate's past posed a threat a couple of months back and we're just making sure they didn't have any friends who might want to take up their cause now that they're gone."

The fact that he used the word "gone" was an ominous sign, but I ignored that as my concern for Matty and his family grew. I stopped, forcing Hawke to stop as well and when he faced me I said, "There's a security firm out here – they're really good. I know the guys who own it. If you need help, I could talk to them."

Hawke studied me for a moment and then said, "Thank you. We're covered right now, but if we need any more guys, we'll take you up on that."

I nodded and began walking again. My thoughts drifted to where they'd been for the last three days and once we reached the stairwell to the garage, I found the courage to ask, "Did he ask you to do this?"

"Do what?"

"Walk me to my car," I murmured. I glanced at Hawke who was watching me curiously. "Two days ago you also forgot something in your car and yesterday Matty's grandfather conveniently happened to be leaving at the same time I was and also happened to be parked on the same level as me."

I hadn't talked to Magnus DuCane who, at forty some years old, seemed nothing like any grandfather I'd ever known. The man had the build of a football player and the only hint of his age were the threads of silver in his dark hair.

We'd reached the bottom of the stairs where I'd been attacked nearly two weeks earlier. "Mav told you what happened, didn't he?"

Hawke studied me for a moment and then reached past me to open the door to the garage itself. "He told me," he finally confirmed.

Disappointment went through me as I wondered what else Mav had told this man about me. But I couldn't help but feel a sliver of gratitude too. Because even though I'd felt a modicum of control return to me after learning the self-defense moves, I was still terrified every time I entered this same stairwell. And the idea that Mav was still looking out for me even when he wasn't around...

"Did he leave?" I asked as Hawke and I walked to my car.

"He took this week off," Hawke responded. "I think he had plans to explore the coast. Head down to California."

"But he's coming back," I said, hoping I'd managed to hide the mix of disappointment and eagerness in my voice.

"Not sure," Hawke responded as he glanced around the parking garage. I bit back the urge to question him further.

"Thanks," I managed to say as I climbed into my car.

"See you tomorrow."

My throat hurt too much so I just nodded and closed the door. I wasn't sure what I'd expected after I'd dismissed Mav like I had. I'd been humiliated and horrified that he'd found out what I'd done to survive as a kid and all I'd wanted to do in that moment was escape and go hide somewhere until I could pull myself together. But now?

I missed him.

The revelation was so startling that I could only sit there in my car, the key in the ignition, my foot pressing the clutch down.

How was that even possible?

I didn't even realize Hawke was still in the garage until he tapped on my window. I swallowed hard and rolled the window down.

"Everything okay?" Hawke asked.

"Yeah," I said quickly as I started the car. "Thanks." Even to my own ears, my voice sounded unnaturally scratchy and uneven.

I hated how the man seemed to be able to look through me, so I quickly rolled my window up, gave him a brief wave and a smile that I had no doubt he could see through and backed the car out of its spot. It was a monumental effort to keep my attention on the road for the short drive home that was made longer because of the evening rush hour traffic. I forced myself to think about other things like needing to find a job for the rest of the summer so I could have as much money saved up before school started in the fall, but it was a wasted effort because my thoughts kept going back to Mav and the way he'd looked at me when I'd handed him the motorcycle helmet.

He'd looked so…hurt.

Which hadn't made sense, so I was sure I'd seen something that wasn't there. Only I couldn't shake the feeling that he'd somehow seen my need to escape his presence as a rejection of sorts.

My phone going off was a momentary distraction and I felt my gut clench as I searched it out. A mix of relief and disappointment went through me when I saw the name *Dom* appear on the screen. I knew I needed to answer it, but even as I let my thumb hover over the answer button, I couldn't make myself press it. I suspected he was calling to invite me to dinner this weekend and based on what Brennan had told me the day I'd been assaulted, it was likely the welcome home party that Dom and Logan were trying to put together for me.

I knew I couldn't keep putting him off, but the idea of spending an extended amount of time with Dom, Logan and the rest of what once had been my surrogate family left me cold. If they knew what I'd done…

The shame was like hot coals searing my insides and I actually felt a wave of nausea roll through me. I opened the windows in hopes of taking in enough air to stave off the impending panic attack. If I could just get home before it hit, Baby would be there to ease me out of it. My frequent panic attacks right after Dom had taken me off the streets were the reason he'd gifted me with the big dog. Because the security I couldn't find in another person's arms, I could easily find in my dog.

Except there had been one set of arms that had made the pain in my chest recede, that had made the air rush back into my starved lungs…

I remembered the words Mav had whispered in my ear as his big arms had held me close and his broad chest had blanketed my back. I hadn't understood a word he'd said since he'd been speaking a different language, but just the sound of his deep voice in my ear had given me something to concentrate on and I'd focused on how right it had felt to have our bodies perfectly aligned rather than the terror that came with feeling like I couldn't breathe.

The pressure that had slowly been building in my chest began to ease and I let my mind wander to all the many times Mav had touched me, both a few days ago and the day of the assault. Except for that moment in the garage when I'd reverted back to my old ways, I hadn't felt dirty when Mav had touched me. I hadn't wanted him to stop. I hadn't obsessed over saying or doing something to inadvertently turn him on. Even after he'd admitted that he knew I'd sold myself for money, I hadn't sensed the disgust that he should have felt.

And yet I'd still run from him.

I shook my head and tightened my fingers on the steering wheel. It didn't matter. It would have been foolish to pursue something with the man, even friendship. Because just like with Dom, Logan and the rest of my family, he'd be disgusted if he found out the truth.

But those thoughts lasted about as long as it took for me to form them because at that exact moment I was pulling onto my street and there was no way to miss Mav leaning negligently against a car that was parked right in front of my apartment.

I barely managed to take my eyes off of him long enough to get my car parked behind his and get out of it, grabbing Matty's Spiderman doll as I did. And when he began walking towards me, I had to fist my hands to keep them from shaking. I resisted the urge to throw my arms around him and instead crossed my arms in front of me, tucking my hands under my armpits as best as I could with the doll clutched in one of them. "Hi."

"Hey," Mav murmured, his eyes pinning me in place in a way that his touch couldn't. My body was thrumming with excitement at how close he was standing to me and I desperately wished he'd lean in and kiss me.

"Hawke...Hawke said you were on vacation."

"No," was all Mav said and then he leaned in. Not to kiss me, but to brace his hand on the car next to my head. The move had his body just inches from mine and I automatically dropped my arms. Because if he did take what I could see in his eyes that he wanted, I needed my arms free so I could wrap them around him in case he tried to change his mind.

"Is that dinner invitation still open?" Mav whispered.

I swallowed hard and nodded. "Yeah," I said after what seemed like forever to find my voice.

"Good," Mav responded and then he was straightening and I felt the loss instantly. I turned around long enough to lock my car and I forced myself not to look back as Mav followed me to my apartment. Even though he was at least a couple feet behind me, it felt like his body was brushing mine with every step I took. Though I'd been with more men that I could count, I'd never once felt desire. Sure, there had been times when my body had physically responded, but that had been nothing like what I was feeling now. My skin felt itchy and too tight for my body and it felt like sparks of electricity were going off deep inside my body. My earlier panic had completely dissipated the moment I'd seen Mav and now all I felt was an incredible rush of heat and longing that was so fierce, I actually felt a moment of fear that there was something seriously wrong with me.

By the time we reached the landing at the top of the stairs and I felt the heat of Mav's body at my back, I was a knot of need, and instead of turning the key in the lock once I managed to get it inserted, I just held there and tried to get control of my erratic breathing.

"What's wrong?" Mav asked.

I could only shake my head as my brain and my body warred with one another.

"Eli," Mav whispered.

If he hadn't touched me at the same time, I would have been fine. I would have been able to just collect myself, turn the key in the lock and go inside and make dinner for him like it was something I did every day. But when his fingers settled on my upper arm, I let out a rush of air and turned around and leaned back against the door.

Mav's head was already slightly bent and I wondered if he'd known what I was thinking or if he'd been planning to kiss the back of my neck like he had that day in the garage after he'd spoken the foreign words to me.

We both just held there and I knew just by the way Mav was watching me that if I wanted this, I'd have to take it. The concept was so foreign to me that I wasn't sure I could go through with it.

But when Mav shifted just the tiniest bit like he was going to back away, I reached up to snag him by the back of the neck and I held him there as I lifted enough so I could brush my mouth over his. The contact lasted a split second, no more. But the impact was devastating.

Because I'd long ago learned to stop wanting something I couldn't have.

Only my body didn't care because the electricity that was lighting up every one of my cells, the fire that was threatening to consume me – it all collided together in a rush and I was leaning in for another taste before I could even consider what it might cost me.

Chapter Seven

Mav

Nothing I'd conjured up in my head could have prepared me for how good Eli's lips felt. Every pass of his lips over mine was brief and hesitant and while I ached to taste more of him, my brain maintained a shred of sanity as his lack of experience became more evident. I could tell he wanted more as his mouth started to brush mine with more urgency and his fingers dug into the back of my neck where he was still holding on to me, but it wasn't until he separated from me just the tiniest bit and brokenly whispered, "I don't know how to do this," that my suspicion was confirmed.

He'd never kissed anyone before.

A rush of primal need surged through me as I realized I was this first for him, but I tamped down on the need to slam my mouth down on his and claim him the way I wanted. "That was fucking amazing," I responded and it was the complete and absolute truth. I ghosted a kiss over his trembling lips before saying, "Can I show you?"

Eli clearly understood what I was asking because he nodded. He squeezed his eyes closed as I kissed him again and when I ran my tongue over the seam of his lips, he let out a startled gasp and

88

reflexively opened his mouth even as he pulled back from me. With the door at his back he had nowhere to go, but instead of plunging my tongue into his mouth like I wanted, I kept up the tender kisses. Every time I gave his supple mouth the tiniest of licks, he sucked in a breath. But instead of closing his lips, he let them part just a little more each time and when I finally dipped inside, he let out a big sigh and I felt his free hand come up to rest on my shoulder, the Spiderman doll pressed against my shoulder blade.

I bit back the rush of lust that went through me as the sweetness of Eli's taste dripped over my tongue and focused instead on giving him what he needed. The first time I stroked my tongue over his, he flinched, but by the third and fourth time, his tongue was seeking mine out. Within a matter of minutes, Eli was hungrily kissing me back and as I experimentally drew back, he followed until he was pressed flush against my body. I wrapped my arms around him to hold him in place as I finally kissed him the way I'd been longing to and he eagerly met every thrust of my tongue. My cock filled fast and when I tried to put some space between our bodies so we could both catch our breaths, Eli refused to release me and his tongue was pushing into my mouth. My good intentions fled as my body lit up like a brush fire and I slammed Eli back against the door and held him there with my body. I grabbed his ass with my hands and lifted him enough so his mouth was level with mine and I used my hips to hold him against the wood as I began thrusting against him.

The excited, needy whimpers spilling from Eli's throat were killing me and if it hadn't been for a catcall coming from the street, I would have been reaching for his zipper then and there. Eli and I separated long enough so that we could both look towards the front of the building where a guy walking his dog was watching us and giving us a thumbs up. While the man continued on his way, the spell was broken and Eli tugged free of my grip. I expected him to panic or try to escape me, but instead he leaned back against the door and brushed his fingers over his mouth. His eyes were bright with desire and something else, but before I could question him, he turned around and unlocked the door. I was sure he was going to tell me he'd changed his mind about dinner, but instead of closing the door, he left it open as he walked into the apartment. I followed him in and watched him drop down to wrap his arms around Baby before getting up and going to the kitchen. Baby came to greet me and while I ran my fingers over his sleek body, I kept my eyes on Eli who was pulling things from the refrigerator.

He finally stopped and looked at me and then smiled. It wasn't a smile I'd ever seen from him before, but I liked it and I couldn't help but grin myself. I should have been regretting the kiss because knowing what I now knew about Eli, I was even more certain that any kind of relationship, physical or otherwise, would mean something more to him than it would to someone else…someone like me.

But I couldn't bring myself to wish it hadn't happened. Even now, I was barely refraining from striding up to him and finishing what we'd started.

"Do you want something to drink?" Eli asked. "I have beer, soda, water."

"A beer would be great," I said as closed the door behind me. Eli handed me the bottle of beer and our eyes held for a moment before he dropped his gaze and started working on dinner. "What are you making?" I asked.

"Chicken Enchiladas. Is that okay?"

"Sounds great," I said. "Can I help?"

"No," Eli responded, casting me a look over his shoulder. "It's pretty easy to make. And besides," – he shot me another quick grin – "It's my mother's secret recipe. If I told you what was in it, I'd have to kill you."

I chuckled and said, "Fair enough." I dropped down into one of the kitchen chairs and focused my attention on the big dog who dropped his massive head in my lap. "How did you end up naming a dog like this Baby?" I asked.

"He came with the name," Eli said as he worked. "He used to belong to Dom. His wife named him that."

"Dom gave him to you?"

Eli nodded. "After Dom found me…"

His voice trailed off for a moment and I saw him pause what he was doing. But then he seemed to shake off whatever had brought him down and said, "After Dom found me, I started having panic attacks. Baby was able to bring me out of them. When Dom brought my mom back to Seattle and helped us find a place to live, he told me he didn't have time to give Baby all the attention he needed and asked me if I'd take care of him for a while."

"He sounds like a great guy," I said softly.

"He is…they all are."

"They?"

"Dom, Logan, Dom's brothers, their partners and kids – it's a big family," Eli said with a small laugh.

"I'll bet you missed them when you left."

Eli glanced at me. "You know about that?"

I was glad that he didn't appear angry at the reminder of the research I'd done on him. "I know the basics. Your mom got married and you left for college a couple years later. Johns Hopkins, right?"

Eli nodded. "Yeah, they had a great pre-med program."

"And a great medical school. Why come back here to go to medical school? I mean, you got accepted to one of the finest medical schools in the country and your mom and her husband had moved to DC…"

There was a slight pause as Eli worked, but he didn't look at me and it took him a while to answer. He finally said, "It's a different world out there."

I waited for him to expand on his statement, but he remained mute as he started chopping several green onions.

"Can I ask you something?"

"Okay," Eli answered quietly. I hated hearing the reservation in his voice.

"The guy who stopped by here the other day…Brennan. Is he your boyfriend?"

Eli stopped what he was doing and turned to face me, butcher knife in hand. "What?"

Jealousy wasn't a great color on me, but the idea of Eli and the good looking young man together had been driving me crazy from the moment Brennan had entered the apartment like he'd had every right to do so. And while I'd suspected I'd been the first one to ever kiss Eli, I wasn't completely sure and it didn't mean he wasn't pursuing a relationship with the other man. I dropped my eyes to focus on the hand I was still running over Baby's head. "I mean, it's okay if he is. That kiss-"

"Please don't," Eli suddenly interjected and I snapped my eyes up at the desperate plea.

"Don't what?" I asked.

"Don't say it shouldn't have happened." Eli walked towards me, the knife still in his hand. He finally remembered the knife when he reached me and lowered it to the table.

It was what I'd been about to say, but not because I meant it. But because I'd been trying to pass it off as something inconsequential. I straightened in the chair and barely noticed when Baby removed his head and flopped to the floor near my feet. "Why not?" I whispered as I bit back the urge to reach for Eli who was standing so close, his legs were nearly touching my knees.

"Just don't, okay?"

I nodded. "Okay." And then I was reaching for him and when I tugged him onto my lap, he came willingly and without hesitation. Neither of us spoke as we just stared at each other and I wasn't sure which of us moved first, but when our mouths finally met, I felt all the tension drain from my body. I let my hands coast up and down Eli's back as his fingers threaded through my hair. The kiss was deep but unhurried and we took turns exploring each other's mouths. Eli finally pulled back, his face flushed with color.

"Brennan is a friend…a brother really," Eli murmured. "There's no one…no boyfriend. There never has been."

I shouldn't have been glad to hear that, but I couldn't deny the thrill that went through me. But even as my body ached to take more of what Eli was very clearly offering, warning bells began ringing in my head. He'd basically confirmed my guess that he wasn't the kind of guy to just fuck around and since I wasn't the kind of guy to do anything but fuck around, there was no place for us to go. I was trying to figure out the right thing to say when Eli tensed up and I had no doubt he'd picked up on my hesitation. He slipped off my lap and I instantly missed the feel of his warm body.

"Are you okay if I make the enchiladas a little spicy?" Eli asked casually as he grabbed the knife off the table and returned to his preparation.

"Sure," I managed to say, but my brain was working in overdrive as I realized how badly I'd fucked this up. My plan had been to just watch Eli from a distance as I'd been doing from the moment I'd dropped him off three days earlier. The rental car had made surveillance easier and had allowed me to grab a couple of hours of sleep here and there while Eli was volunteering at the hospital. Since I couldn't have eyes on him in the hospital, I'd asked Hawke to make sure Eli didn't walk unaccompanied to his car each day and while the other man hadn't questioned my request, I hadn't missed the curiosity in his voice when he'd agreed. I hadn't told Ronan or anyone for that matter that I'd forgone my vacation so that I could keep eyes on Eli since I didn't want to have to explain my motives to anyone. Hell, I didn't want to have to explain them to myself. But when Hawke had called me an hour ago to tell me how upset Eli had seemed after he'd told Eli he wasn't sure if I was coming back to Seattle, I hadn't been able to stop myself from interacting with him again.

The tension in the air was stiff and awkward and I was desperate to get Eli talking again. And if I was lucky, smiling too.

"Why the volunteering?"

Eli glanced at me and I clarified, "Why are you volunteering in the ICS unit at the hospital?"

"I was thinking about pursuing pediatric oncology as a specialty. One of my professors at Johns Hopkins suggested I work with the kids a little bit before deciding for sure. Mentally and emotionally speaking, it's one of the hardest specialties out there."

"So why pursue it?" I asked.

Eli paused in what he was doing, but didn't face me. "Kids like Matty, they have to be so strong, you know? They need as many people in their corner as they can get. I want to be one of those people."

I glanced at the Spiderman doll Eli had put down on the kitchen table.

"That kid," I said with a chuckle as I reached for the doll.

I caught Eli watching me as I studied the doll. "How do you know him? Matty and his family, I mean."

"Hawke and I work together," I hedged.

Eli turned to face me, but instead of asking what I did, he said, "Hawke said Matty might be in danger."

"It's just a precaution. Chances are the friends of the guys who tried to hurt him and Tate and Hawke won't try anything. We're just covering all the bases."

"Were you there?"

Since I had to be careful about how much I said, I merely nodded. But inside my gut was churning because to this day, the memory of having to throw my knife just inches over Matty's head so it could divert the path of the bullet that had been meant for Hawke left me cold inside. Hawke had done his part to make sure Matty didn't move, but it had still been way too close.

"That kid idolizes you," Eli said and I was surprised when he came up to me and took the doll from my hand and examined it. "I like how he calls you Thor."

"I know," I said with a laugh. "It's the hair," I added.

Eli didn't join me in the joke. Instead he looked at my hair and then dropped his eyes to mine. "No, it's not."

My insides tightened at that and I was tempted to drag him down on my lap again. Better yet, I wanted to lay him down on the table and feast on every part of his body.

"Why did he give him to you?" I asked as I motioned to the doll in the hopes of distracting myself from my thoughts.

"I think he thought I was sad."

"Were you?"

Eli's eyes shifted to me for a moment before returning to the doll. "He's observant, isn't he? For someone so young." That was all I got before Eli carried the doll over to the kitchen counter and set him near the coffee pot. We didn't speak again until he'd put the food in the oven. He grabbed himself a beer from the fridge and dropped down in the chair next to mine. "Can I ask you something?"

I nodded.

"The words you spoke to me in the garage. What language was that?"

I stiffened at the unexpected question. It was a part of my life I never talked about and even the idea of bringing it up now made me feel sick. Eli seemed to notice my discomfort because he quickly said, "I'm sorry, I shouldn't have asked that." His body went stiff with tension and I could see him shutting down so when he made a move to get up, I grabbed his hand to keep him from moving.

I didn't know why, but I wanted to give him something of myself. I just hadn't thought it would be this part that I'd let him see.

Chapter Eight

Eli

"It's Lakota."

I relaxed as I realized Mav wasn't going to dismiss my question, but I was disappointed when his fingers eased their hold on my wrist and then disappeared entirely. I was still reeling from our second kiss and as much as I needed time to just process what it all meant, I found that now that I'd had a chance to touch Mav, that was all I wanted to be doing.

"You're Native American?" I asked.

"I'm half Native American…on my mother's side. My father was white…or at least my mother thinks he was."

I didn't miss the bitterness in his voice and I knew I was treading perilously close to a sensitive subject so I resisted asking the question I really wanted to and said, "Would you say them in English?"

Mav hesitated for so long that I was tempted to take back the question, but I held my tongue as he seemed to physically brace himself. His voice was rich and deep as he spoke, but I didn't miss the pained tone.

"Oh, Great Spirit, whose voice I hear in the winds.

And whose breath gives life to all the world.

Hear me! I am small and weak.

I need your strength and wisdom.

Let me walk in beauty, and make my eyes

Ever hold the red and purple sunset.

Make my hands respect the things you have made.

My ears sharp to hear your voice.

Make me wise so that I may understand

The things you might teach me.

Let me learn the lessons you have hidden

In every leaf and rock.

I seek strength, not to be greater than my brother.

But to fight my greatest enemy, myself.

Make me always ready to come to you

With clear hands and straight eyes.

So when life fades, as the fading sunset.

My spirit may come to you without shame."

Once he was done, Mav refused to look at me, but I sensed it was more because he was lost in thought rather than anything else.

The words clearly meant something to him. "Is that some kind of poem?" I asked.

"It's a prayer…to Wakan Tanka, the Great Spirit. The Lakota culture has deep roots in faith and believe in thanking the Great Spirit for everything on Earth."

"Did your mother teach you that prayer?"

Mav lifted his eyes and shook his head. "She wasn't around much when I was growing up. A friend taught me. I was hoping…" His voice trailed off and he dropped his eyes.

I knew I should let it go, but the pain coming off the man in front of me was palpable and I felt an almost unbearable need to take it from him. "You were hoping what?" I asked as I leaned forward and settled my hands over his where they were fisted on his lap.

"I was hoping to impress my grandfather. He ran the museum and cultural center on the reservation and was really traditional." Mav let out a harsh chuckle. "I spent hours and hours getting it perfect."

"What happened?"

"Like I said, traditional. Pure blood only."

I didn't need any more details to know the encounter had had a detrimental effect on this man. His bitter tone and stiff body were enough to tell me his childhood probably hadn't been a good one.

"Did you live on a reservation?"

Mav nodded. "Off and on when I was a kid."

"Where?"

"Pine Ridge, South Dakota."

"Does your mom still live there?"

"No, she took off when she was eighteen. Got pregnant with me and went back for a while before leaving again. I met my grandfather for the first time when I was six. She left me with him every time she'd meet a new guy. Sometimes she'd come back for me and take me with her for a little while, but as soon as the next guy came along, she'd take me back to the reservation. Last time I talked to her, she'd hooked up with some car salesman in Jersey or something."

"You don't talk to her much?"

He shook his head and then gently pulled one of his hands free of mine so he could grab his beer and take a long drink. "She calls me when she needs money."

"And your grandfather?"

"Still on the rez as far as I know," Mav murmured. "Haven't seen him since I was sixteen."

I could tell Mav was nearing the end of his patience with the topic so I did the only thing I could think of and leaned forward and kissed him. "Thank you," I whispered against his lips before kissing him once more. I went to pull back again, but he gently grabbed me by the back of the neck.

"For what?" Mav asked.

"For telling me," I murmured before brushing my lips over his. "For coming to dinner." Another kiss. "For being there that day in the stairwell." Every kiss grew a little deeper than the last and by the time I whispered, "For being my first kiss," Mav had his free arm around my waist and was pulling me to my feet as he stood. His eyes held mine for several long seconds, and then his mouth slammed down on mine and he took complete control of the kiss.

Like when we'd been outside, his big palms skimmed my ass before kneading both globes and then he was lifting me. He set me on the table and immediately used his body to maneuver me so I was lying flat on my back. I registered glass breaking on the floor and realized it was one or both of our bottles of beer. Not that I gave a shit because Mav's mouth was consuming mine so ferociously that nothing outside of the two of us existed. Mav grabbed hold of my hands and pinned them to the table and held me that way as his mouth plundered mine. When he pulled back from me, I tried to follow, but with him holding me down, I was completely helpless to do anything but lay there as he stared at me. I should have been frightened by the power he held over me in that moment, but all I was was incredibly turned on. My dick was already hard and pressing painfully against the confines of my pants and the need that was firing through my body was bordering on this side of uncomfortable.

"Please, Mav," I whispered when it seemed like he wasn't going to do anything other than hover over me, his emerald eyes fixed on mine.

"Please what?" Mav asked, his voice hoarse.

"I don't know," I said honestly. And I didn't. I knew I needed relief and while I knew where this encounter was leading, I still couldn't fathom that any sexual act would take away the growing coil of want that was burning through my gut. But I knew without a shadow of a doubt that the only one who could give me what I needed was this man.

Mav leaned down to kiss me and I felt him transfer both my wrists to just one of his hands above my head. His tongue continued to play with mine as his long fingers skimmed down my chest, abdomen and groin. The touch was too fleeting and I tried to buck my hips up in hopes of encouraging him to continue the contact. But instead, his hand flattened on my belly and then began pushing the hem of my shirt up. I jumped when his palm came in contact with my skin and then I was moaning into his mouth as he used his thumb to test the muscles there. His mouth left mine to trail a path of kisses down my cheek and neck while his hand pushed my shirt even higher. I struggled to pull my hands free, but not because I was afraid. But because I was so desperate for more of him.

I was about to start begging him some more when I felt his hand slide back down my stomach and not stop there and I tensed up in anticipation. I cried out in relief when his hand rubbed over my dick, but when he pulled his hand away just as quickly I yelled, "No, please, don't stop!"

"Shhh, I'm going to take care of you," Mav said against my mouth and then he was kissing me again. I felt his fingers fumble with the button and zipper on my pants for a moment and then his big hand was plunging into my pants and underwear in one swift move. If he hadn't still been kissing me, I would have screamed at the pure pleasure that raced through me when his rough palm encircled my dick. Electricity sparked under my skin and shimmied up my spine as Mav began stroking me with hard, long drags of his rough hand. I was on sensation overload as he worked both my mouth and my cock at the same time and I didn't even have time to say anything before my orgasm slammed into me without warning a few seconds later.

I'd jerked myself off plenty of times over the years, but it was nothing like what was happening to me in that moment. I had no control of my body or even my mind. Nothing existed except for the wave of pleasure that crashed through me as the coil of need inside of me snapped. My body jerked and thrashed uncontrollably as hot liquid sprayed all over my abdomen and groin and I felt tears prick my eyes as Mav whispered, "So fucking beautiful," in my ear.

I hadn't even realized he'd stopped kissing me at that point and that the low keening sound I was hearing was coming from me. The orgasm seemed to go on forever and it wasn't until my body stopped spasming that I finally dragged in the air I so badly needed. Mav's mouth was back on mine, but his kisses were short and sweet. His hand still had a hold of my dick, but he was gently massaging me through the aftershocks that were still hitting my sated, tingling body.

I suspected the entire encounter hadn't lasted more than a couple of minutes, considering how quickly I'd come after Mav had touched my cock, but it felt like hours before the aftermath of my climax had eased enough for me to come to my senses.

"You okay?" Mav asked as he released my hands and ran his fingers through my hair. His hand was still down my pants, but he wasn't stroking my ultra-sensitive dick any more.

I managed a nod and did my best to kiss Mav back when his lips sought out mine again. He kept the kiss brief and then I watched in fascination as he brought his other hand up to his mouth and began licking the sticky, white fluid from it. I'd always hated the taste of cum, but watching Mav consume mine like it was some kind of delicacy had me wondering if things would be different when I tasted his.

When.

I couldn't even be sure there would be a when. I'd interrupted Mav earlier when he'd been about to say our kiss had been a mistake, but I had no doubt that was what he'd planned on telling me. It was true that I hadn't ever been in any kind of relationship before, but I was smart enough to know that not every kiss, even what seemed like an epic one to me, was anything more than just that…a kiss. Even what had just happened between us didn't mean it was anything more than a random sexual encounter.

After Mav cleaned off his hand, he pulled me up to a sitting position. I couldn't tell what he was thinking, but it was impossible to miss the bulge in his pants. Guilt went through me that I hadn't even once though about Mav's pleasure as he'd been bringing me mine. I automatically reached for the button on his pants, but he stopped me by grabbing my hands in his.

"You don't want me to…" I asked awkwardly.

Mav studied me for a moment and then lifted my hands to his lips. He kissed the backs of each one before releasing them and leaning forward to seal his mouth over mine. When he pulled back he said, "This was about you. Only you."

I felt tears threatening to fall at that so all I managed was a nod because I didn't trust myself to speak.

"Why don't you get cleaned up and I'll clean up out here?"

I looked down on the floor and sure enough, our activities had caused both bottles of beer to hit the floor. Luckily only one had broken and it was in large pieces instead of hundreds of tiny ones. "Are you sure?"

Mav nodded and helped me stand. I could feel my cum cooling all over my stomach and seeping into the fabric of my underwear. "There are some cleaning supplies under the sink," I murmured as I turned to head towards my bedroom. With my passion cooling, the embarrassment started to seep in and I was eager to escape Mav so I could regroup. Once I reached my bathroom, I stripped off all my clothes and got in the shower. As I washed myself, memories of Mav's touch started to return and I actually felt the hunger building deep inside of me again. I shook my head in amazement and then quickly finished cleaning up and changed into fresh clothes. I had no idea how we'd go back to any kind of regular conversation after what had just happened, but there was no way around it so I headed back to the kitchen. The floor was clean and the broken glass gone by the time I got back. But I didn't see Mav. I felt a surge of panic that he'd left, but then I sensed his presence and looked to my right towards the living room. And then all my panic came rushing back.

Because in Mav's hand was the picture on the bookshelf – the one I kept turned over for a reason. And I knew just by looking at the expression on Mav's face that he finally had the answer he'd been looking for from the moment we'd encountered each other in that stairwell.

Chapter Nine

Mav

I shouldn't have looked at the picture.

I'd known even as I'd walked towards the bookcase, my eyes zeroing in on the overturned picture frame, that it would destroy what little trust I'd managed to build with Eli. But I'd done it anyway because as beautiful and perfect as the last few minutes with him had been, none of that negated my first priority.

His safety.

I hadn't planned any of what had happened with Eli. Maybe it was because he'd initiated the kisses between us that had started it all. Maybe it was hearing him admit that I'd been the first one to kiss him. I hadn't known and I hadn't cared. All I'd cared about was getting my hands on him. I'd been close to coming myself as Eli had bucked and jerked beneath me as I'd pulled his orgasm to the surface, but the prospect of being able to watch him as he came had made it possible for me to hold off. Sure, I'd been painfully uncomfortable afterwards, but it had been worth it because I'd never seen anyone be so completely consumed with pleasure the way Eli had been.

But all that pleasure was gone now and the old fear was back. And even if it hadn't been written all over Eli's face, the way Baby was pressed up against Eli's legs, his big tongue licking over Eli's lax fingers, was evidence enough.

We both held there for several long seconds and then Eli finally stepped forward and took the picture from me. He didn't look at it as he returned it to its spot on the bookcase. But instead of turning it over, he left the picture upright.

"Why couldn't you just leave it alone?" Eli whispered.

"Look Eli, I get it," I said as I reached out to put my hand on his shoulder. "He's your father…"

"Stepfather," Eli cut in and then he was stepping away from me. "And you don't get anything."

"Then explain it to me," I said. "If he's done this before-"

"No," Eli bit out. "I told you it was a misunderstanding. It was a one-time thing. He was upset."

"About what?"

But Eli shook his head and then wrapped his arms around his body. "I want you to leave," he said softly, though he refused to look me in the eye when he said it. I ignored him and closed the distance between us, but the second I touched him he yanked himself away from me and shouted, "Get out!"

"Eli-"

The young man was clearly in a rage because he shoved at me hard with both hands and bit out, "I don't want you here!" I managed to grab Eli's arms before he could lash out at me again, but when he whispered, "I don't want you," something inside of me cracked and I released him. The pain in my chest began radiating out in waves and I actually had to bend over and force in several deep breaths before I could get control of myself.

"Mav…"

I ignored the mix of shock and worry I heard in Eli's voice and began hurrying towards the door.

"Mav, wait, please!"

Eli went around the other side of the loveseat and placed himself in my path, but I was in such a fury that I easily pushed past him. Even as the wound inside of me began to bleed, I managed to stay calm.

Until Eli grabbed me.

"Mav-"

I turned on him without warning and grabbed him by the upper arms. Fear flashed in his eyes as I forced him back several steps until his back hit the wall near the hallway leading to his bedroom. But he didn't fight me or try to escape and I could feel his fingers biting into my arms where he was holding on to me.

"I'm sorry," Eli whispered as he shook his head.

Anger flooded my entire system, but more so because of the pity I saw in his eyes. He knew what his words had done to me.

"Fuck you, Eli," I spat and I quickly released him and tried to step back.

But Eli held on to me and dragged me as close as his limited strength would allow. "Mav, please, I'm sorry," he murmured and it wasn't until I felt his hand close around the back of my neck that I realized at some point he'd let go of my arm and I hadn't even noticed. The pads of Eli's fingers began massaging the base of my neck, and it wasn't until my lips were hovering near his that I realized I hadn't fought his effort to pull my head down.

"I didn't mean that," Eli said softly and then his lips skimmed mine. "I swear I didn't mean it."

He kissed me again, but as much as I wanted to take what he was offering, his dismissive words still rang in my ears.

I don't want you.

When Eli went to kiss me again, I turned my head to the side so his mouth couldn't make contact with mine. I could tell my actions were distressing him because as I pulled back, his eyes filled with tears.

"Mav," he whispered pleadingly.

I shook my head. It was too late.

It was too fucking late.

"Eli?"

Eli and I both turned at the sound of the man's voice as the front door swung open. While I'd never seen the man who filled the doorway in person, I knew immediately who he was and as his gaze shifted from me to Eli's tear-stained and still bruised face, I knew exactly what he was thinking.

"What the fuck is going on here?" the man snarled as he stormed into the apartment. I didn't bother resisting as he grabbed

111

me by the shirt and shoved me backwards against the wall. "What the fuck did you do to him?"

"Dom!" Eli shouted and then he was trying to put his body between mine and the other man's. Part of me wanted to tell Eli to back off because I was actually itching for a fight and Dom Barretti was clearly the kind of man who could give me what I wanted, but I remained quiet as Eli got the other man's attention.

"He's a friend, Dom!" Eli said quickly.

Dom released his hold on me just a little bit as his eyes drifted to Eli's face. "He hurt you," Dom muttered.

Eli shook his head emphatically. "I'm upset because I said something to him I shouldn't have."

"And that bruise?" Dom said as he finally released me and stepped back. Eli kept his body between us.

"Some guy tried to mug me last week. Mav" – Eli motioned over his shoulder at me – "stopped him."

Dom was clearly still suspicious, but he gave me the slightest nod and took several more steps back, presumably to give me and Eli a bit of privacy to finish our conversation. But since we were already finished, I pushed past Eli, ignoring the way he whispered my name, and left the apartment. My insides burned as I hurried to my rental car.

I don't want you.

My throat felt tight as I climbed behind the wheel. I tried to draw in several deep breaths so I could get myself under control, but my anger won out and I slammed my hands down on the steering wheel. The fact that I was this out of it was proof enough that I was in too deep and as I pulled the car away from the curb, I fished out my cell and hit the speed dial. I only drove around the corner so my car would be more hidden, but had enough of a view that I could still see Eli's apartment.

"What's up, Mav?" I heard Ronan say when he answered my call.

"I need you to have someone look into something for me," I said.

Ronan was quiet for a moment before saying, "Okay."

"Subject's name is Eli Galvez," I said even though my mind rebelled at using that word to describe Eli.

"Is this the kid who visits Matty?"

"Yeah," I said. I gave Ronan a rundown of the attack on Eli and that he'd admitted the man was his own stepfather. To Ronan's credit, he remained silent, but I didn't take that for lack of interest on his part. "He said the guy doesn't have a history of abuse – that it was a one-time thing."

"You don't believe him?" Ronan asked.

"Can you get someone over here to sit on his place?" I asked, ignoring Ronan's question.

"You're there now?"

I nodded and then said, "Yeah."

"I'll see what I can do," Ronan finally said. "You good there for a bit?"

No.

"Yeah."

"Okay, I'll call you back in a few."

I nodded. "Ronan."

"Yeah?" Ronan asked softly and I didn't miss the curiosity and concern in his voice.

"Can you talk to Memphis about putting me on a case?"

Ronan was quiet for a moment before saying, "Seattle no longer appealing to you?"

"You know me," was all I said. Within seconds of hanging up on Ronan, I saw Eli's door open, but instead of Dom leaving the apartment, it was actually Eli himself who was trotting down the stairs. It had been less than five minutes since I'd left.

I kept my distance as I followed Eli's car and I was surprised to find that he was driving much more aggressively than he normally did. I felt my heart drop out of my chest when I finally realized where he was going.

My hotel.

I pulled the rental car to a stop along the curb across from the hotel and shook my head in disbelief. Having Eli search me out was the last thing I'd expected. I waited several minutes to see what would happen when Eli realized I wasn't in my room, but instead of seeing his little sedan sputtering out of the parking garage, there was nothing and after fifteen minutes, my concern started to ramp up and I got out of the car and hurried into the hotel. It took just minutes to get to my room, but I was on edge the entire time as I worried that I might have missed something. What if Eli had been intercepted between my room and his car? What if his stepfather had confronted him again?

But all my panic dissipated when I saw Eli sitting on the floor in front of my hotel room door. His head was hung and he was resting his arms on his bent knees. The position reminded me of the day I'd found him in the stairwell. When he looked up at my approach, I saw a mixture of relief and concern go through him and he scrambled to his feet. I came to a stop within a couple feet of him, but I couldn't find my voice.

"I…I thought you might have left town," Eli murmured.

"What are you doing here?" I finally asked as I searched out the room key.

"I wanted to tell you how sorry I was-"

"You did that," I cut in and then moved past him to open the door.

Eli shifted back and forth on his feet. "I didn't mean what I said."

"It doesn't matter," I said, but to my surprise, Eli moved between me and the door, grabbing the handle from me, but not pushing the door any farther open.

"I don't believe you," Eli whispered. "I think it matters more than you want to admit."

I didn't respond as I studied Eli, but he never took his eyes off of me. I braced my hand against the door and added enough pressure to force Eli to release his hold on the handle. I leaned down just enough so I could keep my voice low as I said, "Make sure you understand what happens if you walk through this door…what you're agreeing to."

I nearly groaned when Eli parted his lips just a little bit so his tongue could dart out and wet them. "You'll want answers," he finally said.

"For starters."

Eli's breathing ticked up a notch before he turned and walked into the room. I felt my cock swell with anticipation as I followed him inside and closed the door. He jumped a little when the door locked, but then he turned to face me.

"Sit," I murmured as I motioned to the couch.

Eli did as I told him which had my body ratcheting up with need so I went to the fridge and got him a bottle of water. Because I didn't trust myself to sit next to him on the couch, I sat in the armchair after handing him the water. Since my warning to him about other things besides just talk happening between us had been an empty threat meant to scare him off, I willed my body to settle down. I'd get the answers I needed, pass the information on to Ronan and get the hell out of this place.

"Tell me about your stepfather," I said.

Eli dropped his eyes and remained quiet for several seconds before finally speaking. "His name is Jack Cortano. Colonel Jack Cortano."

"He's in the military?" I asked, more to keep Eli talking than anything else since I already knew the basics about the man.

Eli nodded. "He used to be the base commander at JBLM before he took a job in DC."

I knew that JBLM stood for Joint Base Lewis-McChord, a joint Army and Air Force base south of the city. "How did he and your mom meet?" I asked since Eli had fallen silent again.

"My mom worked in the accounting department at Dom's company. He was meeting Dom for lunch one day when he met my mom."

"He and Dom are friends?"

Another nod. "They were in the army together. He stayed in after Dom got out to start his business but they stayed friends."

"How old were you when he and your mom started seeing each other?"

"Fifteen. He proposed to her a few months after they met."

"Did you two get along?" I asked.

A pained expression crossed Eli's features before it slipped away and he nodded. "I'd never had a dad before and he reminded me so much of Dom." Eli rubbed at his eyes and although I didn't see any tears falling, I had no doubt the move was meant to deter them. "Even though he had kids from a previous marriage, he treated me like his own, you know?" Eli whispered. "He took me to ball games, fishing trips, all of the same stuff he did with his real sons. I even started calling him Dad. And my mom…"

Eli shook his head.

"He made her so happy. He encouraged her to get her GED, helped her learn English. She got to quit her job so she could go to

117

school full time and get a degree in psychology. She works with veterans and their families now."

"In D.C.?" I asked.

"Yeah. She and my stepfather moved there after he got a job at the Department of Defense."

"Was that when you were enrolled in Johns Hopkins?"

Eli nodded. "They moved down there my sophomore year."

"You mentioned other kids?"

"I have two stepbrothers. Nick and Caleb."

"Do they live with their mother?"

"No," Eli said as he shook his head. "She died in a car accident about a year after Jack married my mom. Caleb and Nick came to live with us after that."

"Did you get along with them?"

"They never seemed to like me much. I think they knew about my past because Nick used to call me a cocksucker whenever our parents weren't around."

I stemmed the anger that went through me. "Did your stepfather know about your childhood?"

Eli swallowed hard and nodded. "He used to always tell me it didn't matter. That no one would ever touch me like that again. Dom...Dom used to say those exact words to me."

I nodded in understanding. Jack Cortano had clearly become the father Eli had wanted Dom to be...had needed him to be. "Had your stepfather ever hurt you before?"

"No," Eli whispered, his eyes downcast. "He never raised a hand against me, never yelled at me, nothing. What happened in the stairwell…"

Eli shook his head.

"What set him off? He said something about 'staying away from him.' Do you know who he was talking about?"

"Caleb."

"Your stepbrother?"

Eli nodded. "Caleb called me the day before and left a message. The connection was really bad because I couldn't understand most of what he said, but I could tell he was crying. I tried calling him back but it kept going to voicemail. So I called Jack and asked him if Caleb was okay. He told me Caleb was having some problems right now, but that he was getting him some help. He…he asked me to give Caleb some space."

Eli lifted his eyes to look at me. "But I couldn't stop worrying about him so I called my mom. She's in Germany right now doing some work at the military hospital over there. She couldn't tell me much except to say that my stepdad was dealing with it. I called Caleb back and left him a message telling him to call me if he needed to talk. That was the morning of the attack."

"Jack confronted you in the stairwell," I ventured.

Eli nodded. "He was waiting for me by the door that led to the floor my car was parked on. He started screaming at me for not listening to him. I tried to tell him I was just worried about Caleb and he grabbed my arm and twisted it. Said he didn't want his son

119

around someone like me. Then he hit me and told me to stay away from him. He hit me again after we heard you call out and then he left."

Even now the image of a battered Eli huddled in that stairwell had my stomach twisting in anger.

"What about your other stepbrother? Nick."

Eli dropped his eyes again. "Nick overdosed a few weeks ago."

"I'm sorry," I whispered. I could tell that even though they hadn't been close, Eli wasn't unaffected by the young man's death.

"I thought that was why Caleb was calling me. He took Nick's death pretty hard. He was the one who found him."

"How old is Caleb?"

"Seventeen. Nick was nineteen."

"Do you still have Caleb's message?"

Eli nodded and pulled his phone from his pocket. He pressed several buttons and then handed me the phone. I put the phone on speaker and then hit the play button. The voice that came on was garbled, but it was clear the speaker was crying.

"Eli? Eli…Nick, it wasn't…I don't know…"

Several long seconds of pure static followed where there was no other audible noise before the young man's voice cut in again. "Eli, I'm sorry. Please."

I reached for my own phone and dialed Daisy's number. When the young woman's voice came on the line, I said, "Daisy, I'm going to send you an audio file. Can you see what you can do to clean it up?"

"Sure, you've got it."

"I also need you to run a trace on the phone. See if it's been used in the past couple of weeks and where it is right now."

"Is there a case number?"

"No," I said simply and was glad when she didn't press me.

I hung up and forwarded the voicemail message along with Caleb's number to her. I returned my attention to Eli who was looking at me with a mix of awe and hope.

"We'll find him, Eli. Make sure he's okay."

Eli nodded. "Thank you."

"So after your stepfather assaulted you in the stairwell, did you hear from him again?"

"No," Eli said.

"Until the attempted break in," I reminded him.

"It couldn't have been him," Eli said. He reached for his phone again and began looking for something. "My mom sent me this picture this morning of the two of them at an event that night. She flew home from Germany for it because it was a fundraiser she'd put together."

Eli handed me the phone. The picture showed the very well dressed couple posing for cameras and I scrolled up to check the date.

"He couldn't have been at that event and here just a couple hours later trying to break into my place," Eli said hopefully. "It had to have been just some random thing."

I didn't bother to mention that Jack could have hired someone since all it would do was scare Eli and I had no proof. And from what Eli had told me, it sounded like the man had been the perfect father up until a couple of weeks ago. With the death of one son and the breakdown of another, he clearly could have been driven over the edge with grief and fear and had taken his anger out on his stepson.

"So you didn't go to Dom because of his friendship with your stepfather," I ventured.

Eli nodded. "You saw him tonight. Dom's always been protective of me. It would kill him to know Jack was the one who hurt me."

I understood perfectly, but it wasn't something I necessarily agreed with. I was saved from having to say anything because my phone beeped. I scanned the message from Daisy and glanced up at Eli. "Caleb's phone is turned on. It's near 5th and Washington in Alexandria, Virginia."

Eli let out a sigh of relief. "That's Jack and my mom's house. That's good, right?"

I nodded absent mindedly as my mind worked. The kid's voice in the message hadn't just been upset – he'd been terrified. "You have a picture of Caleb on your phone?"

After a moment's hesitation, Eli said, "Um yeah." He got his phone back out and scrolled through it until he found what he was looking for. When he handed me the phone, I scanned the family picture in which Eli was conspicuously absent. My gaze settled on the younger of the two boys. He looked like the all-American boy next door with streaky, styled blond hair and bright blue eyes, but something about his wide smile wasn't quite right. I glanced at the older boy who looked a lot like his brother. But unlike Caleb, Nick was doing nothing to hide his disdain. For what, I wasn't sure.

I sent the picture to myself and then went a step further and programmed my number into Eli's phone. I left it on the contact screen when I handed it back to him and when he saw my name, he sent me a slight smile that made my insides jump.

"I'll have someone check this out," I murmured as I motioned to the picture on my phone.

Eli nodded. "Thank you."

We both fell silent for a moment and when I finally got up the nerve to tell him it was time for him to go, Eli shifted so he was sitting on the edge of the couch and said, "Mav, do you think we could try dinner again sometime?"

The hopeful tone in his voice had me cursing myself. "I'm not so sure that's a good idea," I hedged, hoping he'd get the hint.

He didn't.

Eli's face fell and he started twisting his hands around the water bottle he had yet to even open. "Is it because of what I said?" I flinched when Eli's pretty brown eyes held mine. "Because I didn't mean it. I do…I do want you."

Fuck. We were exactly where I'd been afraid we'd end up after I'd kissed him the first time. I dropped my hands and ran my fingers through my hair. I hadn't even noticed how loose it had gotten from the rubber band I used to tie it back. I pulled the band free and dropped it on the table. "We want different things, Eli," I finally said, hoping it would be enough to get my message across.

Eli bobbed his head slightly as he got what I was saying and I felt like a complete shit.

"You only want to fuck me," he whispered.

I waited for the many reactions I deserved. Outrage, hurt, disappointment. But Eli didn't say anything as he got up and carefully put the water bottle down on table. Except he didn't leave.

"If that was all you wanted, why didn't you do it when you had the chance?" Eli asked and I held my breath as he moved until he was standing in front of me.

Over me.

"On the table," he murmured as he placed his knee on the cushion between my slightly splayed legs. I was forced to lean my head back as he put his hands on either side of my head to brace himself. "I wanted you to," he said huskily as he lowered his body until he was straddling my groin and his mouth was just inches from mine.

"Wanted me to what?" I asked stupidly as I struggled to keep track of the conversation.

"Fuck me," Eli breathed against my mouth. "It never felt so good before."

"What didn't?"

"Having someone touch me like that. Like all you cared about was making me feel good."

I let my hands slide up Eli's jean-covered thighs and felt him tremble in response. But his lips stayed where they were and as much as I wanted to lift my mouth to meet his, I was desperate to hear what he had to say next.

"Can I touch you like that, Mav?"

Fuck, I wasn't going to survive this. Even now it felt like the impression of the zipper of my pants would be permanently imprinted on my dick.

I think I managed a nod, but I wasn't actually sure until Eli let go of the chair with one of his hands and skimmed his fingers over my lips. He teased my flesh for several seconds before trailing his hand down my chin and along my throat. He let the pad of his finger press against my pulse and another smile drifted across his mouth. "Your heart's racing."

If he only knew. My entire body felt like it was on fucking fire.

Eli's hand eventually left my throat and I both saw and felt him thread his fingers through my long hair. I nearly came on the spot when he grabbed my hair and twisted his hand enough so my hair was wrapped around it twice. The idea of him doing the same thing to me while he was fucking me had me bucking my hips up

125

against him and I had no doubt he knew my train of thought because, just like that, his eyes glazed over with lust.

"Would you let me do that to you someday?" Eli whispered against my mouth as he gave my hair a little tug. The bite of pain had me closing my eyes as a groan of pleasure escaped my lips. I managed a nod and was rewarded with Eli lowering himself all the way down onto my lap. He rocked back and forth a couple of times as his lips pressed against mine, but he didn't actually kiss me. Instead, his mouth followed the path his fingers had taken and when he reached my pulse, he let his tongue slide over my skin.

"Jesus," I ground out as I dug my fingers into his thighs before sliding them around to cup his ass. I tried grinding his hips back and forth against me in a desperate effort for relief, but Eli resisted my moves and pulled free of my hold. Before I could even process what was happening, he lifted enough so he could slide his hand over my erection. I dropped my head back against the cushion as he caressed me and I held my breath when I felt his fingers working my button loose. I managed to come to my senses enough to watch him lower the zipper, but the second his hand closed around my cock, I reached up and dragged his mouth down to mine for a searing kiss.

Eli kissed me back without hesitation as he began stroking my dick with long, heavy drags. I forced myself to pull back from the kiss as I remembered the incident in the parking garage when we'd been in a similar position. I held his face still as I studied him closely.

126

"It's me," Eli murmured as his gaze held mine. Relief flooded my system and I yanked him down for another kiss. But when I tried to sit up so that I could have more control over the situation, Eli suddenly slipped from my lap.

But not to get up.

Not to escape.

No.

He dropped to his knees in front of the chair and reached for the waistband of my pants. I was too stunned to react right away, but when he looked up at me expectantly and gave me a little tug on my pants, I lifted my hips. Eli worked my pants down just enough to release my dick and then his tongue was blazing a path along my upper thigh. I watched in rapt fascination as my cock twitched every time Eli's lush tongue made contact with my heated skin, but when he just continued to tease me, I couldn't stop the hoarse plea that escaped me.

"Eli, please."

Eli lifted his eyes to watch me for a second and he held my gaze when his tongue reached out to lick my leaking crown. I jumped at the electricity that shot through my balls and it took what little control I had left not to grab Eli's head and shove into him the way I wanted. Since I had no place to put my hands, I grabbed the armrests and held on for dear life as Eli teased me with little licks all over my aching shaft. When he finally did take me into his mouth, I was shaking with unbridled lust and I knew I wouldn't last long.

Unlike his first kiss, there was no hesitation as Eli sucked me deep into his throat, his tongue exploring the heavy veins that ran the length of my flesh. Concern went through me and I lifted my head and said, "Look at me."

Eli immediately looked up at me as he continued to torment me and when I saw only passion and desire in his gaze, I relaxed. "Keep watching me," I ordered gently as I lowered one of my hands to his head before letting it drift farther down until it was resting against his throat. My insistence that he keep his eyes on me made it more difficult for him to deep throat me the way he had been, but I didn't care since the sight of his pleasure-filled eyes was doing to me what no blowjob ever could have.

I managed to keep the connection with Eli as I felt the first tremors of my orgasm start to hit me, but when Eli suddenly closed his eyes and sucked me in as hard and as deep as he could, I let out a hoarse shout and jammed my hips forward, ramming into him before I could stop myself. I tried to pull back, but Eli's fingers curled around my hips and then drifted lower until the tips were biting into my ass and his entire upper half was wrapped around my groin. My control snapped at that point and I wrapped my hands in his hair and held on as I began fucking his mouth in earnest. My orgasm spiraled beyond my control very quickly and even my warning that I was going to come didn't slow Eli as he hollowed out his cheeks with every drag. The climax hit me so hard that I actually felt tears sting my eyes as the pleasure flooded my entire system all at once. I knew I was being way too rough with Eli as I held him in place while I rammed my cock down his throat as jet after jet of cum shot out of me, but I couldn't stop the need to empty myself inside of him, to claim him…to mark him. I managed to ease my hold on him when the orgasm finally released me from its grip.

"Eli," I whispered as I used my hand to lift his chin. His mouth was still wrapped around my half hard cock and while his skin was flushed red from the rough taking, he made no move to release me and my whole body shook when his tongue curled lovingly around my length. The sight of my cum dripping down his chin where it had escaped his mouth was beyond erotic and I reached down to catch the sticky fluid. Eli released my dick long enough to wrap his mouth around my finger and then his tongue was doing to my digit what it had just been doing to my cock. Even as aftershocks continued to wrack my body, I was getting turned on all over again. I leaned down and wrapped my hands around his upper arms. My mouth was on his before he even made it back onto my lap.

Eli kissed me fervently as his hands closed around the sides of my face to hold me in place. I palmed his ass as we kissed and then searched out his erection. I'd been too far gone to notice if he'd come, but one brush over the hard flesh nestled behind his zipper gave me my answer and I quickly got his pants loose and down. I gave him a couple of hard tugs which had him moaning in my mouth.

"Lift up a little," I murmured as I lowered my body on the chair. It took Eli several seconds to understand what I wanted, but the moment I looked up at him and opened my mouth expectantly, he sucked in a breath and then reached for his swollen cock and maneuvered it to my waiting mouth. He wasn't as big as me, but his thickness still stretched my lips wide and I had to fight my gag reflex as he pressed all the way to the back of my throat. He found his rhythm quickly, but I could tell from his desperate pants that it wasn't enough and I pulled off his dick just long enough to whisper, "Fuck my mouth, Eli."

Eli stilled and looked down at me. His hands were braced against the back of the chair as he held himself above me.

"I want it," I said reassuringly when I saw the hesitation in his gaze. My Eli knew more than he should about giving pleasure but next to nothing about taking it.

When he finally nodded, I sucked his cock back into my mouth and gave him several brutally hard drags that had him moaning. Pre-cum leaked onto my tongue as he began to fuck me carefully. I'd pulled his pants down enough so that I could feel the firm skin of his ass beneath my fingers and since he was still holding back, I ran one finger through his crease until I found his pucker. The second I brushed the pad over it, Eli froze. I was worried I'd gone too far, but when I looked up, I saw him watching me with a mix of raw need and confusion. I continued to play gently with him as I showered his cock with attention. When he finally began rocking back on my finger before thrusting forward into my mouth, I applied more pressure to his hole as I massaged him.

"Oh God," Eli whispered as he became more frantic and his cock thickened deliciously in my mouth. I loved how he kept his eyes on me as he began fucking me in desperation. I released his dick just long enough to wet my finger and then I sucked him down again and he instantly resumed his hurried pace. When I returned my finger to his entrance, Eli put enough pressure on it that his hole collapsed and I was able to push my finger in to the first knuckle. He let out a guttural shout and shoved into my mouth hard, his slit hitting the back of my throat. Since my finger wasn't very wet, I didn't push it any farther into Eli's trembling body, but he didn't notice or he didn't care because he was eagerly fucking my finger and mouth now and when he came a minute later, he screamed my name as his cum filled my mouth and spilled down my throat. I played gently with his dick as the aftershocks rippled through him. I carefully eased my finger from his body and as soon as it was free, Eli lowered himself and sealed his mouth over mine. He only kissed me for a minute or so before he dropped his head onto my shoulder and wrapped his arms around me. I let my hands rest on his ass, unable to stop myself from massaging the smooth flesh. Eli's breaths came in heavy drags against my throat as he tried to recover, but I didn't realize until a good ten minutes later that he'd actually fallen asleep against me. I needed to wake him up. To send him on his way. To tell him it had been fun, but that it couldn't happen again.

I didn't do any of that.

I didn't do anything but close my arms around him and enjoy the feel of his heart beating against mine.

There'd be enough time to deal with reality later.

Chapter Ten

Eli

"You made me lose twenty bucks."

I glanced at Brennan as he dropped down in the chair next to me. "What?" I asked as tried to cover up how distracted I was by picking at the piece of cake someone had placed in my hand at some point without me even noticing.

"I had a bet going with Logan that you would be a no-show again," Brennan said with a chuckle and I automatically looked up to search out Logan Barretti, Dom's husband. "Of course, he had insider information about a certain little visit Dom made to your place a few days ago."

The day I'd last seen Mav.

The day Mav had shown me more pleasure in a matter of minutes than I'd never known in my entire life.

The day I'd finally taken another man into my mouth and actually wanted it…and enjoyed it.

My heart flip flopped painfully at the reminder and I tried to focus on what Brennan was saying. I hadn't actually spoken to Dom more than a few minutes before I'd left my apartment to find Mav and apologize for hurting him. And I'd had no doubt that that was exactly what I'd done when I'd lashed out at him and told him I didn't want him. I'd seen it in his eyes the moment I'd spoken the lie, but the true depth the impact of my words had had on him hadn't become apparent until Mav had bent at the waist and struggled to breathe.

As if I had physically struck him.

When Mav had left, I hadn't been able to focus on anything Dom had said to me. I'd only heard bits and pieces about him being worried about me, and all I'd managed to get out was telling him that I needed to go and that I'd call him later. I hadn't even remembered to turn my oven off. Fortunately, Dom had realized it before he'd left and when I'd called him later that night to explain my abrupt departure, he'd told me I could explain it in person when I attended my welcome home party this weekend. I'd known better than to ignore the subtle order and so when Saturday afternoon had rolled around, I'd forced myself out of bed and made the trip to San Juan Island. But despite my physical presence in Dom and Logan's beautiful island house, it didn't mean I was there mentally.

Maybe if things hadn't ended with Mav the way they had.

And I had no doubt that they'd ended.

Because I'd woken up in his hotel room alone. I'd been curled up on the same chair we'd had our encounter in and there'd been a blanket draped over me. But Mav had been nowhere to be found. No note, no text, no nothing. If I hadn't seen his small overnight bag sitting on a chair near the bed, I would have guessed he'd checked out. When I'd gone to my car, his Harley had been

133

gone. I'd managed to go to the hospital the rest of the week for my volunteer duties, but my heart hadn't been in it. And when Hawke had walked me to my car each night, I hadn't argued or asked if he knew where Mav was.

I may not have ever had any relationships in my past experience to draw from, but I knew enough from what Mav had said in the hotel room. He wanted to fuck me, not date me. And apparently, he wasn't even all that interested in fucking me either.

"Hey," Brennan said as he gave me a little nudge.

"Sorry," I murmured as I tried to pull myself from my sad reverie.

"No problem," Brennan said gently, but he gave up trying to draw me from my funk. I managed to make conversation as other members of the family came to greet me, but by the time I was done, I was barely holding it together. I'd specifically returned to Seattle to be closer to these men and women who'd changed my life, but now that I was here, I felt like an interloper. To them I was Eli Galvez, the kid who'd struggled to overcome a shitty past to have a bright future as a doctor. They had no idea of everything I'd done and been in the years that had passed. They had no idea the secrets I had kept…was still keeping. I was a fraud and I had no right to immerse myself in their world.

It wasn't until Sweetie, Logan and Dom's German Shepherd, pushed her muzzle into my hands that I realized my stress levels were increasing. I hadn't brought Baby with me because he wasn't overly fond of spending long periods of time in the car, but now I was regretting it. My skin felt itchy and I subtly glanced at my watch to see when I could make my escape. To my dismay, I'd only been at the party for a couple of hours and guessed that I had to put in at least another hour before I could start making my excuses about needing to leave.

"Here," I heard Dom say and I looked up to see him standing in front of me, a bottle of soda in his hand.

"Thanks," I murmured.

"Let's take a walk."

I nodded and followed him to the back door. Tanner, Dom and Logan's eight-year-old son came barreling after us and threw himself into Dom's arms. "Papa, can we play football now?"

Dom hugged Tanner and then lifted him high over his shoulder so that Tanner was hanging precariously over his back. "In a little bit," he said as he gave the boy a swat on his bottom.

My chest constricted as I watched Dom right the boy and then hold him for several long seconds against his chest. Tanner seemed used to his father's prolonged hugs and didn't squirm to get away. When Dom finally released him, I wasn't surprised when Tanner wrapped his arms around my middle and said, "Welcome home, Eli."

And then he was off like a shot to rejoin Logan who was holding his and Dom's young daughter, Sylvie. I watched as Logan cast Dom a sidelong glance. It was a look I'd seen a thousand times and that hadn't dimmed in the nearly nine years they'd been together. It was a look I'd once hoped I would one day share with someone.

I had to tear my eyes away from the two men as they silently communicated and I ended up walking outside ahead of Dom. I waited for him to catch up and then followed him down to the water where there was a large beach as well as a dock, where a massive boat was moored.

"I spoke to your dad today," Dom began.

I swallowed hard and forced every bit of normalcy into my voice as I could when I said, "Oh yeah?"

"Yeah. He seemed worried about you. Said you seemed a bit distracted these days."

I flinched at that, but kept my mouth shut. My insides felt like they were going to explode though.

"He was hoping I could convince you to move back home. Says he knows a guy at Johns Hopkins who can reinstate your admission."

I kept my attention on the dock as we began walking towards the end of it.

"I'm sure your mom is missing you," Dom added.

"The UW is a better fit," I murmured non-committedly.

"Eli, you know we're all glad you're back..."

Dom let his words hang in the air and I was glad when he didn't finish them. I knew it would be next to impossible to keep anything from this man, but my hope was that he wouldn't push for answers and that once I started school, I'd have the excuse of the heavy workload to explain away my demeanor.

"How did things work out with your guy?" Dom asked once we reached the end of the dock. "Mav, right?"

I nodded and forced a swallow of soda down. "He's not my guy," I managed to say. "We're just friends."

"Whatever I walked in on didn't look like it was just about friends."

"Dom..."

"Okay, okay," Dom said as he put his hands up in supplication. "Can't blame a guy for worrying," he said with a chuckle. "You want to protect your kids from the harshness of life for as long as you can, you know?"

I nearly bent over in pain at that and I actually dropped my soda. It hit the dock with a splat, spraying all over our shoes. "Shit," I bit out as I tried to get control of my shaking hand. Luckily, Dom was distracted by trying to grab the bottle before it rolled into the water so he didn't notice my predicament.

Fuck. How many times had I wished Dom had seen me as his own kid?

And now it was just too fucking late.

"You okay?" Dom asked, his voice heavy with worry as he snatched the bottle up and glanced at me.

"Yeah," I said quickly. "Sorry."

"You sure?"

I nodded. "Yep. I've just been a little tired. You know, with what happened to Nick, the move…"

Dom nodded. "Your dad says Caleb's been struggling, but that they found him a good therapist and that he seems to be back on track now. And your mom is keeping busy with the VA."

I managed to nod in agreement even though my skin felt like something was crawling just beneath the surface. "It's been tough," I said and I automatically began walking back towards the house.

I needed to get the hell out of there.

"Dom," I said as we reached the shore. "Do you mind if I head home? I'm really tired and I need to check on Baby."

Dom studied me for a moment and then nodded. "Yeah, sure."

I glanced back at the house and then managed to mumble, "Can you say my goodbyes for me?"

I was already walking towards the side of the house so that I wouldn't have to go through it and see everyone again when I heard Dom say yes and wish me a safe trip home. By the time I reached my car, I could feel the bile churning deep in my belly and it didn't start to ease until I reached the ferry dock almost twenty minutes away. My fingers wouldn't stop shaking as I got out of the car and went up to the top level of the boat to watch the approach to the mainland. I heard my phone beep with a text message, but bitter disappointment curled through me when I saw that it was Brennan asking if I was okay. I sent him a quick text back telling him I was good and that I'd call him later. Instead of putting the phone away, I pulled up Mav's contact and stared at his phone number.

What would he do if I called? Texted?

Would he answer or ignore me?

Was he still even in town?

I jammed the phone back in my pocket and drew in several long breaths of air in the hopes it would help calm me, but even the long process of getting the car off the ferry in Anacortes did nothing to ease my jitters. And two hours later when I pulled into the city, I bypassed my apartment. In my mind I knew where I was going even though I told myself how stupid it was. The sight of Mav's hotel did nothing to ease my anxiety, but when I saw his Harley sitting in the familiar spot in the parking garage, I finally took my first real breath.

Maybe it would have been smarter just to leave things at that. To know that he was still in the same city. To hope that maybe our paths would cross at the hospital and I could find some way to draw him into conversation.

Except his voice wouldn't be enough. His touch wouldn't be enough. I needed more. I needed to be the me that only he seemed to be able to draw out. I needed to not feel sick with guilt or fear or doubt for just a few minutes.

I had several chances to turn around between the car and his door, but once the idea had taken root inside my brain, it was all I could think about. I needed Mav, pure and simple. I didn't understand why he made me feel different. I didn't know how things would go between us. I didn't even know for sure that he would talk to me. But none of that kept me from rapping my knuckles on his door and waiting with bated breath. Relief went through me when the door unlocked and then opened. Mav's dark green eyes looked me up and down as he leaned against the open door, but he didn't say anything and neither did I. When he finally stepped back and put his hand on the door like he was going to close it, I wanted to die inside. But when all he did was open it wider and move out of the way to let me in, I knew anything that happened going forward would be my choice. I just had to take the step forward.

So that was what I did.

* * *

I couldn't stifle my cry of relief when Mav's mouth closed over mine. He hadn't said a word, hadn't pointed out that what was about to happen was a one-time thing, that it wouldn't mean anything. And the kiss…

God, I felt everything in the way his lips caressed mine. He was both gentle and insistent, but there was no rush in the way he kissed me. One of his hands came up to caress my neck as the other pressed against my lower back, urging me closer to him. I lifted my arms to wrap them around his shoulders and felt the dampness of his hair which was hanging loose. I let my fingers tangle in the softness of it and when Mav released my mouth long enough to skim his lips along my jaw and down my throat, the emotion became too much and I had to bury my face against his shoulder. I hated that I couldn't get a grip on myself, but if Mav noticed, he didn't say anything. He just held me tighter and kept pressing soft kisses to any part of me he could reach without having to relinquish his hold on me.

I didn't know how to tell him how afraid I'd been that I'd never have this moment with him. This moment where it was just the two of us. This moment where he made me feel whole without even trying.

So I didn't say anything. Instead, I searched out his mouth and tried to tell him that way. He met every one of my kisses with the same gentle sweetness, but his hands were busily stroking all over my back and ass. Our cocks brushed against one another every time we shifted even a little bit and within minutes, our kisses turned deep and needy. Mav's fingers curled around my ass and lifted me and I instinctively wrapped my legs around his waist. The position felt awkward at first until I realized the move had put my mouth just a little higher than his. I took complete advantage and stole into his mouth with my tongue. I used my hands to brush his long hair back from his face and when I ended the kiss, he tried to follow me. I let my fingers roam over his face, testing every texture. His brow, his nearly perfectly straight nose, the little bit of facial hair covering his jaw, his smooth lips. And then I held his eyes with mine as I leaned in and brushed my lips over his in the briefest of kisses. I did it over and over, never taking my eyes off of him. And I knew the instant he saw what I'd wanted him to see, because he sucked in a sharp breath and pulled back just a little to study me a second before he slammed his mouth down on mine and took complete control of the kiss, of me, of everything.

I had no fear as Mav walked us both to the bedroom and I barely noticed when he laid me down on the soft comforter because his mouth was consuming mine. I still had my legs wrapped around his waist as he settled his weight on me, but the second I hit the bed, his hands found mine and he linked them together with his and held them above my head. His hips rocked against mine feverishly as he kissed me over and over and I knew it wouldn't take much to push me over the edge. I had no idea if Mav sensed how close I was or if he was in the same boat, but he suddenly released my hands and lifted off of me enough to limit the contact between our groins.

"No," I whispered before I could stop myself, the neediness in my voice off the charts. Fuck, I was such a raw mess of need that I was certainly going to scare him off, especially considering this whole thing was just supposed to be about sex. I bit into my lip hard to keep myself from begging him not to leave me.

Mav watched me for so long that I began to truly worry that I'd ruined the whole thing. But instead of stepping back, he reached out and used his thumb to free my lower lip from the death grip my teeth had on it. The rough pad swiped over the tender flesh several times, easing some of the sting. And then he leaned over me, bracing himself on his other arm. Our mouths were mere centimeters apart, but he didn't kiss me.

"Don't hide from me," Mav said softly and then he did kiss me. A quick brush of his mouth over mine. "You don't see it, do you?" he asked.

"See what?" I somehow managed to get out.

"How fucking beautiful you are…how perfect."

I felt tears sting my eyes at his words. I didn't even realize I was shaking my head until he said, "Yes," and then kissed me again. Longer. Deeper. "Tell me what has you so afraid," he breathed against my mouth.

Maybe if he hadn't been brushing his fingers through my hair as he said it or if he hadn't kept pressing tiny kisses against my lips, I could have held it together. But his words, his touch – they cracked open something deep inside of me and I couldn't stem the tears that fell. "I'm afraid you'll leave me," I whispered as I closed my eyes. "I'm afraid this will all be some cruel dream and I'll wake up any second alone again…"

Humiliation coursed through me as tears slipped unchecked down my face. But instead of pulling back, Mav used his fingers and his mouth to soak up my hot tears and when I finally settled, I heard him whisper, "I've tried."

"Tried what?" I asked, my voice sounding dry and scratchy.

"Leaving."

I stiffened at that, but when I instinctively tried to move away from him, he dropped all his weight down on me. One of his hands closed over one of mine and his long fingers began stroking back and forth over my palm as if trying to soothe me.

"Every day for the last three days I packed my shit, checked out of this room and got on my Harley and pointed it in a different direction, not caring where I ended up," Mav said quietly as he continued to pepper my mouth with small kisses. "And every day I turned around and came back and got this same room and waited and hoped."

My stomach dropped out as I realized what he was saying. I shook my head in disbelief. "You didn't call or text…"

Mav kissed me again, deeper this time. He lifted just long enough to whisper, "I leave so I don't get left," and then his mouth sealed over mine and I knew he was done talking. His final words hung in my brain as he began to kiss me, desperately, as if the admission had opened some kind of floodgate for him. I met every demanding kiss with equal fervor and when he pulled me upright so I could sit astride him as he sat back on his heels, I wrapped both my arms and legs around him so there was practically no space between us. Mav reached behind his neck with one arm and managed to pull his T-shirt off in one clean sweep. He tossed the garment aside and ran his hand through his hair to push it back, giving me an unfettered view of his broad chest. I sucked in a breath at the sight of the large tattoo that spanned the upper half of his body.

A phoenix.

"Oh my God," I breathed as I let my fingers trail over the bird's broad wings and long body. While the color was mostly black with hints of red in the wings and long tail, the detail work was very intricate and beautifully done and it felt like at any moment the beautiful creature would continue its ascent from the fiery ashes from which it had been born.

"It's beautiful," I said as I explored every curve and line. I looked up to see Mav watching me intently. "You're beautiful," I whispered as his dark eyes held mine. He didn't say anything, but the arm wrapped around my waist tightened imperceptibly and then he was drawing me up against his chest for another kiss. We were both breathless and desperately rubbing against each other for relief when he pulled back.

"I need you," he finally said and I heard the tremor in his voice. For any other man I had no doubt the words would have been easy ones to say, but for Mav, I suspected they cost him so much more.

I leave so I don't get left.

I couldn't make sense of what could have happened to this beautiful man to make him think I would ever turn away from him, but I knew that was exactly what he was afraid of. I clasped his face with both my hands and told him the one thing I knew he needed to hear more than anything else in that moment.

"Yes."

Chapter Eleven

Mav

Yes.

Logically I had known that would be Eli's answer since everything he'd just said was proof that he needed me as much as I needed him, but hearing the word released the stranglehold I had on my emotions.

I would get this moment with him. This one night.

It would be enough to sustain me when I was forced to let him go for good. Because I wasn't foolish enough to believe Eli really wanted *me*. He wanted something I could give him in this moment...escape, relief, the ability to forget – I wasn't really sure which and I didn't care. But eventually he would do what all the others had done and turn his back on me. He'd be kinder about it, of course. He'd say he was too busy with school or family or he wouldn't say anything at all and I'd be forced to watch him silently withdraw from me.

It didn't matter because long before that happened, I'd figure out how to do what I hadn't been able to these past three days – walk away from him.

I managed to use one hand to work Eli's shirt off of him before I lowered him back down to the bed. But unlike before, he didn't look tense and on edge. Instead he just lay there and let me have my fill of him. He was definitely a lean guy, but he also had considerably more muscle definition than I'd expected. I'd had the sense to turn on the wall lamp next to the bed before I'd climbed into the shower so even as darkness fell outside, I could still make out his features and the warm hue of his bronzed skin. I let my hands skim over his sides and relished in the way he sucked in his breath as I touched him. I teased his nipples a little bit before I leaned over him and ran my tongue across one of them. Eli let out a gasp and then I felt his fingers thread through my hair. He held on to me as I nipped at the turgid flesh before turning my attention to the other one. I explored the rest of his torso with my hands and quickly followed with my tongue. By the time I reached his belly button, Eli was squirming beneath me and trying to guide me farther south. I dipped my tongue into his navel before letting my mouth drag over the bulge that was still covered by his jeans.

"Mav," Eli grunted as he tried to increase the pressure where I was nuzzling him.

"Take yourself out," I ordered as I sat up and reached behind me to work his shoes and socks off. There was no hesitation as Eli fumbled to get his pants open. His cock was so hard he had to gently pry it free of the confines of his pants and underwear. I helped him work the clothes completely off, but was careful not to touch him. Once he was naked, I knelt between his spread legs and reached down to lift them so they were bent at the knee, his feet flat on the bed.

"Show me where you want my mouth," I said softly as I began stroking myself through the athletic pants I'd thrown on after my shower. The loose fabric did nothing to hide my erection and Eli was clearly more focused on it rather than my words because he didn't react at first. When I stopped stroking myself, Eli lifted his eyes to mine in confusion and I repeated my order. His cheeks flushed with color even as his hand reached for his cock. He fisted himself and began slow drags up and down his shaft as his eyes fell back to my hand which I was once again rubbing along my stiffness. I didn't miss how he matched his strokes to mine.

"Where else?" I asked after I let him play with himself for a good minute. Pre-cum leaked from his crown and stuck to his abdomen in glistening, sticky streaks.

Eli's eyes flipped up to mine again and his mouth parted as if he were going to say something, but he didn't. His hand tentatively dropped lower until he was cupping his balls and gently rolling them in his palm. I was having trouble staying on track because the sight of him playing with himself was a thousand times more erotic than I could have imagined. I lowered my own pants to free my cock, but ignored the rock hard flesh for my own balls.

"Where else?" I managed to ask as Eli began brushing one finger back and forth over the soft flesh just behind his balls. Since I wasn't expecting him to actually do it, I nearly swallowed my tongue when Eli's long fingers disappeared into his crack. I was about to reach for him so I could split him open to get a better view, but he surprised me yet again when he lifted his legs up and folded them in on himself, exposing his hole and the fingers that were gently massaging it. I forgot about my own aching dick and lowered myself so that I could run my tongue over one ass cheek, then the other, never taking my eyes off the sight of Eli fingering himself. I reached up with one hand to gently pull his fingers away, but instead of replacing them with mine like I was tempted to do, I stuck his fingers in my mouth and covered them with saliva. Eli let out a little moan as I sucked on his digits just a bit before placing them back on his eager hole.

He needed no instruction on what to do next. I kept licking closer and closer to his opening as he began pushing one finger inside of himself. I glanced up long enough to see he had managed to brace himself with his free arm so he could watch me watching him. I'd been with plenty of guys in my time, but I'd never seen someone so lost in their pleasure before. The intimacy of what was happening, the taboo aspect of it, either didn't register or he didn't care because he didn't hesitate to keep working his finger farther into his body. I began placing little kisses on his hand as he fucked himself and when he needed more moisture, he eagerly sought out my mouth. By the time he had two fingers jammed deep inside his body, I was humping the bed looking for some relief of my own. I finally dipped my head and began running my tongue in circles around his stretched opening and the second Eli pulled his fingers free, presumably to add a third finger, I stiffened my tongue and stole into

149

his quivering entrance. Eli's reaction was instantaneous. Besides the hoarse shout that exploded from his lungs, his still wet fingers clamped down on my head and fisted in my hair until it was nearly painful.

I feasted on Eli's ass like a starved man and when I finally pulled my tongue free of his trembling body, his hole was stretched wide. I quickly wet my fingers and pushed one inside of him. His muscles instantly clamped down on the digit and he shoved hard against my hand, trying to get more inside. Since my finger was as far in as it could go, I added my middle finger to the mix and twisted my wrist back and forth until Eli was whimpering for more. He used one hand to hold his leg back so I would have room to work while his other hand was frantically jerking at his cock. I kept up the motions with my fingers as I leaned down to lick over his balls. Eli let out a swift curse and bucked up against my mouth, impaling himself even farther on my fingers. His feet were flat on the bed and he was using them to leverage his body to get the angle and depth he wanted and needed. I sucked each of his balls into my mouth and played with them for a while as I eased off on the finger fucking, but when I spit out his balls so I could suck his dick into my mouth, Eli screamed my name and snagged me by the hair again. He fucked my mouth without reservation which was a clear sign of how close he was so I swiveled my fingers until I found the knot of nerves I was looking for deep inside of his body. The first stroke over his prostate had him freezing in place. The second had him letting out a loud moan that was definitely mixed with a couple of desperate pleas. The third one had him shooting into my mouth as his ass clamped around my fingers with so much pressure, that I barely managed to keep from spilling my own release on the bed.

The orgasm tore through Eli to the point that he had absolutely no control over anything he said or did. My head hurt in the best way where he was holding on to me as he continued to try to ram his dick down my throat as far as he could even after the last of his seed had left his body and his inner muscles were clenching and unclenching around my fingers as pulse after pulse of pleasure washed over him. When the climax finally released him from its grip, his whole body went lax and instead of holding my hair in a brutal grip, he began stroking it softly back and forth. I kept my fingers inside of him as I gently cleaned the proof of his release from his softening dick. When his inner muscles finally eased their stranglehold on me, I carefully pulled my fingers free of his body. I lifted up and climbed up Eli's body and just stared at the dreamy expression on his face. He pulled me down for a kiss and I felt his legs wrap around me as we made love to each other's mouths. I loved knowing that even as tired and as sated as he was, he still wanted me close.

My own body was tight with need and while my plan had been to get Eli worked up again before I actually fucked him, Eli clearly had other ideas because he kept shifting his hips so that my hard cock was sliding through his crease, grazing over his hole. At one point my cock hit his opening just right and I actually began to push into him a little bit before I could stop myself. It was only when

151

I told Eli that I needed to ready myself that he actually released his hold on me and I couldn't help but smile and kiss him for that. It felt like forever before I managed to strip off my pants and search out a condom and lube from my bag which was on the floor next to the bed. My fingers struggled to get the latex on even though it was a task I'd done countless times before. I glanced at Eli to make sure he was still okay and was surprised to see him watching me with rapt fascination. With his splayed legs open wide in invitation giving me a teasing glimpse of his reddened, fluttering entrance, I nearly dropped the condom all together. I actually had to take my eyes off of him to focus enough to roll the condom down my painfully sensitive length. I slathered lube on my shaft before adding some to my fingers. I crawled up Eli's body, settling my fingers at his opening and covering it generously with lube before wiping my hand on the bedding.

"Tell me you want this," I said as I placed the head of my cock against his slick hole.

Eli reached up to tenderly push my hair behind my ear. "I don't have the words to explain how much I want this," he whispered.

My heart constricted painfully at the open emotion in his eyes. He'd been brutalized by so many and so early on in his life, but all I saw was complete and utter trust when he looked at me. He'd meant exactly what he'd said.

I sealed my mouth over his as I began to push forward. Eli bore down on me and let out a huff of air when my cock finally began to breach his tight body. His fingers bit into my upper arms as his muscles tried to keep me out and he couldn't stifle a small cry of pain when the outer ring gave way. I held myself still to give him time to adjust and as he tried to catch his breath, I brushed kisses all over his face and mouth.

"So perfect," I whispered over and over again. Eli's eyes were closed, but every time I said the word, he smiled just a little bit and when his body finally relaxed and began to suck me in, his lips sought out mine for a deep, sweet kiss. As badly as I wanted to sink into the tight heat enveloping my aching cock, I kept up the painfully slow pace of rocking gently back and forth into Eli's body until my balls were finally pressed against his ass.

"You okay?" I asked. My own body felt like it was on fire and Eli's lush brown skin was glistening with sweat. He was wrapped tight around me and was physically shaking, though I knew it didn't have anything to do with pain or fear. Because I was in pretty much the same boat.

Eli managed a nod. He was the first to move as he pulled his hips back just a little before sliding them forward. I groaned into his neck at how good just that little bit of friction felt, but I resisted the urge to pound into him. I would let Eli control the pace for as long as he needed.

It turned out that he didn't need long because within a minute of rocking against me, his movements became more desperate. With my weight pinning him to the bed, there was only so much freedom of movement for him.

"Mav," he begged. "Please."

"Please what, baby?" I asked as I licked away the sweat that had formed around his parted lips.

"Fuck me," Eli managed to say and then his mouth was fastening over mine. I'd never been so physically close to a man as I fucked him, but the idea of even separating the slightest bit from Eli was unacceptable to me so I slid my arms beneath his back and hugged him tight as I took over. I would have liked to have gone slow, but there was just no way as my dick surged through all the tight heat that was fisting it like a second skin. And with Eli's little grunts of delight in my ear urging me on, I didn't stand a chance. I rocked into him over and over as the lube began easing the way and within a matter of minutes I was pounding into him without reservation, even as our upper halves barely moved as we held on to one another. We didn't kiss or speak as our bodies fed off each other. Besides our breath mingling and Eli's fingers digging into my upper back every time I surged into him, there was very little movement going on from the waist up. From the waist down, the pace was frenetic and raw…almost frantic. I could feel Eli's cock smashed between our bodies, but I couldn't find the strength to reach between us to get him off.

Because I didn't want to risk losing even the little bit of connection it would cost if I moved my hand where it was splayed along his back down to his dick. From the grunts and pants that were spilling from Eli's lips as we fucked, I guessed he might not need the extra stimulation. My theory proved to be correct when Eli began clawing my back in desperation and shouts of pleasure fell from his mouth. In the same instant that he let out a satisfied howl of relief, hot liquid coated my abdomen and Eli's inner muscles clamped down on my dick so hard that I went off just like that. Blackness threatened as my balls emptied and electricity shot up my spine and out to all my nerve endings. I called Eli's name as I began shooting into the condom. I drove my cock into Eli as deep and as hard as I could as I tightened my arms around him to keep him from sliding away from me. The force of my orgasm was so intense that my hips rocked Eli's ass up and off the bed, forcing his legs to bend back in on his body in what had to have been an uncomfortable position. But I couldn't have stopped it even if I wanted to.

Because for the first time that I could ever remember, my pleasure controlled me and not the other way around.

The blissful agony rolled through me in endless waves and even after every drop of cum had been sucked from my body, I was still shoving into Eli in a desperate attempt to ride out the orgasm to completion. I'd lost track of Eli's orgasm in the fray, but he was still clinging to me when my body finally began to relax. I recovered enough to finally look at him, but his eyes were closed, effectively shutting me out of what he was feeling.

"Eli," I whispered, almost afraid at what I would see when he opened them.

He shook his head. "Not yet," he said softly.

"What?" I asked as I leaned down to brush my mouth over his.

"I don't want to wake up yet."

I kissed him again, but when I made a move to pull out of his body, he locked his ankles around my lower half to keep me where I was.

"Not yet, okay?" he said, his voice barely audible. "Just not yet."

"Okay," I murmured as I settled my head against his chest and listened to the sound of his still racing heart. I knew I was too heavy for him, but when I tried to even shift some of my weight off of him and to the side, he tightened his arms around me.

I sighed in relief. He wasn't letting me go…yet.

Chapter Twelve

Eli

I stilled my hand when Mav shifted beneath my touch, but when he didn't wake up, I continued letting my fingers trace one of the snake tattoos that ran the length of his back. When I'd seen them the first time, I hadn't been sure how far past the waistband of his pants the tattoos went, but now that Mav was lying face down on the bed, the comforter kicked down past his ass, I had my answer. Each snake's tail was curved around the globes of Mav's gorgeous backside and like the tattoo on his chest, the artistry was so flawless that it looked like the snakes could come to life at any moment.

We'd both fallen asleep with the lights still on after Mav had finally been forced to withdraw from me so he could get rid of the condom. He'd ended up having to clean me up with a washcloth and maneuver me under the covers because I'd been completely useless after the earth-shattering orgasm that had left me utterly drained. Though I suspected much of that had had to do with the intense emotions I'd been dealing with as Mav had made love to me. I wasn't sure if he saw what we'd done as making love, but it was the only way I could describe what had happened between us. I'd been fucked plenty of times and while I'd never enjoyed it, a couple of my customers had actually been gentle with me…one had even whispered that he loved me as he'd been fucking me. But I'd never been foolish enough to believe the act had anything to do with love. In my mind, fucking had always been about one guy using another to get off and nothing more. But what had happened between me and Mav…it was so much more than that.

It had to be. The things I'd seen in Mav's eyes as we'd become one couldn't be faked.

Could they?

"Don't."

The whispered word had me looking up from Mav's back to see he'd turned his head so he was facing in my direction.

"Don't what?" I asked as I automatically removed my hand from his back.

Mav reached out with his right hand and gently tugged my lip free of the hold I had on it with my teeth. I hadn't even realized I'd reverted to the habit at some point.

"Don't think about whatever has you so worried," he murmured. He reached for my hand and put it back on his back. "Don't stop that either," he added. "Feels good."

I smiled and let my nails gently rake over his back. My fingers caught on some scratches in the middle of his back and I realized I'd been the one to put them there.

"Those felt good too," Mav whispered and I glanced up to see him with a happy smirk on his face.

I held his gaze for a moment before I leaned down and brushed my lips over each scratch. When I lifted, I continued exploring the tattoo. He shivered as I massaged him lightly with my fingers.

"Do they have some special meaning to you?" I asked as I motioned to the tattoos.

Mav curled his arms under the pillow. I hated that his eyes darkened and that he shifted them away from me.

"Some Native American cultures revere snakes, but most hate and fear them. My grandfather believed them to be evil spirits. As soon as I could afford it, they were the first tattoos I got."

"Why two?" I asked.

"Because I'm what's known as a Winkte…Two Spirit."

I stilled my hand and looked at him. "Two Spirit?"

"Someone who has both masculine and feminine spirits."

"Because you're gay," I ventured.

Mav nodded. "Two Spirits are also revered in some cultures. They're believed to be gifted by the Creator to view the world from two perspectives."

"But not yours," I said in understanding.

"My grandfather believed in the cultural definition that Winktes are non-men." Mav's voice was casual and light, but I didn't miss the hint of bitterness beneath the words. "Two spirits, two snakes, two ways to say fuck you," he said simply.

"And the phoenix?" I asked as I let my hand drift lower until I was caressing his ass. Mav closed his eyes and sucked in a breath.

159

"Had it done five years ago."

"What ashes were you rising from?" I asked as I slid my finger over Mav's crease.

Mav didn't answer until I stopped moving my hand. His eyes opened and he watched me for a long time before saying, "The kind that burn you over and over again."

I nodded in understanding because I didn't need specifics. I knew exactly what he was talking about. I resumed my caress and shivered when Mav kept his eyes on me. I had planned on just exploring Mav's perfect body, but the more I touched him, the more my need began to flare to life deep inside of me. "Turn over," I said softly as I pulled my hand back. Mav's glittering green eyes held mine as he did what I told him. I wasn't surprised to see that he was hard as a rock. I ignored his cock and dropped my lips to skim over the tattoo. I traced the outline of it with my tongue, but when I reached one of his nipples, I couldn't resist the urge to taste it. Mav let out a little growl so I did it again and then gently nipped the sensitive flesh. I felt Mav's fingers wind through my hair as he held me in place, but he didn't resist when I moved my attention to his other nipple.

I took my time working my way to Mav's dick and by the time I got there, a small pool of pre-cum had formed around his navel. I licked the surprisingly sweet fluid up and then ran my tongue down the length of his shaft. I hadn't expected to like the taste of pre-cum, but just like with Mav's cum, I was finding myself quickly becoming addicted to his unique flavor.

As I explored Mav's cock, his hand left my head and I nearly jumped when it closed over my ass. He squeezed gently and then began massaging me. I enjoyed his touch for a few seconds before I returned my attention to his dick. The proof of how turned on he was continued to leak from the head and I eagerly lapped it up before I sucked the entire crown into my mouth. I was rewarded with hard fingers curling around one of my ass cheeks. I moaned around Mav's cock which had him shoving his hips upwards. I captured the base of his dick with one hand to keep him from burying himself down my throat and continued to torture him with light licks and short sucks that wouldn't be enough to actually get him off. The only problem was, he was teasing my ass in much the same way because his fingers had made their way to my opening, but weren't doing more than pressing against it for a mere second or two before running up and down my crease.

I quickly understood the game because the more pressure I added to Mav's dick, the more I was rewarded with longer touches. And when I finally deep throated Mav, a slick finger was pushed deep inside of me. While I had started off in control of our encounter, I realized quickly that the tables had been turned on me and I was the one desperate for more as I began impaling myself on Mav's finger even as I tried to maintain the intense suction that was causing my cheeks to ache. But when Mav began striking my prostate, I pulled off of him and quickly said, "Don't make me come yet," before I dropped back down on him. As badly as I needed to get off, it wasn't a finger I wanted jammed deep inside my ass when that happened.

Mav teased me a bit more with subtle touches over my gland, but not enough to make me go off like I had just a couple hours ago when he'd touched me there for the first time. I was about to protest when Mav's finger slipped free of my body, but when I felt him grabbing my hips and maneuvering me into a new position, I eagerly continued showering his swollen, leaking cock with the attention it wanted. Mav continued to move me until I was straddling his upper body, my ass nearly riding his face. I had a split second to process what was happening when his big hands split me open, and with the first swipe of his tongue over my hole, I was already shaking with excitement. I forgot all about Mav's cock as I ground my ass against his seeking tongue and when I felt it push into me, I let out a rough shout. I grabbed my cock and began stroking it as I rode Mav's mouth. By the time his tongue left my body and his mouth began gently suckling my hole, I was beyond desperate for relief and I quickly snatched the bottle of lube off the nightstand. In one swift move I had Mav's dick lubed up and was turning around.

"Eli-" he began to say, but I cut him off with a hard kiss. My body was so tight with need that I could think of nothing else as I reached around my ass and found Mav's cock. I lifted my mouth from Mav's long enough to rise up and lower myself down onto his stiff length.

"Eli...Fuck!" Mav shouted as my body began taking him in inch by agonizingly slow inch. The pressure and burn had me seeing stars and needing more so I lifted just a little before dropping down hard, taking several more inches in all at once. Mav's fingers bit into my thighs and his head was pressed back against the pillow, eyes closed, mouth parted as grunts escaped his lips.

I finally stopped moving when he was buried all the way inside of me, but it wasn't until Mav whispered, "Eli, we need a condom," that I realized why it felt so much different this time around. I should have been horrified at my own irresponsible actions, but the feel of Mav's hot, bare skin massaging my inner walls was just too good and I didn't give a fuck. I lifted up and dropped back down on him several times before I lowered my upper body and kissed him hard.

"I'm sorry," I breathed between kisses. "It's so good, Mav," I managed to get out. "I need it like this. I've been tested and I'm negative," I added. "I swear."

Mav's hands were gripping my ass hard enough that I knew I'd have bruises, but he wasn't trying to stop me as my hips began rolling back and forth over him. No, he was urging the motion on.

"Me too," he growled.

I took that to mean he'd tested negative too, but I knew it wasn't the only thing I needed to hear. "Do you want me to stop?" I asked and I forced my body to stop moving so I could give him the time he needed to think. I knew being bare inside of me might mean something to Mav beyond the protocols of just responsible sex. It sure as hell meant a lot more to me, but just because I wanted something more with this man, didn't mean I had the right to expect him to give it to me.

"No," Mav said as he shook his head. He opened his eyes and shook his head again. "Don't stop," he whispered.

Relief coursed through me and I began moving again even as I gently kissed him. I rocked back and forth on him several times before I straightened my body and then began lifting up and down. Mav helped me by holding my hips, but he went a step further and began thrusting up into me every time I lowered myself. The coil of need grew and grew as his hot flesh thickened even more inside of me. One of Mav's hands began jerking me off, but it didn't last long because Mav suddenly snarled and lifted me completely off of him. In one swift move, he shoved me face first down on the bed and then yanked my hips up. He drove into me with one plunge and began fucking me so hard, my entire body began sliding up the bed. I tried to get purchase with my hands, but even as I fisted them in the bedding, Mav pressed all of his weight down on me and began ramming into me. His body kept mine from moving so I could only lay there and take it.

And I fucking loved it.

It was raw and brutal and so primal that it felt animalistic. I should have been frightened by how rough the act had become, but I wasn't. Because even as Mav rutted into me, his mouth was seeking mine out and his lush tongue was sliding over mine. Between kisses he was saying my name. His arm was wrapped around my neck, holding my head up so he could access my mouth more easily and when he wasn't kissing me, I heard and felt his grunts of pleasure even as my ass began to burn. The pleasure/pain sent me to a whole other level and I began begging Mav for even more as my orgasm began to crawl up my spine.

I climbed so high and so fast that I actually began to fear what would happen when I fell, but when I whispered Mav's name, he licked the shell of my ear and said, "Let go, baby. I'll catch you." Then he changed the angle of his hips just a little and as soon as his cock slid over my prostate, I came. The climax was so intense that I let out a harsh scream and then bit down on Mav's forearm which was still holding me in place. Mav shouted in my ear and shoved into me hard as hot liquid began to fill me up. The burn of his release caused tears to streak down my face as another round of pleasure swept through me. Every time Mav humped into me, I felt another ripple of electricity fire throughout my entire body and more heat coated my insides. And through it all, Mav was right there in my ear telling me how beautiful I was and how good I felt. By the time our orgasms had subsided, Mav was still buried deep inside of me and he was kissing the back of my neck as I lay beneath him, too exhausted to do anything except revel in the knowledge that a part of him would stay with me long after he was forced to leave me.

Chapter Thirteen

Mav

Light was just beginning to filter through the sheer curtains when Eli began to stir. His back was pressed to my front and I had one arm pillowing his head while the other was wrapped around his chest. A glance at the clock showed it wasn't even five a.m. yet.

I hadn't been able to fall asleep after I'd somehow found the energy to get Eli and myself into the shower after we'd made love the second time around. I also hadn't been able to stop touching him even after I'd gotten us settled back under the covers. There'd been an awkward moment where Eli had started to press up against me, but then had pulled back as if worried it might not be what I wanted. He'd been right…and wrong.

I hadn't wanted to touch him anymore. Part of me hadn't even wanted him to stay. But the second he'd tried to physically withdraw from me and put more distance between us, I'd snagged him around the waist and pulled him back against me. I hadn't been able to force myself to loosen my hold on him until I'd felt his fingers link with mine where they were pressed against his chest. He'd fallen asleep minutes later and I'd done exactly what I'd told myself I wouldn't. I'd touched him.

Endlessly.

With my lips, with our joined hands, with my other hand…I hadn't been able to control the urge to constantly feel his warm, soft skin – to prove to myself he was really there.

And I'd obsessed over the fact that part of me still lingered deep inside Eli's body. That I'd become a part of him that he could never escape.

Not once had I ever fucked a man without a condom.

Not once.

The implications were almost too much for me to handle. From the moment I'd opened the door last night to see Eli standing on the other side, his expression pained and desperate and a reflection of what I'd been struggling with myself in the three days since I'd last seen him, I'd pretended all the reasons I should send him away didn't exist and I'd let him in. I hadn't been lying when I'd told Eli that I'd tried to leave Seattle. The second I'd gotten on my Harley every morning, I'd felt a rush of relief go through me. But it had only lasted mere minutes and as I'd put the city skyline behind me, the knot of anxiety had begun to build and build until I could focus on nothing but the need to get back to Eli. I'd purposefully not checked in with Ronan about who was watching Eli and if they'd seen anything suspicious. And when Daisy had called me yesterday morning to talk to me about the progress she was making with cleaning up Caleb's voicemail, I'd told her to talk to Ronan and had hung up on her before she could question me. I'd both dreaded and hoped that Eli would reach out to me and I'd hated myself for it. Because it put me right back on the reservation with my grandfather. I was once again a confused, lonely, desperate kid trying to figure out how to make a man look at him with something other than disdain in his eyes.

I felt Eli's fingers begin trailing back and forth along my arm where I was holding him. His fingers stopped on the abrasion on my forearm and I felt his head tilt so he could look at the place where his teeth had marked me. I'd been out of control when I'd been fucking Eli a few short hours ago. There was just no way else to describe it. Feeling the heat of his welcoming body surrounding my naked flesh had just been too much. Add in the knowledge that I'd be branding him as mine and I hadn't stood a chance in hell of keeping myself separate from him. I'd needed everything from him as I'd made our bodies one. Every touch, every whispered plea...I'd been desperate to make sure he'd held nothing back from me as I'd shown him the rightness of our being together. And then I'd filled him and it still hadn't been enough.

Eli gently caressed the abrasion for a minute and then he was carefully pulling free of my hold. I released him and expected him to look at me, but he didn't. He sat up and scooted to the edge of the bed and stared out the window for a long time before finally standing up. I couldn't take my eyes from his beautiful body as he walked to the window and pushed back the curtains enough to look outside. He stood there for a while before taking a deep breath and turning back in my direction. His eyes connected with mine, but he didn't speak. Disappointment flooded my gut as I watched him begin to collect his clothes. Once he was fully dressed, I waited for him to walk out of the room. I wasn't sure if he was going to even say goodbye as he left, but as much as I wanted to curl up on my side and close my eyes so I wouldn't have to watch him go, I forced myself to keep looking at him.

No way in hell was I going to let him see that I felt like my insides were being torn apart.

But once Eli had dragged his socks on, he didn't reach for his shoes. Instead he kept his gaze on me as he walked to my side of the bed and sat down. I held my breath as he reached out to skim his fingers across my cheek. Then he leaned down and brushed his mouth over mine in a chaste kiss.

"Morning," he said quietly, a small smile gracing his beautiful lips.

"Morning," I managed to return even though my insides were knotted so tight, I could barely breathe. A gentle brush off was a thousand times worse than a quick dismissal.

Eli kept his hand on my face and his thumb stroked back and forth over my cheek. There was a dreamy, contented look in his eyes that I both loved and hated. I didn't want this to be fucking easy for him.

"I have to go let Baby out," Eli finally said as he lowered his hand from my face and placed it alongside my body so he was hovering over me.

I was going to bite out a dismissive comment, but I held my tongue and merely nodded.

Eli leaned down and held his lips just above mine. "Will you come with me?" he whispered.

I couldn't find my voice to respond to that because my brain was too busy telling me it was some kind of trick. He'd gotten what he wanted – we both had. Yeah, he'd begged me last night not to leave him, but that had been in the throes of passion. Things were different in the light of day.

They were always different.

"We could go have some breakfast," Eli continued. He seemed to struggle for a moment before saying "Please Mav, I don't want this to end yet."

Yet.

Because it would have to sometime.

I knew I was only prolonging the inevitable, but I nodded anyway and as soon as Eli's lips brushed mine, I felt the panic leave my body. When Eli tried to pull back, I snagged my hand around the back of his head and held him there while I plundered his mouth. The same neediness that had driven Eli the night before had now invaded me and I sat up, taking Eli with me. I dragged him against me as I kissed him over and over and he didn't hesitate to kiss me back. I wasn't sure if he sensed my internal struggle, but as my need for him grew, his hand slipped under the blanket and closed around my dick. I gasped against his mouth and held there as he began gently jerking me off. Emotion coursed through me as he stroked me over and over. He acted like we had all the time in the world and he never once reached for his own dick. At some point I grabbed his face with both my hands and for the life of me I couldn't let him go as I pressed our foreheads together. My breathing began to grow heavy as Eli continued his sensual torment and as the orgasm slowly built, I closed my eyes. Neither of us spoke and Eli never once tried to escape the hold I had on him.

It was all about me.

For the first time in my whole goddamn life, I was being put first.

I let out a ragged moan as I came and I couldn't contain the harsh sob that escaped me. I managed to keep the tears that threatened at bay, but as I loosened my hold on Eli, I felt his free hand close around the back of my head as his lips skimmed my forehead. His other hand was still gently stroking my dick, drawing out my pleasure as my body tingled with sensation. I had no idea how long he held me like that for before his lips gently pressed against mine. "Let's take a shower," he suggested.

I managed a nod and could only watch in satisfaction as he lifted his hand to his mouth and licked my cum off of it before grabbing my lax hand and pulling me to my feet. As we began walking towards the bathroom, Eli reached behind his neck with his free hand to pull his shirt off, but when it came time for me to release his other hand long enough so that he could get rid of the shirt, I actually struggled to loosen my fingers enough to let go of him even for a second.

God, I was so fucked.

"We're finally sharing a meal together," Eli said with a chuckle as he bit into the bagel that was loaded with generous amounts of cream cheese.

I smiled and took a sip of my coffee. "I was really looking forward to those enchiladas," I said.

Eli's eyes held mine as they turned serious. "Tonight," he said. "I can make them at your place."

My place.

Fuck, why did I like the sound of that so much? And why did the idea of spending another night with Eli – a date night no less – sound like the best fucking idea I'd ever heard?

My throat felt too tight to speak so I nodded. Eli's wide smile was like a balm to my soul.

"I have a shift at the hospital this afternoon, but I can be at the hotel by six."

I picked at the blueberry muffin I'd ordered as I nodded again, but then I said, "Maybe I'll come with you. Visit with Matty for a bit." I glanced up to see Eli still smiling.

"Okay."

Eli took the small piece he had left of his bagel and fed it to Baby who was lying at his feet. After getting to Eli's place, we'd walked the dog a couple of blocks to a café that had an outdoor seating area where the dog was allowed. Since it was still early, there weren't any other patrons in the patio section so Baby had free roam of the place, but he never left Eli's side.

I was reaching for my coffee when my phone rang and when I pulled it out, I saw Ronan's name on the caller ID. It had been days since I'd talked to him since I'd put a moratorium on hearing about the surveillance being done on Eli at my request.

"Hey," I said when I answered.

"Are you going to stay with him for the day or do I need to call Dante to relieve me?"

Shit. I hadn't even considered the fact that Ronan might be the one watching Eli in my absence. He obviously would have followed Eli to my hotel which he and Seth were also staying at so they could continue to help Hawke and Tate with shifts taking care of Matty. But since I hadn't called Ronan to tell him Eli was going to spend the night with me, he would have had to spend the whole night in the parking garage or across the street so he could follow Eli whenever he left.

"Fuck, I'm sorry Ronan," I murmured.

"Don't worry about it," Ronan said. "What's the plan?"

I glanced up at Eli who was watching me with curiosity. My decision was easy and I kept my eyes on Eli when I said, "I'm staying with him."

"I've got some information on his case. Do you want to hear it?"

I glanced around our surroundings and finally spotted a nondescript sedan at the end of the block. It wasn't one of Ronan's regular cars so I could only assume it was a rental. The fact that I'd missed that we were being followed was very telling as to where my head was at.

"Yeah," I said and I glanced at Eli again. "Can you join us?" I asked as I made another decision that likely was going to destroy the progress I'd made with the young man across from me.

Ronan was quiet for a moment, probably surprised by the request, but he murmured a quick "Sure," and then hung up.

"Ronan's joining us?" Eli asked, the confusion clear in his voice. He knew Ronan from his visits with Matty, but that was the extent of it.

"I work for Ronan," I said.

Eli nodded. "Security stuff," he said. "Like what Dom does."

Definitely not what Dom did since I had no doubt the man followed the letter of the law and I hadn't believed in that shit in a really long time. "Sort of," I hedged since I really didn't want to get into that with him. "I asked Ronan to have someone keep an eye on you the last few days," I admitted. "Before that I was watching you myself."

Eli stiffened. "You've been following me?"

I nodded. "Since the day you asked me to teach you to fight."

"I…I didn't see you."

"You weren't meant to," I responded. "Eli, I'm sorry, I was worried-"

Eli held up his hand and shook his head and I fell silent. "Why did you stop?"

"What?"

"You said you had Ronan have someone else follow me. That means you stopped watching me after that day in your room when we…"

If the situation wasn't so serious, I would have smiled at the way Eli's cheeks flooded with color when he tried to find the words to describe the day we'd sucked each other off.

"You left me there," he added, the hurt in his voice clear.

I dropped my eyes and shook my head. "It wasn't supposed to happen," I admitted. I lifted my gaze and looked at him. "None of this was supposed to happen."

Eli tensed up and his eyes fell. I was glad I'd chosen the chair next to him rather than across from him because it made it easy to grab him when he started to push his chair back. I dragged him forward and kissed him hard and didn't release him until he began to kiss me back. "Look at me," I demanded.

It took him several long seconds to finally lift his eyes and I hated how shuttered they'd become. I tightened the hold I had on the back of his neck and forced out the words I'd been so terrified to tell him this morning when he'd been leaning over me to say good morning to me. "Eli, last night was the best night of my entire life," I whispered harshly. His eyes finally opened up a bit more and I realized I had his complete attention. "My entire fucking life," I said firmly. "And that scares the ever loving shit out of me."

Eli finally nodded and then brushed his lips over mine before reaching out to wrap his arms around my neck. I sighed in relief as I curled my arms around him and drew him as close as I could.

Neither of us stirred until Baby stood up and pressed against Eli, his golden brown eyes focused on the man walking towards us. I forced myself to release Eli and ignored the look of curiosity Ronan shot me before he reached out his hand to let the Rottweiler sniff it. He waited until the animal seemed satisfied that he wasn't a threat before taking the chair across from me. Since I refused to release Eli's hand which I'd grabbed at Ronan's approach, Eli shifted in his chair so that he could face Ronan without putting anymore distance between us.

"Hi Eli," Ronan said kindly. It was something about Ronan I would never get used to. From the day I'd met the man five years ago, he'd been as cold as ice. An emotionless, soulless man whose sole focus was his job. He'd never shown pity or mercy and he'd delivered brutal justice without so much as an afterthought.

Until Seth. Until one young man he'd known for the better part of a decade had given him the strength to let go of his past and merge the man he'd become with the man he'd once been.

But as strange as the new Ronan – or rather the "real" Ronan – was to accept, I found that I liked him. A lot. And I hadn't even lost an ounce of the respect I had for the man who'd given me a new purpose in a time in my life when I'd had nothing left.

"Hi," Eli said with a nod of his head.

"Did Mav tell you he asked me to look into your situation with your stepfather and brother?"

Eli nodded. "He told me he would have someone check it out. I didn't know he meant you, though." Eli glanced at me and then squeezed my hand before returning his attention to Ronan. "Thank you," he said softly. "And thank you for helping him watch out for me."

Ronan gave him a slight nod and then surprisingly settled his hand on Baby's head. The big dog had clearly taken a liking to the man because he was pressed up against his leg. "Caleb's phone hasn't moved since the day Mav asked our tech person, Daisy, to trace it. The last call he made with the phone was to you."

Eli stiffened and asked, "What does that mean?"

"Your brother is okay, Eli," Ronan quickly said since he likely knew the direction Eli's thoughts had taken. Eli's relief was palpable, but before he could ask anything else, Ronan continued. "It took some digging, but we've found Caleb. The day he called you he was admitted to an inpatient psychiatric hospital."

"What?" Eli whispered hoarsely.

"We were able to hack his medical records. It says he was admitted because he threatened to hurt himself."

"Is he okay?" Eli asked. I could feel the tremor in his hand so I pulled him up against my side, not caring what Ronan thought.

Ronan nodded. "One of my guys had been watching the house. When we found out where Caleb was, I asked him to get inside the hospital to make sure Caleb was okay. He saw him this morning. He's heavily sedated, but he's okay."

Eli turned his head into my chest. "He kept saying he was fine when anyone would ask him if he was okay. No wonder my stepdad was so upset."

I stroked my hand over Eli's head. "He's getting help. That's what matters." I looked up at Ronan. "Who did you send?"

"Jace."

I nodded. I knew Jace well. The man had great instincts. "What about Caleb's voicemail?"

"Daisy sent it to a guy she knows who used to do audio forensics for the FBI. He's working on it now." Ronan fell silent for a moment and then motioned his head to the side. I understood the silent request and stroked my hand over Eli's hair.

"Baby, can you get me another coffee?"

Eli straightened and nodded. He brushed his mouth over mine and said, "Black, right?"

I smiled and nodded and then he asked Ronan if he wanted anything. Ronan declined and as soon as Eli commanded Baby to stay and was out of hearing range, Ronan started talking.

"I've asked Jace to keep an eye on Eli's stepdad. We'll know if and when he leaves DC. But I still think we should keep eyes on Eli."

I had already come to that conclusion myself, but my decision was based on more emotional reasoning rather than logic. "Why?"

"Cortano's clean," Ronan said. "Too clean," he added. "But he's got some guys on the books that aren't. Guys from his early days in the military who've had less than stellar careers and hire themselves out to the highest bidder."

"Mercenaries," I murmured.

"I've got Daisy monitoring the ones we know about, but there could be ones we missed."

I nodded in understanding as fear settled in my gut.

"Hey," Ronan said and I realized I'd dropped my eyes at some point. "He's going to be okay," Ronan said softly.

I managed a quick nod. "What else?"

"I'm worried about Barretti," Ronan said.

"Dom?" I asked and quickly shook my head. "No way, I've seen him around Eli. He'd lay down his life for him in a heartbeat," I said adamantly.

Ronan glanced over his shoulder to make sure Eli was still inside the café. "Mav, Cortano helped Barretti get some international security contracts with the government that are worth billions."

"What do you mean 'helped'?"

"Cortano has connections with several people who sit on the Committees that award the contracts. Barretti Security Group was doing fine before, but when Cortano put in a good word for them and they got those contracts, their net worth quadrupled. Dominic Barretti and his brothers would lose big if Cortano got the government to pull their contracts."

"When did this happen?"

"The first contracts were awarded eight years ago, but more have been added and they get renewed every couple of years."

I shook my head in disbelief. No way could I fathom that the man who'd nearly kicked my ass when he'd thought I'd laid a hand on Eli would betray him like that. "No," I said again, going with my gut. "No way he'd do Cortano's dirty work for him."

Ronan studied me for a moment and then said, "And his brothers? You so sure about them?"

I wanted to say that yes, I was sure, but the reality was that I wasn't. Eli hadn't talked much about his surrogate family. And money made men do terrible things to even those they claimed to love the most.

"Surveillance of Eli continues," I finally said. "For anyone who might be a threat," I added, acknowledging the ugly truth that the threat might be much closer to home than I would have liked.

"We don't have the resources to watch all of Barretti's men, but I'll bring in a few more guys to watch the ones in Eli's inner circle. And I'll have Daisy monitor them for communications with Cortano. Hopefully this really was just Cortano overreacting to the stress of what was happening to his kid, but I think we need to play it safe and assume there's more going on."

I nodded even though I felt sick to my stomach. If anyone in Eli's family turned out to have ties to whoever tried to break into Eli's apartment the other night, Eli would be heartbroken.

"I take it I should tell Memphis to take you out of the rotation for a while?" Ronan said.

I looked up at him and finally remembered that I'd asked him to have Memphis find me a case that would get me out of Seattle. I saw Eli headed back our way so I merely nodded and tried not to think too much about the look of satisfaction that passed across Ronan's face. He stood just as Eli reached our table.

Eli sat down and passed me my coffee before taking the hand Ronan extended. "I'll see you around," he said to the younger man. "I'm not supposed to tell you this, but Matty is planning to let you win big today at Tic Tac Toe and he made Seth promise not to get too jealous since Seth has yet to manage to beat him."

Eli and I both laughed at that and to my surprise, Eli held on to Ronan's outstretched hand as he stood back up. He gave a very startled Ronan a quick hug and I saw Ronan swallow his surprise and hug him back before releasing him. "He's a lucky kid to have all you guys in his life," Eli murmured before he sat down again. Ronan smiled, gave Baby a brief pat and then left the patio.

"Everything okay?" Eli asked as his fingers closed over my hand which was resting next to the fresh cup of coffee he'd brought me.

"All good," I managed to say, though lying to Eli made a sour taste flood my mouth. "I was thinking we should have another lesson today," I said.

Eli's eyes sparkled with mirth as he said, "I'm up for that."

I chuckled when I realized what he was talking about and I leaned down to kiss him. "A self-defense lesson," I murmured against his mouth.

"Okay," he said softly as he teased my lips with his. "Do I get something if I knock you on your ass?"

An unexpected surge of lust went through me at his words and I said, "My ass."

Eli straightened a little. "What?" he asked in all seriousness.

I kept my voice low even though there was no one around to hear us. I put my hand on Eli's thigh as I said, "You knock me on my ass this morning and tonight after dinner, you can have my ass."

I let my fingers graze Eli's cock as I spoke and he let out a guttural moan before he slammed his mouth down on mine. When I finally dragged my mouth from his so that we wouldn't end up doing something that would get us arrested, I said, "Deal?"

"What happens if I don't knock you on your ass?"

I opened my mouth to answer, but Eli interrupted me and said, "Shit, I don't care," he said as he stole another kiss. "I come out on top either way."

I laughed at that. "You'll definitely start out on top, but it's up to you if you stay there or not."

Eli growled and reached for the mug of coffee he'd just brought me. "Where are you going?"

"To get a damn to-go cup," Eli barked and I watched him dart back into the shop as fast as he could, not caring as some of my coffee spilled over the edge of the mug. I chuckled and settled my hand on Baby's head when he rested it in my lap.

Yeah, I was fucked all right. In more ways than one.

Because Matty wasn't going to be the only one letting Eli win today.

Chapter Fourteen

Eli

"You won!" Matty yelled in exaggerated delight and he held up his hand and gave me five.

"I can't believe it," I said with a laugh as my eyes lifted to meet Mav's. My stomach dropped out at the look I saw there and I found it difficult to swallow after that. I wasn't sure, but it felt like something had shifted in our relationship this morning after I'd jerked him off. It should have been such a simple thing – a quick, down and dirty act meant to get Mav off and nothing more. But that wasn't how it had started and it definitely wasn't how it had ended.

As soon as I'd asked Mav to come with me this morning to let Baby out, I'd sensed a profound change in him…like he was finally letting his guard down and letting me see the real him and not just the parts he wanted me to see. But letting those walls fall had come at a price too, and his vulnerability had made my heart ache. The way he'd kissed me had been unexpected and as amazing as his mouth had felt against mine, there'd been an edge of panic in every brush of his lips. Like he was afraid to stop. My instincts had taken over and I'd begun trying to ease his fear by bringing him pleasure. But his reaction hadn't been at all what I'd thought it would be.

Yes, he'd gotten off. But I hadn't missed the whimpers that had bubbled up from his throat. And I'd finally understood that as strong and powerful as Mav was, he was plagued with the same raw neediness I'd been experiencing the night before. Except my need had been sated by the way he'd made love to me, the way he'd held me and spoken to me and told me how beautiful and perfect I was. I just hadn't known how to give that back to him. But when that sob of relief had slipped from his throat as he'd come, I'd known I'd done something right. The way he'd lovingly washed my body in the shower, and I his, had been proof that whatever darkness had been rolling through him when I'd first woken up had subsided…for now.

I'd been surprised to learn that Mav had been following me and then had turned that responsibility over to someone else, but it hadn't bothered me as much as it probably should have. Maybe because I was used to overprotective men. Maybe because I liked knowing what it meant. But all of the conflicting emotions I'd been struggling with had slipped away as soon as Mav had told me that being with me the night before had been the best night of his entire life. I'd made the decision then and there that I was going to fight for whatever this thing with Mav was, because every second I spent with him was better than the last. I'd had some great moments in life, but few compared to what I'd found in his arms, his touches, his looks.

"Here," Matty said as he handed me the magic marker. I wrote a big letter E on the bottom corner of the page and when I looked up, I saw Matty nodding at his grandfather, Magnus, who was sitting in the far corner of the room. The older man nodded back and got up and reached behind his chair.

"Close your eyes," Matty ordered softly and I quickly complied. I heard some commotion next to me, but kept my eyes closed. I was sitting close to Matty's bed so I felt his little body shift on the mattress and then his hand touched my arm as he steadied himself. Something lightweight dropped on my head, but I pretended not to notice as I awaited further instruction.

"Okay, open them," Matty said gleefully.

I opened them to find Matty sitting on his knees, his fingers clasped in front of him. I reached up to feel what was on my head. I knew what it was even before I carefully pulled it off and I couldn't help the sting of tears that burned my eyes as I studied the carefully colored paper crown with my name on it.

"Oh wow," I whispered and I didn't even have to pretend that I was choked up.

"Do you like it?" Matty asked. "I colored it myself."

I nodded, needing a minute to get myself together. "I love it," I managed to get out before I reached out to wrap my arms around him. He hugged me as hard as he could and then took the crown from me and put it back on my head.

"Don't tell Seth," he whispered, even though Seth wasn't in the room. "He might get sad. I'm going to let him win tomorrow," Matty added.

I nodded. "I won't tell him." I glanced at Mav who was still watching me with the same look of pleasure on his face. I noticed

Dante over his shoulder. The young man was standing in the doorway of the room, but his eyes weren't on me or Matty. I followed his dark gaze to Magnus who had returned to his chair. I didn't miss how the older man shifted uncomfortably at Dante's intense look, but kept stealing glances his way.

I didn't have much time to dwell on the interesting turn of events because Dante quickly slipped back out of the room and a few moments later, Tate, Hawke and an older woman with long red hair entered. Mav immediately stood and moved out of the way so Matty's fathers could reach his side. I also stood and walked around the bed to give them space. Concern went through me at the sight of Tate's puffy red eyes, but when he kept smiling at the woman who was clutching his hand in hers and who had equally puffy eyes, I realized whatever was happening was a good thing and not a bad one. I went to Mav's side and took his hand when he held it out.

"Bye, Matty," I said as I gave him a wave.

"Bye, Eli," he returned as he reached out to hug Tate.

As Mav led me from the room, I heard Tate say, "Buddy, I have someone really special I'd like you to meet, okay?"

"Okay, Daddy," Matty said with absolute trust.

Mav and I passed Dante, but the young man didn't look at us as he scanned the hallway. In all the times I'd interacted with Dante, albeit briefly, he'd always had an easy smile on his face…like he didn't have a care in the world. There was no smile today and as I glanced over my shoulder, I saw Magnus leaving the room. His and Dante's eyes met for a long moment, and I could practically see the

186

air sizzling with electricity around them. But then Magnus hardened his jaw and began walking the opposite direction and he didn't once look back at Dante.

I returned my attention to Mav as he led me towards the parking garage. "Do you know who that was with Tate and Hawke?" I asked. I loved that he had yet to release my hand. Many of the nurses and doctors I had met in the weeks since I'd started volunteering at the hospital murmured greetings as they passed us, but none looked at me and Mav with judgement or disdain. Several actually even ventured a smile when their eyes lit on Mav's and my joined hands.

"Tate's mom, Layla."

"His mom?" I asked in surprise.

Mav nodded. "Tate's father kidnapped him and his older brother when Tate was really little. He never knew about her until Hawke and Ronan found her a couple months ago. They've been talking on the phone a lot, but Tate was scared to meet her until now. He and Hawke met her this morning at the airport and were planning to bring her to meet Matty if everything went well."

"Why was he afraid to meet her?"

Mav's hand tightened on mine as he said, "Tate's been rejected by everyone who was supposed to love him. I think he thought she'd do the same thing."

"You guys remind me of Dom and his brothers," I murmured.

Mav looked at me. "How so?"

"You guys are making a family for Matty. For yourselves," I said. I glanced up to see that Mav's expression had fallen and I pulled him to a stop just before the door leading to the stairwell. "What?" I asked.

"Nothing," Mav said and tried to tug me forward, but I held my ground.

"No, tell me. Please."

"I'm not part of that," he finally said after a long, drawn out silence.

"Part of what?"

"I work with them, that's it," he clarified.

I finally got what he was trying to tell me, but I suspected he was actually trying to tell me something else and that had me worried. "You don't consider them family?" I asked.

Mav sighed and looked like he'd rather be anywhere else. "They're good men…great ones. And you're right, they are a family."

"But you're not a part of it."

"Don't do that," Mav grumbled as he dropped my hand.

"Don't do what?"

"Don't feel sorry for me. Not everyone needs what they have. What you have."

I struggled with how to respond since I didn't want to fuel his growing irritation and ruin the night we had planned, but I suspected we were treading dangerously close to yet another turning point in our relationship. I could press him and try to figure out why he didn't feel like a part of a family that clearly included him whether he wanted it to or not, or I could back off and drop the whole thing and we could continue pretending it wasn't a glaring sticking point. I finally settled for somewhere in between.

"I don't have it," I admitted. "That big family," I clarified.

"Dom Barretti loves you, Eli. I have no doubt the rest of the Barrettis do too."

I nodded. "I know they do," I said softly, suddenly wishing I hadn't brought the topic up. There was no way I could make Mav understand without seeming like a jealous, petty child. "We should get going so Baby doesn't make a mess in your hotel room," I said quickly as I tried to push past Mav. It had been Mav who'd suggested we take the dog back to the hotel with us this morning and I hadn't argued since it meant I could spend an entire uninterrupted night and morning with him.

Mav caught me around the waist and held me there as he bent down to brush his lips against my ear. "They love you, Eli."

I closed my eyes at that and finally said the words that made acid churn in my belly. "They shouldn't." With that, I managed to escape Mav's hold and hurried down the stairs. He caught up to me at the landing and grabbed my arm, but instead of questioning me further, he kissed me hard and used his body to pin me against the wall.

The kiss was brutal and greedy and I eagerly returned every desperate swipe of his tongue over mine. I was panting when he finally released my mouth, but held me against the wall with his big body, his hard cock pressing against mine. "I think you should collect your prize as soon as we get back to the hotel," Mav murmured against my mouth. His teeth gently caught my upper lip in their hold before releasing it and soothing the skin with his tongue.

"Even though you let me win?" I bit out as my dick swelled painfully and pushed against my zipper.

We'd ended up working out for nearly two hours in the gym at the hotel this morning, but mostly because we'd ended up getting distracted so often. It had helped when other guests had come into the gym to work out, but the second they'd left, Mav and I had been all over each other and at one point he'd started jerking me off as he'd had me pinned on the mat beneath him. He'd only stopped when a wide eyed, older woman had coughed to get our attention to let us know we were no longer alone. By the end, I had actually learned some additional moves, although I'd been too horny to really care and while I had managed to throw Mav over my shoulder when he'd grabbed me from behind, I'd had no doubt that he'd helped with that quite a bit. He'd declared me the winner and then dragged me up to the hotel room. We'd showered together and jerked each other off, but had run out of time to do much else since I was due at the hospital.

"You want a rematch?" Mav asked as he teased my lower lip in the same way he had my upper one.

"Fuck, no," I groaned and then I grabbed his hand and practically dragged him to his waiting Harley. I used the ride back to the hotel to run my hands all over his thighs and ass, not caring who saw us and when he got me into the hotel elevator, Mav returned the favor by lifting me and pressing me against the wall and grinding his cock against mine. I was half temped to tell him I'd changed my mind when we got to the room and ask him just to fuck me right there against the door, but my eagerness to know what Mav's tight ass would feel like as it engulfed my cock had me barely acknowledging my dog as he greeted us. I promised the confused animal I'd take him out later as I dragged Mav to the bedroom and slid the double doors shut so Baby wouldn't crawl into bed with us like he was prone to do at home.

Mav separated from me long enough to ask, "Where do you want me?" and I barely found my voice long enough to speak when he made a move to start stripping off his clothes.

"Slowly," I murmured as I leaned back against the doors.

Mav's eyes lit up with molten desire at my order and I filed that away. It would definitely come in handy tonight. "Shoes first," I said and instead of staying where I was, I walked to one of the big plush chairs in the corner near the bed and sat down to enjoy the show. Mav worked his boots off along with an ankle holster of some kind that I hadn't even known he wore and then he took his socks off too. Since I hadn't actually ordered him to remove the socks, I shot him a questioning look which had him hardening his jaw. But I knew it also excited him to know I was in charge because the bulge in his pants grew even more impressive.

"Shirt," I said. "Turn around first."

Mav turned around and slowly pulled his shirt off. Saliva filled my mouth as I watched the snakes shift and dance along his back with every rippling flex of his muscles.

"Turn back around," I ordered when I'd taken my fill. Mav turned around, shirt still in hand. When I nodded, he dropped it to the floor.

"Button and zipper, but nothing else," I murmured as I shifted in the chair, trying to find some more space in my pants. Being sexually aggressive wasn't something I'd ever even conceived of, but it was like an all-consuming drug.

Mav's fingers were slow and deliberate as he unbuttoned the jeans and the slow descent of the zipper had my dick notching up with every little click of the teeth separating. "Come over here," I said when Mav had released the hold on his pants. As turned on as Mav was, he didn't lose any of his confident swagger as he approached me and stopped until he was almost touching my legs.

"Take yourself out," I managed to say, though my mouth felt exceedingly dry.

Mav took his time pulling his cock out and the sight of the clear fluid trickling down his engorged shaft had saliva suddenly flooding over my tongue. "Taste yourself," I said as I lifted my eyes to his. Mav's gaze held mine for a split second before he ran his fingers over the head of his dick. I couldn't take my eyes off his hand as it slowly lifted to his mouth. His tongue lapped out to lick the fluid off, but I barely let him have a taste before I said, "Now kiss me."

192

Mav stopped moving his mouth, presumably to make sure he didn't obliterate the taste of himself and then he leaned over me and slid his mouth against mine. But to my frustration, he kept his tongue in his own mouth and I was too impatient to order him to do anything else so I shoved my tongue past his lips and slid it over his. I sighed when his flavor hit me. We ended up kissing for several minutes before I remembered our little game and I had to force myself to let him go. But before he could step back, I said, "On your knees."

Heat flashed in Mav's eyes as he hovered over me and I could hear his breathing ratchet up a notch. He was playing the cool character, but I now knew better. I held Mav's eyes as he dropped to his knees between my spread legs. His hands were resting on my thighs, but he didn't move them. "Take the rubber band out of your hair," I said as I let my eyes scan the length of Mav's chest and then down to his bobbing cock that was now glistening with pre-cum. Mav's black hair slipped over his shoulders as he tossed the rubber band to the floor. I couldn't stop myself from reaching out to let my fingers play with the slight curls on the end.

"Undress me," I murmured as I released his hair and leaned back. Mav took his time working my shoes and socks off and then his big hands skimmed over my belly before searching out the very last button on my shirt. I hadn't given much thought to my clothes when I'd grabbed a fresh change of them when we'd picked up Baby, but now I was insanely glad I'd picked a button down shirt because the feel of Mav's fingertips brushing my skin as he separated my shirt with every button he worked free was heaven. By the time he reached the top button near my neck, I was struggling to get enough air and I was suddenly desperate for him to finish so I could give my next order. I leaned forward to help him work the shirt completely off of me and then I sat back and waited. I held my tongue as Mav slowly began working my pants free and I realized at some point he'd become the one in control because by the time my pants and underwear were gone, I was writhing with need.

"Suck me!" I demanded harshly.

I was glad that Mav seemed eager to do my bidding because I'd lost all interest in playing around and when he sucked me to the root on the first pass, I let out a hoarse groan. I thrust up into his hot mouth, pulled back and then did it again. I'd ordered him to suck me, but in reality I was fucking his mouth. On my third pass, I fisted my fingers in his long hair and held him still as I shoved my cock as far down his throat as I could. He gagged slightly, but when I gentled my hold and pulled my hips back, his hands grabbed them and yanked them up. Fingers bit into my ass as Mav swallowed as much of me as he could. But I was too close and there was no way I was going to miss out on the chance to get inside of him, so I had to forcibly pull him off with what I was sure was a painful hold on his hair. I leaned down to kiss him hard and then I lowered my arm over his shoulder and ran it along his back. His tongue began licking my dick gently, but he didn't take me back in his mouth. My fingers skimmed down his lower back and then dipped past the waistband of his pants and underwear and into his crease. I stretched until I was able to reach his hole.

I couldn't see the puckered flesh, but it fluttered beneath my touch. I removed my finger long enough to wet it with my mouth and then I put it back against his opening and began massaging him. Mav groaned and began pushing against my hand with his ass so I gave him what he wanted and carefully pushed my finger inside of him.

"Yes," Mav whispered. His head was in my lap, his hands resting on my hips, but he was just lying there enjoying what I was doing to him. I loved the way his soft hair felt against my thighs. I toyed with his hole for a while, but the position didn't allow me to get my finger completely inside of him so I removed it and then settled my hand on his head.

"Do you want me inside that pretty little hole, Mav?" I asked gently as I stroked his hair.

Mav just nodded against my lap, his face nuzzling my aching dick with the movement. I lost all interest in ordering him around so I leaned down and pressed my lips against his ear and whispered, "Take everything else off and get the lube and a condom and lie down on the bed on your stomach."

I stayed where I was as Mav lifted off me. His eyes met mine as he began to get up and while they were still heavy with lust, they were filled with something else too. He brushed his lips over my mouth and then rose and went to the nightstand. But all he pulled out was the bottle of lube and I felt my insides clench at what that meant. I'd thought going bare last night had been a one-time thing – something he'd given me only because I had begged him to.

Mav placed the bottle on top of the nightstand, stripped his pants and underwear off and then lay down in the middle of the bed, his head resting on the pillows. He turned his head so he was watching me. I stayed where I was for several long seconds just so I could drink my fill of him. I began playing with myself as I let my eyes roam his body and when I saw that Mav was enjoying the show, I decided to give him more of one. I didn't spend too much time working my dick because I was already too close to the edge, so I massaged my balls for a little while and then ran my hands all over my chest. I tweaked my nipples several times and heard Mav groan, but it wasn't until I lifted my legs and put my feet on the edge of the chair that Mav went completely still. I shifted my ass forward until I knew he would have the perfect view and then I went to town on my hole. By the time I was fucking myself with two fingers, Mav was humping the bed and gripping the pillow beneath his head and I was doing everything in my power to make sure I didn't come. I forced myself to stop impaling myself on my fingers, but I kept them inside myself as I caught Mav's eyes and held them.

"Do you want to fuck me, Mav?"

Mav nodded.

"Say it."

"I want to fuck you, Eli," Mav nearly snarled.

I removed my fingers and let Mav take in the sight of my stretched hole for a moment before I climbed to my feet and went to the bed. I knelt next to him and leaned down until my mouth was just above his ear. "If you don't come while I'm fucking you, I'll let you fill me up again," I whispered.

Mav groaned and closed his eyes. He managed a nod, but he definitely wasn't looking so sure of himself any more.

I got back up and went to the foot of the bed so I could study Mav's gorgeous ass. "Spread your legs," I murmured as I reached out to trail my hands up his calves. Mav did what I said, exposing his hole. I licked my lips in excitement and then put my knee on the bed. I crawled up between Mav's legs, but only enough so I could get the position I wanted. It meant my lower half was hanging off the bed, but I didn't really care because for what I had in mind, I didn't need my dick just yet. I let my hands massage over the snake tattoos that curled over his smooth skin and then followed with my tongue. Mav flinched when I licked him, but then he stilled again. I took my time working my way to his hole and when I finally licked the puckered, wrinkly flesh, Mav let out a strangled moan. Since I'd never done anything even remotely close to this to another man, I was running on pure instinct. I kept licking, kissing and sucking on Mav's hole until it relaxed enough that it began to open a little bit and then I dipped my tongue inside of it.

"Yes!" Mav shouted so loud that I almost stopped what I was doing. But when he added "Eli, please," I did it again and then I took a deep breath and began pushing more than just the tip inside of him.

Chapter Fifteen

Mav

I ended up crushing the pillow against my mouth as Eli's tongue sank into my body. I'd been expecting Eli to prepare me with his finger like he had when I'd been on my knees in front of him, but I hadn't expected this. It was something I'd done on only the rarest of occasions and I'd never had it done to me because it was just way too intimate. And I couldn't help but wonder if I would have enjoyed it as much if it had been one of the many random strangers I'd fucked over the years. Hell, I didn't have to wonder. I knew for a fact that it was only this good because it was Eli.

I hadn't told Eli that it had been a long time since I'd bottomed – nearly twenty years in fact – because I'd already sensed his nervousness about taking me and he'd admitted it to me in the shower after our self-defense lesson. I'd reassured him that I'd like whatever he did to me and that nothing he did would hurt me, but I'd hedged on the details when he'd asked me if I'd ever been fucked before. The only time I'd ever bottomed was when I was fourteen and my best friend, Travis and I had been experimenting with sex. I hadn't found any pleasure in the act while Travis had, so after the one disastrous attempt, I'd ended up topping the few times we'd fucked.

But giving myself to Eli was just a foregone conclusion and even if I didn't get as much pleasure from being the one getting fucked as I did when I was doing the fucking, I didn't care because I remembered the way Eli had fisted my hair the day we'd fucked each other's mouths for the first time and I'd been so turned on by the idea of him being inside of me, controlling me, that I couldn't imagine it would be anything like it had been with Travis.

As Eli continued to feed on my ass, I spread my legs wider and lifted my head to look over my shoulder. The sight of him buried between the globes of my ass was too much and I had to close my eyes and drop my head again so that I wouldn't come on the spot. Watching Eli play with himself had done a number on me and his offer to let me fuck him when he was done with me was too much of a lure to let go before then. I wanted his tight ass fisting my cock again. I wanted to watch his eyes go wide as my cum burned his insides.

I was relieved and disappointed at the same time when Eli stopped tormenting me and then crawled up my body, his cock nudging my ass. "I need you, Mav," Eli whispered against my ear as he began humping me, his pre-cum covered dick sliding through my crease and brushing over my hole.

I managed a nod because I was afraid to trust my voice. Eli's mouth found mine and he kissed me long and hard as he reached for the lube. He shifted on my back, but instead of lube covered fingers pressing into me, it was the head of his cock. I wasn't worried that he hadn't prepared me with his fingers because his tongue had

199

loosened me enough that he had no trouble pushing the head of his dick inside me. The burn was fierce, but I pushed back against him anyway and forced my body to relax as more of him slipped inside of me. Eli was lying on my back so I felt his heat seeping into me as his hands caressed my shoulders and sides. His hips flexed against me as he pulled out a little before pushing back in.

"Are you okay?" Eli asked, his voice heavy with worry even as his cock began to work its way into me with more force. He was clearly caught between his body trying to instinctively get what it needed and his fear of hurting me.

"Don't stop," I urged as I turned my head in hopes that he would kiss me. "It feels so good," I said truthfully as the burn began to ease. Eli kissed me and then his hands were searching mine out where they were clutching the pillow. I released the pillow and let him link our fingers together and then listened to the grunts that fell from his lips as he continued to thrust into me in short little punches until he was fully seated. He held there a moment as his lips pressed against my neck and then he began sliding in and out of me in smooth strokes. The ridges of his cock felt amazing against my inner muscles and the building friction soon had me shoving my cock deep into the bedding. It was only the reminder of what I could look forward to if I held off that had me mentally thinking of anything that would keep me from coming. Luckily, Eli's inexperience proved to be a benefit because he was clearly enjoying the newfound pleasure too much to linger and torture me. He slammed into me hard over and over as his hands released mine and he grabbed my shoulders as if to hold me down. And then one of his hands was in my hair, twisting it around his fist until his fingers were pressed against my scalp. I nearly came when he dragged my head backwards just a little bit and held me like that, the sharp tugging of my hair as he pounded into me causing electricity to dance up my spine.

I moaned over and over as Eli used me and when he began crying out against my shoulder where his mouth was buried, I let out a strangled grunt because he started filling me a second later, his hot cum scalding me. He thrust into me over and over again as the orgasm drove him on and on. The fingers that weren't fisted in my hair were digging into my shoulder so hard I had no doubt I'd have bruises in the morning, but I loved every second of it. And I loved when Eli kept pushing into me even as his orgasm began to wane. The grip on my hair eased and then Eli was brushing it aside so his lips could reach my skin. Soothing kisses rained down over every part of me he could reach and even though I was still painfully hard and desperate for relief myself, I basked in how cherished his touch made me feel. When he finally pulled free of my body, I immediately missed the fullness.

Eli slid down my back, his hands skimming over my sweat slickened skin. His hands settled on my ass and with my legs still splayed open wide, I knew exactly what he was seeing because I could feel it. His cum leaking from my body. Eli kept massaging me with his fingers and I lifted my head so I could watch him watching me. He was covered in a sheen of sweat and his black hair was slicked back off his wet forehead. His half hard cock was covered with a layer of lube and his own cum. His eyes lifted to mine for a moment before going back to my hole and I knew exactly what he had planned long before he did it.

It should have disgusted me, but it didn't.

Not even close.

I let out a muffled moan as Eli leaned down to lick over my opening and he briefly dipped inside for a moment before he climbed back up my body and searched out my mouth. I opened without hesitation as he shared himself with me. When we'd consumed every last drop, Eli said, "Turn over."

He lifted enough to let me move onto my back and then he grabbed the lube. I watched him reach behind himself to work some lube into his body. I'd expected him to do it quickly, but he lingered and began riding my abdomen as he finger-fucked himself. My painfully hard cock was nudging his hand as he impaled himself on his own fingers. I let my hands massage Eli's thighs as I watched himself work himself over and wasn't surprised when his cock began to grow stiff again. I was about to reach for his dick when Eli pulled his fingers free and then searched out my cock. He had enough lube on his fingers to slick me up a little bit and as he pressed me against his hole, I felt him swipe the head through some of the lube that had collected around his opening. I expected him to take it slow as he took me inside himself, but instead, he bore down on me with such force and intensity, that I was bottoming out inside of him in one smooth glide. Eli bit into his lip at what I assumed was an intense mix of burn and pain. I held myself still inside of him even though I wanted to move more than anything. Eli finally let out a deep breath as his body relaxed and then he placed his hands on my chest to support himself as he began rocking back and forth over me.

As frantic as I was to come, I was entranced by the way Eli moved his body over mine and I kept myself still so I could just feel everything he was doing to me. The heat and pressure on my dick were incredibly intense, but the friction wasn't enough to get me off because Eli was limiting his movements. But that didn't mean nothing was happening to me, because it was.

It absolutely was.

Eli's rocking and the occasional swivel of his hips were causing jolts of pleasure to flash through me. They didn't build to something bigger, they just rolled through me, one after the other. The sensation was incredibly pleasurable and unlike anything I'd ever known. I'd always been so desperate to come, that I'd never basked in what came before. And that didn't even include the satisfaction I felt at watching Eli as he took his own pleasure. His hands stroked all over his body, much like they'd done when he'd been sitting in the chair, teasing me. His back was arched beautifully and his eyes were closed as his hard cock bobbed against his abdomen with every roll of his hips. He leaned back and put his hands behind him, resting them on my legs. The shift in position had more of me sinking inside of him. The bursts of pleasure began to increase in intensity and frequency as Eli picked up the pace and within minutes, I was seeing stars as I rode the edge of my orgasm.

I knew Eli was in the same boat as me because the easy, gentle rocking of his hips changed and he began slamming his body up and down on mine. He straightened and grabbed me by the neck, urging me up. I needed no more invitation and sat up, grabbing him around the waist with one arm while I braced myself with the other. I shoved my hips up as he dropped down and he let out a strangled cry. His hands were gripping my neck as we began to frantically fuck one another. Eli's cock was trapped between us so he let go of me with one hand and shoved it between our bodies. I could feel him jerking himself off just as hard and as fast as I was fucking into him. I shifted the angle of my hips just a little bit and was rewarded with a harsh scream as I slid over Eli's prostate.

"Mav!" Eli shouted as his hand moved down to my shoulder and dug in tight. I nailed him again and again with every powerful lunge and just as my orgasm steamrolled through me, Eli let out a wail and threw his head back as his cum splashed over both of us. I kept fucking Eli through my orgasm as endless sprays of cum tore free of my body and filled Eli's pulsing channel. I closed my eyes, the orgasm spreading through my every nerve and cell and I cried out in relief and grabbed Eli's waist with both hands as I pumped into him over and over until there was nothing left to give him. Aftershocks rocked through me making me twitch deep inside Eli's body and I could feel my own cum engulfing my dick in glorious warmth. I fought to catch my breath as I pressed my head against Eli's chest and I reveled in the way his arms went around my shoulders and he rested his cheek on the top of my head. I could feel his fingers stroking through my hair.

I didn't want to move or talk or even breathe in that moment because I didn't want to disturb the perfect simplicity of it.

But the silence was shattered in more ways than one when Eli whispered the words I'd never thought I'd hear in my entire life…and wasn't sure I'd ever wanted to.

"I love you, Mav."

Chapter Sixteen

$\mathcal{E}li$

I woke up when I heard Mav's phone ring, but I didn't move from my position when I felt his arms release me so he could answer it.

"Hello?"

I couldn't hear what the other person was saying, but whoever it was spoke for a long time before Mav finally said, "Where?"

I felt the bed shift and finally turned over to see Mav sitting on the edge of the mattress. The blanket had fallen away to reveal his lower back and ass and I resisted the urge to reach out and run my fingers over the snakes that I was perversely coming to think of as mine.

"Yeah, okay," Mav murmured and then he hung up the phone. But he didn't put it down and he didn't move from his position. His shoulders were hunched and his hair was a tangled mess.

Probably from the several times we'd made love again throughout the night.

I could tell from the light filtering through the curtains that it was morning and a quick glance at the nightstand clock showed it was almost eight. Baby was lying quietly along the foot of the bed. Since I hadn't let him in, I could only assume Mav had. After I'd destroyed the perfect moment we'd had last night after I'd told Mav I loved him, there'd been a subtle shift in Mav. He'd kissed me and continued to hold me until our bodies had settled, but there'd been a strange distance that had grown between us – but it wasn't something I could clearly put my finger on.

We'd ended up showering after that and then I'd cooked Mav the enchiladas I'd promised him while he'd taken Baby for a walk. We hadn't spoken much as we'd eaten. Mav had suggested watching a movie on TV and I'd been thrilled when he'd pulled me in his arms so that I was pressed against him as we'd sat on the couch and watched. But still, there'd been something missing. He'd started kissing me during a slow part of the movie and when he'd finally turned it off and pulled me to my feet, I'd been more than ready for what was to come next. He'd made love to me slow and deep the first time and he'd actually made me come twice before he'd come himself. In the pre-dawn hours, he'd woken me up by slipping inside my body from behind. He'd brought me to another intense orgasm before taking his own, then we'd showered again. But as soon as he'd gotten done washing me, he'd lifted me into his arms and shoved into me with little warning or preparation. I'd wrapped my legs around him as he'd held my ass open with his big hands, his body pinning mine against the wall and I'd just held on as best I could for the brutally rough ride. My ass had felt like it was on fire from all the fucking we'd done, but I'd still come just as hard as I had all the other times we'd come together.

And still I wanted more.

When Mav didn't lay back down, I sat up and pressed myself against his back. I wrapped an arm around his waist and skimmed my lips over his cheek.

"Everything okay?" I asked.

Mav was quiet for a long time and I felt a chill go through me when he didn't respond to my touch in any way. He almost always touched me back in some kind of way, whether it was with a kiss or just to close his hand over mine. But his back was stiff and unyielding and he actually shifted a little as if trying to escape me even though he didn't get up.

"Um, yeah…I have to leave town for a few days to take care of something. I'll have Ronan take you home."

Mav tried to stand, but I quickly shifted so I was sitting next to him and held on to his hand. "Wait, what is it? What happened? Who was that on the phone?"

Mav wouldn't look at me as he studied his phone. But his expression was completely blank. "The ME's office in Newark. They need me to come ID and claim my mother's body."

I sucked in a breath and covered my mouth with my free hand. "Mav…"

Mav stood before I could hug him like I had planned. He tugged his hand free of mine. "Get dressed. I'll call Ronan," he said as he went around the bed and began scooping up his clothes. I scrambled off the bed and stopped him before he could escape into the bathroom like he intended.

"Mav, please, talk to me," I said as I rubbed my hands up and down his arms. His skin was tight and cold.

"Nothing to talk about."

"I'll come with you," I said as I released him and began gathering my clothes. I started making plans in my head as I yanked on my pants.

"Eli-"

I shook my head and said, "No, it's fine. I'll have Brennan watch Baby and I'm sure I can find someone to take my shift at the hospital. If not, they'll be okay without me for a few days…"

"Eli."

I kept talking since I knew what the tone in Mav's voice meant. "Do you think Ronan would mind taking Baby home for me so Brennan can pick him up?"

"Damn it, Eli! I don't want you to come!"

I froze at that because I hadn't expected him to come right out and say it. His voice was cold and dead. I turned around and saw that he'd managed to pull his pants on, but nothing else.

"Mav, you shouldn't do this alone."

"I've been doing this shit alone my entire fucking life! You really think I'm going to change all that for you? Because you're a good fuck?"

Pain ripped through my insides at the words and even though I tried to tell myself he was just lashing out and didn't mean them, I felt tears sting my eyes.

"Just go home," Mav bit out, more quietly this time and then he disappeared into the bathroom. I flinched when I heard the lock engage. I hadn't noticed Baby moving back and forth between us, but when I sat down on the edge of the bed, the dog shoved his nose against my lax fingers. I managed to get dressed despite the sudden physical ache in my body and when Mav didn't come out of the bathroom, I went to the living room to get my car keys and the small overnight bag I'd packed the day before when we'd picked up Baby. I sat down on the couch in the hopes that Mav might come out, which he eventually did a few minutes later, but as soon as he saw me through the double doors leading to the bedroom, he slid them closed. The fact that he didn't lock them meant nothing. Hell, it was probably because they didn't lock. Either way, he'd already locked me out of his heart.

I felt tears gathering in my eyes as I stood and went to the door. "Baby," I called. My dog was standing in front of the bedroom door whining incessantly and I felt tears slide down my cheeks.

He doesn't want us, I said silently to the dog.

"Baby, come," I said quietly and the big dog instantly came to me. I snapped on his leash and pulled open the front door, but nearly had a heart attack when I almost ran right into Ronan. He grabbed me before our bodies could collide and then gently released me. His eyes shifted from me to the bedroom and then back to me.

He looked angry and I tried to discreetly step around him so I could make my escape. But he grabbed my arm and gently forced me back into the room.

"Sit," he said as he pointed to the couch. I wanted to both laugh and cry when Baby instantly sat down at Ronan's firm command.

"He asked me to leave," I started to say, but stopped when Ronan's features grew even tighter. I wiped at my face and went to sit on the couch. Baby came with me and jumped up onto the plush piece of furniture. I was glad to have something to hold on to when he lay down across my lap. I snuck glances at Ronan as he strode to the bedroom doors, but he didn't bother knocking. He just slid them open and walked right in before closing them behind him. I considered sneaking out while Ronan was preoccupied with Mav, but thought better of it. Ronan didn't seem like the best guy to piss off.

But that wasn't the only reason.

No, I stayed because some perverse part of me kept hoping that Mav would walk through those doors, take me in his arms and tell me he was sorry and ask me to stay.

"Not likely," I whispered to myself as I remembered Mav's cruel words about just being a good fuck. More tears welled in my eyes and I didn't even bother to try and stop them as I buried my face in Baby's soft fur.

Chapter Seventeen

Mav

My insides bled as I heard the doors behind me slide open, but I steeled myself for what I needed to do. "I told you I don't want you here anymore."

"It's me."

I glanced up from the browser on my phone that I'd been using to try to find the next flight out and saw Ronan pushing the double doors closed. I assumed his presence meant that Eli hadn't waited for him so I said, "He probably just left. You should be able to catch up to him in the garage."

"He's in the living room," Ronan said, his voice quiet and unreadable.

I turned away because I knew what it meant that the man hadn't just gone and collected Eli like I'd asked. "It's none of your business, Ronan," I murmured as I woke my phone back up and started searching the flights again.

"Just like it's none of his?" Ronan asked.

I didn't respond to that and instead said, "I've got a lot of shit to do."

Ronan stopped next to me and snatched my phone away and tossed it on the bed. "Seth is working on having the plane readied for you and as soon as you're airborne, I'll make the arrangements to have your mother's body transported wherever you want."

I knew Ronan was talking about the private jet he and Seth had recently purchased so they wouldn't keep needing to charter a plane when they wanted to travel somewhere. Since Seth suffered from extreme anxiety, they'd found it more prudent to buy a private jet so that they could travel on their own schedule and bring Seth's dog, Bullet, with them. And it wasn't like the men couldn't afford it.

"That's not necessary," I muttered as the numbness I'd felt ever since the man on the phone had muttered the words that had ensured I'd never hear my mother's voice again. Even if it was just to beg for money.

"What happened with Eli?"

The shift in conversation caught me off guard and a wave of pain flooded my insides as I thought about the terrible things I'd said to him. I'd been desperate to drive him away, but the words had been unnecessarily cruel. And a complete lie.

"Nothing. It's over. I'll need a few days and then Memphis can put me back in the rotation."

"I'll talk to Eli about going with you. If it's his job at the hospital-"

Anger surged through me at that and I shoved past Ronan to grab my bag from where it was sitting on the dresser in the far corner of the room. "I don't want him to come with me and I don't need

213

your help! I'm fine," I snapped as I began jamming the few clothes I'd taken out of the bag the day before back into it.

"Mav, I know you're hurting, but this is what family does-"

"Family?" I spit out. "We're not fucking family, Ronan. We're employer and employee!"

I had my back turned so I didn't see Ronan until he was on me. He grabbed me by the arm and yanked me backwards until I hit the wall. I took a swing at him, but he easily caught my fist and then pinned my arm against my side. Besting Ronan physically wasn't possible, so I didn't bother to struggle.

"The other thing family does is they tell one of its members when they're being a fucking idiot. Now shut the hell up and listen to me."

Ronan's hold on me eased, but he didn't release me and I found I was suddenly too tired to care. I'd let him say his piece and then I'd get the fuck out of this city for good.

"Stop running, Mav," Ronan suddenly whispered.

The drop in his voice was so dramatic that I focused my eyes on him.

"Just stop and look around you for a minute. Hawke, Tate, Matty, Seth, me...you've got us whether you like it or not. We are not going anywhere, no matter how hard you push us away, do you hear me?"

I hated that a little spark inside of me fluttered to life. I hated that even as Ronan released me, a part of me wished he hadn't. I managed a nod, though I wasn't sure what I was agreeing to. I couldn't deal with this shit right now. Maybe not ever.

"Let us help you, Mav," Ronan said gently, too gently.

I nodded again, my throat feeling too dry to actually speak. I pushed off the wall, but found it hard to do anything else.

"Tell me what else you need," Ronan murmured.

"Take him home," I whispered. "Please."

"Mav-"

"I can't have him here, Ronan," I said simply, hoping like hell Ronan would just take my word for it and not ask any more questions.

He studied me for a long time and then nodded. "I'll have Seth text you once the plane is ready."

As Ronan turned to go, I grabbed his arm. Pain spiraled through my belly as I whispered, "Take care of him, Ronan."

"I'll keep him safe," Ronan promised and then he patted me on the shoulder. "When you get back, we'll figure everything out."

I nodded, but said nothing.

Because I had no intention of coming back to Seattle. Not for my Harley, not for the family Ronan had so easily proclaimed me to be a part of, and definitely not for the man I'd somehow managed to fall completely in love with without even realizing it.

* * *

Instead of texting me, Seth appeared at my hotel room door an hour later and informed me that he was driving me to the airport himself.

Seth was close to the same age as Eli and had a similar build, though he was a bit taller and had a head of thick blond hair and bright green eyes. I hadn't gotten to know him until well after he'd gotten together with Ronan, but my initial impression had been that he was a quiet and kind-hearted young man, but also somewhat docile. But the second I'd started telling Seth I would ride my Harley to the airport, he'd pulled my bag from my hand, said that my plan wasn't acceptable and proceeded to walk to the elevator. When I'd joined him, he'd taken my hand in his for a gentle squeeze before letting me go.

We hadn't spoken on the ride to the private airport other than Seth giving me some general information about the trip and that a car would meet me at the airport in Newark and drive me to the ME's office. By the time Seth had pulled up to the small hangar where the jet was parked, I was a jumbled mess of emotions. But it wasn't my mother I was thinking about – no, just one episode kept playing on a loop in my head…the moment I'd reduced every beautiful thing that had happened between me and Eli to a few ugly words.

Because you're a good fuck.

I climbed out of the car and went around the front to collect my bag from Seth. As soon as I took it, he was wrapping his arms around me. I knew the act was meant to offer comfort, but all it did was make my skin crawl.

"Take care of yourself, Mav."

I withdrew from Seth as quickly as I could and murmured, "I will."

"We'll see you when you get back."

I nodded and stepped past him. The pilot was standing at the bottom of the stairs. He shook my hand and introduced himself and told me to make myself comfortable while he and the co-pilot finished doing some pre-flight checks on the outside of the plane.

My insides began to knot up as I stepped into the plane as I realized this was really it – that this time when I left, there would be no turning around.

It's the way it should be, a little voice inside of me whispered.

And then everything just stopped because the first thing I saw when I stepped into the spacious cabin wasn't the huge white leather seats or luxurious décor.

No.

The first thing I saw was the reason I was fleeing Seattle for good.

Eli.

I stood in the doorway of the plane for several long seconds in complete and utter disbelief before I forced myself to step inside. Eli had been sitting in one of the seats in the first row, but he quickly stood when he saw me. He was wringing his hands together and the look on his face could only be described as terrified. I couldn't help but wonder if he was afraid I'd physically hurt him or if he was just waiting for me to inflict more verbal wounds on him.

The brief excitement that had surged through me at seeing him dissolved and was replaced with anger. "Fucking Ronan," I muttered.

"I did this, not Ronan," Eli said, his voice shaky. "I told him to bring me here when he said he'd arranged a plane for you."

I had no doubt that Ronan hadn't put up much of an argument.

"You're not coming with me," I said as I turned to look out the door to see if Seth had left yet. Irritation went through me when I saw that he was leaning against the front of his car, along with the pilot and co-pilot.

Yep, I'd been played.

"Go," I said as I motioned to the door.

"I'll follow you," Eli said.

I lifted my eyes at that and saw that Eli had moved closer to me and the terror in his eyes was gone and had been replaced with a grim determination.

"I'll find the ME's office in Newark and wait there until you show up. And when you push me away again, I'll figure out where you're going next and I'll follow you there too. I don't care how many times you tell me you hate me or that you don't want me or that what we had together didn't mean anything," Eli said angrily. "I. Am. Not. Leaving. You."

I hated the sudden rush of warmth that filtered through me at his last words.

"Fine," Eli suddenly said and although there was a thread of hurt in his voice when he said it, he straightened his back as he stepped past me and I had no doubt he would do exactly what he said. I snagged him by the waist and stepped forward until Eli's back was pressed up against the wall of the plane. His arms came up to grab mine as I held him there with my body.

"It won't change anything," I said as I shook my head. "I'm not coming back here."

Pain flooded Eli's eyes and he dropped them. I hated myself for what I was doing, but I couldn't escape the self-preservation instincts that had kicked in. If I spent any more time with this man, I'd never be able to walk away and I wouldn't survive it when he did. Not *if* he did, *when* he did. Because I had no doubt it would happen someday. He'd see the things in me that all the others had and when he turned his back on me, I wouldn't be able to put the pieces back together again.

"You won't even try?" Eli asked brokenly.

"Try what?"

"To love me?"

I closed my eyes, but it did nothing to ease the ache in my chest. "No," I lied in desperation. I needed him to get the fuck off this plane and go home, because even now, the urge to tell him the truth was fucking killing me.

I risked opening my eyes and saw that Eli was staring at my chest. I'd expected to see tears or pain, but all I saw was the same emptiness I'd seen that day in the parking garage when he'd thought

219

I'd wanted sex in exchange for self-defense lessons. I reached up to cup his face in the hopes of bringing him back to me, but quickly dropped my hand. "Eli, go home," I urged gently, though my insides were screaming at me not to let him go.

Eli turned away from me to head towards the entrance, but when he whispered, "I'll see you in Newark," I grabbed his arm to stop him.

I let out a loud curse that had him flinching, but I ignored him and stepped to the door.

"Let's go!" I shouted and didn't bother to wait to see what Seth and the pilots' reactions were. I dragged Eli to the first row of seats and pushed him down in one. Instead of sitting next to him, I went to the back of the plane and searched the cabinets until I found the various bottles of alcohol I'd expected would be there. I grabbed one without even looking at what it was, sloshed a generous amount into a glass and swallowed it in one drag. By the time I picked a seat on the opposite side of the plane, well away from Eli, I started to feel the burn of what had turned out to be scotch. But it wasn't enough to take my mind off the young man who'd somehow invaded every part of my soul in just a few short weeks.

I doubted there was enough alcohol in the world to do that.

Chapter Eighteen

Eli

Five hours and counting.

That was how long it had been since Mav had last spoken to me. But it didn't matter because it felt like just seconds had passed since he'd cut me open and left me to bleed to death.

No.

One word. One word that was proof of what I'd known from the moment I'd woken up one morning in a haze of confusion and pain and realized that I would never have the family I'd started to believe I could have after Dom Barretti had come into my life.

I'd been so determined to follow through on my plan after I'd told Ronan to take me to the airport. There'd only been enough time to call Brennan to ask him to watch Baby for me and to tell the hospital I had a family emergency. Ronan hadn't argued with me when I'd informed him of the change of plans and asked him to take Baby back to my place after dropping me off. He'd simply agreed and reminded me that he'd need my house keys. Once we'd reached the airport, he'd spoken to the waiting pilot for a couple of minutes and given me a brief hug during which he'd whispered a few short words in my ear that had become my mantra as I'd waited to confront Mav inside of the jet.

Fight for him.

Fight wasn't even an adequate word for the battle that had ensued, both with Mav and within myself. I'd wanted nothing more than to get off the plane and go home so I could lick my wounds after Mav had told me he wouldn't even try to love me. And while I'd tried to get off the plane, I wouldn't have gone home. I would have done exactly what I'd said I'd do and followed him, no matter what it cost me.

I wasn't leaving Mav even though he'd already left me. Once I was sure he was okay after dealing with the loss of his mother, then I'd let him go. But that wasn't all I was going to do.

No, I'd had a lot of time on the flight to think and I'd come to the realization that returning to Seattle had been a terrible mistake. I'd thought being around Dom and his family would somehow heal the wounds I'd inflicted upon myself with one terrible decision, but being around my surrogate family had made me realize they were no longer even that to me. I had become an outsider looking in on a life I could no longer have. And even though Dom, his brothers and their partners would never know what I'd done, it didn't matter because I knew.

Five hours was both a lot of time and not enough. Because while I hadn't needed much time to make the decision to leave Seattle for good, I'd had plenty of time to think about what it would be like to try to start over again. When I'd done it the first time when

I'd left Seattle to go to school on the east coast, I'd chosen to see it as a new adventure. This time around, I'd be leaving behind so much more than bad choices. Leaving the family I'd wanted to be a part of more than anything would cripple me. But leaving Mav...I had no way to even describe what that was going to do to me. He'd become the one person I could be myself around. Who would I be now?

"Eli, we're here," I heard Mav say and I looked up from where I'd been staring blankly out the window. I'd glanced at my watch when the pilot had announced that we were beginning our descent into Newark, but I didn't remember anything after that. I was lucky Mav hadn't decided to just leave me sitting there.

My fingers felt numb as I worked the seat belt loose. I grabbed my bag from the seat next to me and stood. Mav hadn't moved and he looked like he wanted to say something, but he didn't and he finally turned and left the plane. I steeled myself for what was to come and followed him.

When I got off the plane, I saw Mav standing at the bottom of the stairs, his eyes on a man standing about a hundred yards away, a big SUV right behind him. The two men stared at each other for a long time. The other man's expression was unreadable from where I stood, but I didn't miss the tension in Mav's frame. When I reached him, he glanced at me and then began walking forward. I stayed a few steps behind and watched the interaction when Mav reached the other man. They studied each other for a long time before the other man put out his hand. Mav hesitated and then extended his arm, but their handshake wasn't traditional. Instead of grabbing each other's hands, their hands wrapped around each other's forearms and held there for a long moment. Then the stranger smiled and stepped forward to wrap his other arm around Mav and pat him on the back. It wasn't a lover's embrace, but rather one of brothers.

When they stepped back, the other man's eyes fell on me and then shifted back to Mav.

"Mace, this is Eli Galvez. Eli, this is Mace Calhoun. We used to work together."

"Hi, it's nice to meet you," I murmured as I held out my hand. I hated that Mav hadn't even attached the nondescript moniker of "friend" to me when he'd introduced me.

Because we weren't even that. I was a good fuck, nothing more, I reminded myself.

"It's nice to meet you, Eli," Mace said as he shook my hand. "I wish it could have been under more pleasant circumstances," he added as his gaze shifted back to Mav. "We don't have to do this right away," Mace said to Mav. "I can take you to your hotel-"

"No," Mav interjected with a shake of his head. "I need to get this over with."

Mace nodded and then reached for my and Mav's bags. He stowed them in the back of the SUV while I climbed into the backseat and Mav sat up front in the passenger seat. None of us spoke as we made the twenty-minute journey to the Coroner's office, but I did hear Mace make a call to tell someone named Detective Adams that we were on our way. I'd purposefully chosen the seat behind Mace so I could watch Mav as we drove and the closer we got to our destination, the more rigid his frame became. By the time Mace was parking the car, Mav's jaw looked like it was going to crack from the pressure.

I followed Mav and Mace into the building and ultimately the basement where it was considerably cooler than the upstairs had been. A portly man in a cheap suit was waiting for us, file folder in hand.

"Mr. James?" the man said as he extended his hand. We'd stopped in front of a large glass window that was covered with a curtain on the inside. I knew exactly what was on the other side of that curtain and I felt my stomach roll.

"Yes," Mav said stiffly as he shook the man's hand.

"I'm Detective Adams. I've been assigned to this case."

Mav nodded and I barely noticed when both Mace and I were introduced to the man because I was focused on how Mav's eyes had shifted to the window. I ached to touch him, to tell him that everything would be okay.

"When you're ready, I'll have the ME pull the curtain back," the detective said.

"I'm ready," Mav said without hesitation and he faced the window. I automatically moved to his side, but I doubted he noticed me. Mace was on his other side. The detective went to an intercom and spoke into it and a second later the curtain was drawn back. I forced myself not to react to the sight of the covered body, but I felt like I was going to throw up when the ME began drawing back the covering to reveal the body.

I hadn't asked Mav how his mother had died, but I had my answer the instant the woman's face was revealed. Because there was a small, almost perfectly shaped hole on her right temple. I shifted closer to Mav when I heard a rush of air escape him.

Pain tore through me for him and without thinking, I automatically reached out to grab his hand. A few moments later, his fingers remained lax in my grip so I began to release him, but the second my fingers loosened, his hand tightened around mine.

"Mr. James, is this your mother, Kim Red Winds?" the detective asked as he read the name from a piece of paper in the folder he was holding.

"Kimimela," Mav murmured. "It's her Indian name. She shortened it to Kim when she left the reservation. It means Little Butterfly," he said dully.

The detective didn't respond, but I saw him jot it down.

"What happened?" Mav asked, his eyes never leaving his mother's bloodless face.

"It was a domestic altercation with the man she was living with. Witnesses said they were often heard arguing and evidence suggests she may have been trying to leave him when he shot her."

"Where is he?" Mav asked, his hand tightening on mine.

"Dead. He took his own life shortly afterwards."

Even though Mav's hold on me bordered on painful, the rest of his body showed no reaction whatsoever.

"Mr. James, the ME will need some information on what you would like done with the body. Have you selected a funeral home yet?"

"No funeral home," Mav said. "I'm taking her home."

* * *

"Come in," I called when I heard the knock on the door. I'd been sitting out on the balcony of the guest room in the townhouse Mace shared with Cole and Jonas, the two men he lived with and who I had already guessed were his lovers based on the single master bedroom Mace had shown us when he'd given us a tour of the place.

I'd been surprised that Mav had agreed when Mace had suggested we stay with them rather than at a nearby hotel, but I'd figured out why he'd said yes as soon as we'd gotten to the spacious townhouse. Because when Mace had shown us to the bigger of the two guestrooms, Mav had declared the room mine, leaving Mace no choice but to offer him the second guestroom on the other side of the hall.

Mace pushed opened the door. He had a couple of towels in his hand which he placed on the bed. Behind him trailed a small, fluffy tabby cat that promptly jumped up on the bed and lay down on top of the towels.

"Digger," Mace murmured as he reached for the cat.

"No," I said quickly. "Leave him."

"You sure?" Mace asked as we both watched the cat curl itself into a ball, its tail wrapping around its body. I hadn't missed the fact that the animal was missing one of its eyes. From the moment Mav and I had stepped over the threshold of Mace's townhouse, we'd been greeted by several dogs and cats, though I hadn't seen this particular one at the time. Mace had explained that a few of the animals were fosters, but with the way he greeted them and they him, I had to wonder if they would be fosters for long. Because the huge, heavily tattooed man clearly had a soft spot for them.

"Yeah," I said as I stepped forward to run my hand over the cat's soft fur. "I'd love the company," I added before I could think better of it.

"Well, if you need anything else, just let me know. I'm going to get dinner started since Jonas is teaching a late class and Cole won't be back from Connecticut for another hour or so."

Agitation was rolling through me and the idea of being cooped up in the room across from the man who hadn't acknowledged me even once after he'd dropped my hand at the Coroner's office after his mother's body had been covered back up had me unable to sit still for more than a minute at a time. "Can I help?" I asked.

"With dinner?" Mace asked in surprise. "Um, yeah, sure."

I turned to close the balcony door so Digger wouldn't go outside and then followed Mace from the room. I glanced at Mav's closed door. He'd disappeared in there shortly after Mace had finished the tour with the excuse that he had arrangements to see to, but I wasn't certain that was the complete truth since he'd made several calls from the car and I'd garnered enough information from the one-sided conversation to glean several things.

His first call had been to Ronan to let him know we'd arrived and that we'd be flying to Pine Ridge, South Dakota the following day to take his mother's body back to the reservation she'd grown up on. When Mace had asked about the arrangements after Mav had hung up with Ronan, Mav had simply said that Ronan would take care of having the body transported to the airport in Newark as well as to the reservation from the airport near Pine Ridge. His next call had been the telling one because after he'd said his name, he'd asked to speak to his grandfather. He'd been silent as the other caller had spoken, but when he'd said, "Tell him his daughter is dead and I'm bringing her home," and then hung up, I'd known the man had likely refused to speak to Mav. And I knew that whatever tomorrow brought when we reached the reservation, it would be pure hell for Mav.

Once Mace and I reached the kitchen, I threw myself into cutting up the vegetables that needed to be chopped for the salad. Neither of us spoke as we worked, but I didn't miss the way Mace looked at me. When I was finished putting the salad together, I noticed that Mace was making two versions of the same type of casserole. At my curious glance he said, "Cole loves mushrooms and peppers, but Jonas hates them."

I smiled at that. "My uncle does that too."

"Does what?"

"Cooks separate meals for his partners."

229

Mace stilled. "Your uncle is involved with two people?"

I nodded. "Two men. They've been together almost nine years. Ren keeps saying he's tired of making two dinners plus something separate for the girls, but he does it anyway."

"Girls?"

"Their daughters. Two of them."

Mace laughed. "Two daughters? They're screwed."

I chuckled. "The fathers or the daughters?"

Mace smiled. "Both I guess." He went to the refrigerator and pulled out a can of soda and offered it to me. He grabbed one for himself and motioned to the kitchen table.

"Those girls have my uncles wrapped around their little fingers. Ren, Declan and Jagger are the ones in trouble."

"Are they your only family?" Mace asked.

The temporary warmth I'd been feeling at the many memories of the three men trying to figure out how to manage two young daughters fled. Mace must have seen something in my expression because he said, "Sorry, it's none of my business."

"No," I said with a shake of my head. The air turned awkward between us and I felt instantly guilty. The man's question had been a harmless one. I was the one turning it into something more. "They're a big family," I said. "Ren has three brothers. Vin is the oldest and he's married to Mia. They have four kids. Dom's next. He's married to Logan and they have three kids. Rafe is the youngest and is married to Cade. They also have three kids and are expecting another one in a couple of months. There's also Zane and Connor

230

who are raising Zane's younger brother and sister and they have a five-year-old son. Logan's sister is married to one of his best friends and his other best friend is married too."

Mace looked at me for a long time before laughing heartily. "That is a big family. You're a lucky guy, Eli." Mace took a drink and then asked, "Which one of the brothers is your father?"

"What?" I asked in startled surprise.

Mace hesitated. "You said they were your uncles. I just assumed…"

I swallowed hard and shook my head. "No, I'm not really part of the family," I clarified. "I met Dom when I was a kid and he helped me and my mom out. I kind of just hung out with them here and there."

I was glad when Mace didn't say anything. Instead, he got up to check the casseroles and put them in the oven. When he returned to the table I asked, "How long have you and Jonas and Cole been together?"

"A few months. We're still trying to figure everything out," he admitted.

"What do you mean?"

Mace tilted his head. "We know that the three of us were meant to be together, but that doesn't mean the rest of the world sees it the same way."

I nodded in understanding. "Ren, Declan and Jagger went through that. Their family was never an issue of course, but there were plenty of people who told them more than once that what they were doing wasn't natural. Especially when they had kids and started interacting with other parents and stuff."

"How'd they deal with it?"

"They figured out who their real friends were and told everyone else to fuck off," I said. "It's hard for their oldest little girl to understand sometimes why she doesn't get invited to certain kids' birthday parties and stuff," I acknowledged. "But her fathers more than make up for it – those two girls will never doubt how much their fathers love them. And you mess with one Barretti, you mess with them all," I added with a chuckle.

I glanced up to see Mace watching me thoughtfully. "Barretti as in Barretti Security Group?"

I nodded. "You know them?"

Mace shook his head. "I know of them. I work for their competition," he said. "Though I guess you can't really call us that. Your uncles are the global leaders in security. With all those army contracts, there's just no catching up to them at this point..."

I dropped my eyes at Mace's words as my stomach rolled violently. I sucked in a deep breath and said, "Yeah, they're doing really well." I looked up to see him watching me intently. "So, um, you said Jonas is a teacher?"

Mace pinned me with his gaze for several long seconds before saying, "He's an artist. He teaches art classes to underprivileged kids."

"And Cole?"

232

"Cole's doing some consulting work for the Navy along with his father."

The dogs lying on the floor at our feet suddenly jumped up and ran for the front door. Several long seconds later, a dark haired man entered the kitchen. "Did I hear my name?"

The beautiful smile that spread across Mace's face actually made my heart hurt and I felt tears sting my eyes when I watched him stand and embrace Cole and then kiss him softly. "Hey," he whispered.

"Hey yourself," Cole said back and then kissed him again.

I'd managed to get a hold of myself when Mace turned his attention back to me and began making the introductions, but inside I felt like my entire world was imploding and for the first time since I'd gotten on the plane, I wondered if I'd made a terrible mistake.

Chapter Nineteen

Mav

I knew what I was doing was wrong and beyond cruel, but I did it anyway. And not just because I couldn't sleep or because it felt like the few bites of dinner I'd forced down my throat felt like they were going to come back up any second. No, it wasn't any of those things that had me turning the doorknob as quietly as I could in the darkened hallway.

It was because I couldn't fucking breathe.

And it had felt that way from the moment I'd seen my mother's cold, lifeless body lying on a slab of metal with nothing to preserve her dignity but a flimsy blue sheet that looked more like a piece of plastic than anything else. The only thing that had kept me from slamming my fist through the thin piece of glass that had separated me from her had been the long fingers wrapped around mine. I'd been able to suck in enough oxygen from that point on to keep me alive, but I was coming apart inside and I knew there was only one thing that could possibly stop it.

One person, rather.

My expectation was that I would find Eli sound asleep and I hoped that I could just look at him and feel a few moments of peace

– enough to hold me over for the next few hours until I could do it again in the morning when we made our way back to the airport. That was how I'd managed to get through dinner with Mace and his men. Because I'd had Eli sitting next to me and I'd gotten to listen to him make polite conversation with Jonas, Mace and Cole. The dinner had definitely been a quiet affair and no one had tried to draw me into the discussions revolving around Jonas's work with the kids he taught or how the threesome was adjusting to living in a big city like New York. I hadn't seen Eli up until that point – not after I'd told Mace we wouldn't be sharing a room and had disappeared into mine like the coward I was. But how the hell was I supposed to explain that if I spent even a few seconds alone with Eli, I'd give in to my need to touch him? To beg him to hold on to me and never let go, no matter what I said or did.

I'd ventured out of my room long enough to hear Mace and Eli talking and while it had been interesting to learn that Mace and his men were still adjusting to building a life together, my main focus had been on the things Eli had said, specifically his references to not being a part of the Barretti family. I'd wanted more than anything to march into the kitchen and demand he explain why he felt that way when everything I'd seen in the few minutes I'd seen Dom and Eli interacting told me different. But I'd stayed in my hidden spot by the stairs on the other side of the wall and hadn't moved until Cole had come home. I'd joined them for dinner when Mace had asked me, but I hadn't lingered afterwards and within a few minutes of closing my own door, I'd heard the door across the hall close too. Six hours of feeling like my lungs were going to shrivel up and die inside of my body had me sneaking across the hall to get my fix.

Except my fix wasn't quietly sleeping and the second I opened the door, my eyes connected with Eli's. The room was dark, but he hadn't closed the curtains so there was enough light from the city street lamps to see his face. He was sitting in an armchair that he'd dragged in front of the balcony doors which were open, allowing the light din of traffic and street noise to filter into the room. And despite it being early summer, the night air was cool enough that the room was almost uncomfortably cold. Eli was still wearing his street clothes and the bed hadn't been disturbed so I had no doubt he'd been in this exact position for a while.

Eli's eyes held mine as I closed the door behind me. I expected him to say something, to ask what I was doing there, but he just stared at me, his eyes shrouded with sadness. I had no idea how much time passed as we watched each other, but Eli was the first to finally move. He pushed up from the chair and walked around it and towards the bed. Once he reached the side of it, his fingers reached up for the first button on his shirt. He never once took his eyes from me as he slowly worked all of the buttons free and then peeled the shirt off and dropped it to the floor. I held my breath as he reached for the button on his pants. I knew I needed to turn around. To walk back out of the room. To pretend I'd never walked into it in the first place.

I didn't do that. I didn't do anything except stand there and watch as Eli unhurriedly revealed his body to me bit by bit. When he was naked, he didn't move, didn't try to cover himself. He just waited…a silent offering.

One I knew I would take…I couldn't pretend that it wasn't the real reason I'd come to his room in the first place.

My feet felt heavy as I made my way to stand in front of him. I waited for him to say something, to ask questions about what this all meant…to insist that it meant *something*. But he didn't. He just held my gaze for a moment before dropping his eyes so he could search out the hem of my shirt and push it up. He undressed me as slowly as he'd undressed himself and when the last of my clothes hit the floor, I reached for him. He came willingly and matched me kiss for kiss, touch for touch and I finally felt the knot in my chest loosen. I only stopped kissing him long enough to grab the packet of lube from my wallet and then I was lowering him to the bed.

I was too needy to do anything but slather some lube over my length before pushing into Eli's body, but instead of protesting, he held on to me and lifted his hips to meet the powerful thrust that had me bottoming out inside of him in one move. I couldn't stop kissing him as I surged into him over and over and I reveled in the way he clung to me. For all I'd said and done to him, he never held himself back from me as I sought the peace I so desperately craved and when he came apart in my arms, he told me he loved me, setting off my own nearly painful orgasm. When I forced myself to pull free of him and roll off his body, Eli lay there for a few seconds and then

237

climbed to his feet. He didn't say anything as he walked around the bed and disappeared into the bathroom, closing the door behind him. I heard the shower come on a moment later. The dismissal stung and I fought the urge to follow him in there. Except I had no right to expect any different.

I shook my head in disbelief. After everything I'd done and said to him, he'd still told me he loved me.

Self-hatred consumed me as I yanked on my clothes. Eli always had and always would deserve someone better than me. And he'd see that himself in a few short hours when he saw the world I'd come from and that had still rejected me. Then I'd watch him climb on Ronan's plane to go back to a life that didn't and shouldn't include me. And I'd go back to my life the way it had been before I'd ever set eyes on him.

But as I closed Eli's door behind me, I wondered why the hell the idea no longer appealed to me.

Not even a little bit.

* * *

"Morning," I heard Jonas say as I entered the kitchen, my bag in hand. I hadn't expected to find anyone up and about since it was only four o'clock in the morning. He was sitting at the table drinking what looked like a homemade latte. The overhead light wasn't on, but the light above the stove was so I didn't have trouble making out his features. His eyes shifted to my bag. "You know Mace as well as anyone," he said. "You really think he'd let you leave like this?"

238

I didn't even get to answer before I heard the front door open and Mace came into the kitchen. He turned on the overhead lights and leaned against the doorframe. "That was one unhappy cabbie," Mace said. "Had to pay him fifty bucks to take a hike."

I ground my teeth as I watched Mace walk over to lean down and kiss Jonas. "Are you coming back to bed?"

Jonas shifted his gaze to me, then said, "I'll be up in a few. Cole has to be up in an hour anyway so maybe you want to wake him up now and I'll join you in a bit?"

I didn't miss the suggestive tone in Jonas's voice and clearly Mace hadn't either because the next kiss he laid on Jonas was anything but innocent and sweet. When they finally separated, Jonas was smiling happily and Mace aimed a dark look directly at me. "You owe me fifty bucks," he said before leaving the kitchen. Jonas got up and grabbed a mug off the counter along with a full pot of coffee.

He put it down on the table. "I can make you a latte if you prefer," he said as he motioned to the espresso machine on the counter.

I shook my head and sat down, reaching for the coffee. "This is fine, thank you."

Jonas sat back down and studied me as the stillness of the kitchen was only interrupted by the occasional shifting of the dog that was lying at Jonas's feet. The night before was the first time I'd officially met the young man, but I knew quite a bit about him since I'd been Mace's backup on the case that had introduced him to

Jonas. I'd been charged with gathering information on the young artist who'd been a suspect in several sexual assaults against little boys as well as the disappearance of a boy in Boston. While my role had been to pull together the information Mace needed, Mace's job had been to end Jonas's life so he would never hurt another child. And while I'd been assured of the young man's guilt based on the evidence we'd had, Mace had thankfully held back. Because it had ultimately turned out that Jonas had been set up by one of our own guys trying to collect a contract that had been put out on the young man. My own guilt in the role I'd played had kept me from coming back to New York to meet the two men who'd changed Mace's life.

That same guilt was rolling through me now, but it was in good company because it seemed that all I could feel since the moment I'd woken up yesterday morning to answer that fucking phone call was guilt and shame.

"It's not easy, is it?" Jonas asked and I lifted my eyes from where they'd been studying the coffee mug that I suspected one of Jonas's students had made because it had two stick figures on it with art easels and the words *I love Mr. Jonas* were written in red letters above the image.

"What?" I asked.

"Letting someone in."

I didn't respond, but of course that didn't seem to faze the young man. "There's that moment that you always remember…the one where you finally lose all hope," Jonas murmured softly. "And you have to decide to either go on anyway or just let go."

I watched as Jonas began running his fingers over the inside of his wrist. He kept his eyes there as he said, "And then fate steps in and changes everything." Jonas lifted his eyes and let a smile drift across his face as he removed his hand from his wrist. "Of course, then you have to decide if you're going to take what fate is offering you or if you're going to tell her to fuck off," he added with a light chuckle.

He took a final sip of his latte and stood. I watched as he put the cup in the sink and began to walk past me. I wasn't surprised when he stopped next to me, but he caught me off guard when he leaned down to give me a small hug. "Don't tell her to fuck off, Mav," he whispered and then he was gone, turning off the overhead lights. The dog jumped up from the floor to follow him, leaving me alone in the darkened kitchen. It would be easy enough to call another cab, but I didn't. I didn't do anything except refill my coffee and sit there in the silence.

And waited.

Chapter Twenty

Eli

I hadn't had any idea what to expect as we drove past the jagged hills that blanketed both sides of the desolate road that led to the reservation. I hadn't seen much from the air because I'd fallen asleep within minutes of the jet leaving Newark and I hadn't stirred until the landing gear had hit the small airstrip just south of the reservation. Like the previous day, Mav and I hadn't exchanged more than a couple of words from the moment I'd gotten up, my body still deliciously sore from his lovemaking.

I had no regrets about sleeping with Mav again and even though afterwards had been brutal and I'd needed to hide out in the bathroom to use the sound of the shower to cover my muffled sobs, I knew I'd do it again in a second if he asked me. But I knew the chances of that were slim since our time together was winding down with every hour that passed. I had no doubt he'd meant what he'd said about not returning to Seattle beyond the time it took to collect his Harley.

Once we'd gotten off the plane, there'd been two cars waiting for us. A simple sedan that Ronan had rented for us and a hearse. Mav hadn't watched the shipping container that carried his mother's body being loaded into the belly of the plane, and when we'd gotten off, he'd sat silently in the driver's seat until the driver of the hearse had tapped on the window to let us know they were ready to go and that they would follow us. It was nearing lunch time when we drove past the sign indicating we were entering the reservation and within minutes we were driving into a small valley that was nothing more than dust, a little bit of brown vegetation and a smattering of small houses and buildings spread out over a few hundred acres. There was one main road leading into town with a few smaller roads serving as access points to several houses. A feeling of bleakness settled in my gut as we passed one decrepit house after another. Garbage littered the street and front yards along with old appliances, chopped up wood and endless, unidentifiable debris. Junked out cars were all over the place and to my horror, I saw more than one person lying on porches or along the sides of houses. My first thought was that they were dead, but I realized they were just sleeping. Some had blankets, some didn't.

"Oh my God," I breathed before I could think better of it and I instantly regretted it when I remembered that this place had been Mav's home. I shot Mav a glance. He was stiffer than I'd ever seen him and his fingers were curled around the steering wheel so tight that his knuckles had gone bloodless.

There were more people out and about than I would have expected for such a small town and most looked like they weren't up to anything in particular. Many were sitting in broken chairs or on old plastic milk crates in front of their houses or in front of the few stores that lined the main street. Many were holding half empty bottles of liquor in their hands. A few kids were riding their bikes down the street and I saw at least two older boys riding horses bareback with only ropes attached to the animals' halters to help them steer. Stray dogs were sniffing through the garbage and I had to look away when the skinny animals turned on each other and began fighting.

As we made our way past the tiny houses that looked like they would blow over with the next stiff wind, more people began exiting their homes to watch us and I felt an uneasiness settle over me at their blank expressions. "You said you haven't been back here since you left when you were sixteen, right?" I finally asked as I tried to imagine Mav as one of the dirty, scrawny, poorly dressed children riding their bikes alongside our car.

"Yep."

"Was…was it always like this?" I asked, hoping like hell I wasn't insulting him, but still too overcome with what I was seeing to make sense of it.

"Yes," Mav said quietly. "It's been forgotten for a long time."

"Forgotten? What do you mean?"

"The government made the Lakota a lot of promises. Promises they haven't kept in the 200 years since the first treaty was signed. Nine out of ten people in Pine Ridge are unemployed. About the same number of people are alcoholics and about half those people are homeless. The kids that don't kill themselves actually look forward to going to bed every night so they can escape the pain of being hungry all the time."

I swallowed hard as what he was telling me sank in. "How did you survive this?" I whispered in disbelief as I looked around. But Mav didn't answer me and it didn't really matter. I was just glad he'd found a way out, though I hated knowing that it wasn't this cruel, unforgiving place that he'd fled, but a cruel and unforgiving man.

Mav pulled off onto a side street and drove for several miles along a winding dirt road that was more sparsely populated. He stopped in front of a light blue mobile home that in any other place would have been considered unlivable. Several men were sitting on lawn chairs in the front yard and at least half a dozen kids were playing with an old soccer ball. Two women were hanging laundry from a long line strung up between two sparse trees next to the trailer. Three tents were pitched in the front yard. Behind the mobile home I could see what looked like more tents, but they weren't normal ones. They were covered with what looked like burlap tarps or something. In front of them was a big fire pit and off to the side were a couple of long tables.

"Sweat lodges," Mav murmured when he saw the direction of my gaze.

Mav stopped in front of the house, but didn't get out right away. He finally glanced at me and said, "You should stay in here."

"I'd like to come with you," I said softly.

Mav turned to stare out the windshield for a moment and then finally nodded. I got out of the car at the same time he did. He went to talk with the men in the hearse and I saw that they stayed in the vehicle. I walked around the car to join Mav. The children who'd been playing with the ball had stopped to watch us, but instead of approaching us, they hung back, their eyes just as clouded and suspicious as those of the adults I'd seen in town. I fought back the urge to take Mav's hand as we approached the front door where the men were sitting. Only one appeared to be lucid because the others were either swaying back and forth or already passed out. I could see several pairs of feet sticking out of the tents in the front yard. Empty bottles of liquor were scattered all over the place.

"Where is he?" Mav asked the one man who watched our approach in eerie silence.

The man jerked his head towards the door behind him, but said nothing. Mav glanced at the door and then to my surprise, he reached for my hand. I suspected it wasn't so much about needing comfort like in the Coroner's office the day before, but more about keeping me close. I gladly took it and hoped he couldn't feel the slight shudder that kept rolling through me. Things had never been easy for me and my family when it had just been me, my mother and sister, but compared to this place, we'd lived in fucking Shangri-La.

The inside of the trailer was dark and stank of alcohol, rotting food and sweat. Garbage bags sat near the entrance and more were piled on top of the small kitchen table. A couple of men and women were sitting at one of end of the trailer watching an old television set that actually had the old fashioned bunny ear antennas. Another man was passed out on the floor in front of the TV. In the kitchen was a young woman washing a baby in one side of the double sink. The other sink was piled high with dirty dishes, as was the counter next to it.

No one spoke to Mav as we moved towards the back of the trailer and he barely spared them a glance. I had counted at least a dozen adults so far and half that many kids, and I had a strong suspicion that they somehow all lived in this one tiny house. There were three bedrooms in the trailer. The first two had people sleeping on several mattresses that were on the floor, and one had a couple of toddlers playing quietly on the floor with broken, faded toys. I nearly gagged at the stench as we passed the single bathroom and by the time we reached the far end of the trailer, I wanted to cry for Mav. I gripped his hand tightly in mine and he cast me a quick glance. He nodded at me as if understanding my distress, but he didn't say anything.

The last bedroom was the biggest and was empty except for the single man sitting in an old rocking chair in one corner. He was smoking some kind of pipe. His long silver hair was tied in decorative braids and where everyone else had been dressed in either ragged, dirty clothes or only partially dressed, he was wearing clean clothes and had on some kind of leather vest that was fringed with tassels. His braids were tied off with decorative beads along with small feathers.

He didn't speak when he saw Mav, but his jaw hardened when he saw our joined hands. I didn't need to understand the man's language to understand the word that fell from his mouth. Even if I hadn't already heard Mav say it to me when he was telling me about his past, I would have known the slur for what it was.

Winkte.

Two Spirit.

I wanted more than anything to drag Mav out of there as I felt his hand turn cold and clammy in mine.

"Uncle Lyle told you?" Mav asked.

Mav's grandfather nodded.

"I've brought her home to you."

The man did nothing to even acknowledge the statement, let alone thank Mav. He slowly climbed to his feet and took another drag on his pipe before setting it down on a small table next to the chair. Mav didn't wait for him to reach us. Instead he led me back out of the trailer. Several people had gathered around the hearse and were looking in the windows at the back of it. Mav motioned to the two men in the hearse and they quickly got out and went to the back to begin removing the shipping container. Mav never once released me as he went to the trunk of our rental and pulled out a paper bag. I'd seen him with the same bag the night before when he'd disappeared into his room, but I hadn't realized what it was. The first thing I noticed was a picture sitting on top of what looked like some clothing. The picture was worn and faded, but I could make out a young woman with long black hair. A little boy with equally dark

248

hair was sitting on her lap, a huge smile on his face. My heart sank as I realized it was a picture of Mav and his mother and I realized the bag contained the personal possessions the detectives had collected from the crime scene, including the clothes his mother had been wearing when she'd been killed, as well as her purse and all its contents.

Mav only released my hand long enough to hold onto the bag while he closed the trunk and then he grabbed it again. His grandfather had barely made it out of the house when Mav thrust the bag at him. The old man took the bag and then slowly removed the picture and studied it for a long time. I watched in stunned silence as his gaze connected with Mav's just before he dropped the picture to the ground and then stepped past Mav to where the men were pulling the shipping container from the hearse. Mav's grandfather began saying something in Lakota as he stood next to the container and placed his hand on it as he clutched the bag of possessions to his chest with his other arm.

"Let's go," Mav said harshly as he pulled on my hand. As we walked, I reached down and snagged the picture that had gotten stepped on at some point, but wasn't damaged beyond that. Mav noticed me pick it up, but didn't say anything. By the time we were back in the car, Mav's grandfather was leading a processional towards the sweat lodges and the hearse had started the process of turning around.

"Are we coming back for the funeral?" I asked as Mav turned the car around.

"No," he said. "I'm not allowed to attend."

Sadly, the statement didn't surprise me. "We could come back in a couple of days and visit her grave," I offered.

"They won't bury her."

"What will they do?"

"While most present day Lakota bury their dead, my grandfather believes in following the traditions before the reservations were formed. They'll build a scaffold in a tree and leave her body and possessions there."

I shook my head because I couldn't even find words to respond to that. Several minutes of silence passed as we drove out of town, but I found I couldn't contain my need to know more about Mav's former life. "Did...did you live in that house with all those people?" I asked.

Mav nodded. "Uncles, aunts, cousins...one big happy family," Mav mocked, though there was nothing humorous about his expression.

"I'm sorry, Mav. I had no idea-"

"Doesn't matter," he bit out and I knew from his tone that he was done talking about it.

"Are we flying out tonight?"

"You are," Mav said. "The pilots had to fly the plane to Rapid City to refuel, so we'll meet them there."

I barely heard the last part because I was still stuck on the first part of his sentence. "Wait, what do you mean? Aren't you flying back to Seattle to get your motorcycle?"

"No."

No, no, no!

It couldn't be happening like this. I couldn't be down to just a couple more hours with Mav. Pain flooded my chest and I tried to suck in a breath, but that only made the pain worse. "Stop the car," I whispered since that was all I could manage to get out.

"What?"

"Stop the car!" I screamed, but it cost me precious oxygen and when Mav hit the brakes, I stumbled out of the car and immediately fell to my knees. And for the first time since I'd had my first panic attack when I was a teenager, I hoped like hell this one would actually kill me.

Chapter Twenty-One

Mav

I hadn't even gotten the car in park before Eli opened the door and when I saw him fall to his knees, I fumbled with my own door. We were alone on the secluded stretch of road that ran north through the reservation. I had no idea where Ronan had hired the hearse from, but when we'd turned to head north out of town, they'd gone south.

"Eli," I yelled as I hurried around the car. He was still on his knees and his face was stricken as he tried to draw in enough air to breathe. If I hadn't known better, I would have thought he was having an asthma attack that was truly constricting his ability to breathe, rather than a psychosomatic symptom of the extreme stress he was experiencing.

That I had brought on.

"Eli, baby, look at me," I ordered as I pulled him to his feet and leaned him back against the car. I grabbed him by the face to hold his attention and didn't miss the way his hands closed tightly around my wrists.

"I need you to slow your breathing, okay?"

Eli managed a nod.

"Breathe with me," I said as I took in a breath, waited several seconds before taking another one. It took several tries for Eli to match my breathing, but when he did, the death grip he had on my wrists eased, and his flushed skin began to return to normal. It was a good five minutes before he was breathing normally.

"Okay?" I asked as I stroked his cheek with my finger. But instead of answering me, he pushed my hands from his face and stepped past me.

"Eli-" I called as I began to follow him.

He didn't respond, but he shook his head back and forth violently. When he showed no signs of slowing down, I hurried to catch up to him before he reached the longer grass because I knew that it wasn't unusual for rattlesnakes to be lurking in the overgrown brush. As soon as my fingers wrapped around his arm, Eli turned on me and I was caught off guard when he used one of my own moves against me. Luckily he hadn't put enough force behind the punch to truly break my nose as intended, but it hurt like a motherfucker. I was glad when he didn't start walking away again, because I doubted I'd be able to catch him as quickly.

"You're a fucking coward, Mav!" he screamed. "I get that you don't want to be with me, but what about your friends?"

"They're not-"

Eli threw another punch, but I managed to grab his fist before it made contact. "Do you have any idea what I'd give to have what you have?"

"You do," I said as I eased Eli's fist down to my chest. "With Dom-"

"No I don't!" he shouted. "I fucked up any chance of being part of that family a long time ago."

Eli settled and tugged his hand free. His eyes dropped to study his bruised fist.

"What does that mean?" I asked, but Eli shook his head.

"If it's me who's keeping you from going back, then don't worry. I'm leaving Seattle as soon as I can get my stuff packed."

I stilled at that. "What are you talking about?"

"It was a mistake to go back there."

"Why?"

Another shake of his head and Eli was pushing past me. When I grabbed him, he tried to tug free of me, but he didn't lash out like he had before. "Tell me why."

"We're different, Mav," he said softly. "You didn't do anything to deserve what they did to you," Eli said as he motioned back in the direction of town. "I deserve everything I get."

Frustration coursed through me at the lack of answer, but when Eli's face went blank a moment later, I knew I wouldn't get anything else out of him. As soon as I released him, he began walking back towards the car. Once we were back on the road, the exhaustion hit me hard. Coming back to this hell hole had been the hardest thing I'd ever done, second to the moment I'd seen my mother's lifeless body under that sheet. I hadn't been at all surprised by my grandfather's reaction or the fact that he looked exactly like he had twenty years ago. What had surprised me was that I hadn't felt anything when he'd whispered the slur that I'd heard more times than I could count when I'd been a kid. I hadn't even felt the need to tell the man to fuck off like I'd wanted to so many times when I was little, but hadn't had the guts. I'd just wanted to get Eli out of there because I hadn't wanted any part of my former life touching him.

I glanced at Eli to see that he wasn't doing anything more than staring at the dashboard of the car. The picture of me and my mom that he'd picked up off the ground was carefully clutched between the fingers of one hand. I wished I could get him to talk to me, but what the hell could I say? Every single thing I'd said and done in the past twenty-four hours had only inflicted pain on him.

Fuck, could I really leave things like this? Could I really watch him get on that plane and never see him again? And what if I did go back to Seattle? Would it change anything if he wasn't there? Would I accept what I had finally started to believe – that I was finally a part of something that had been denied to me my entire life – only to find that it didn't meant anything if I couldn't share it with the one person who had made me actually want something besides my Harley and an open road?

Before I could think on what I was doing too much, I reached for my phone and called the pilot. When he answered I said, "Change of plans. We'll fly out in the morning."

"Of course, Mr. James. Just text me what time you'd like to depart and I'll take care of the rest."

"Will do," I said before hanging up. I glanced at Eli, but he didn't look like he'd even heard what I'd said. We drove for another hour before the exhaustion became too much. It was still early, barely two o'clock in the afternoon, but it didn't matter if we stopped now or closer to Rapid City. I picked the very next exit that had a motel and pulled off. We'd left the reservation, so the area was a little more populated and there was a small restaurant attached to the motel.

"Are you hungry?" I asked Eli. He shook his head in response, but that was it.

I left Eli in the car while I checked in, but when I started to say two rooms, I glanced back and saw that he was still sitting in the exact same position, seemingly oblivious to his surroundings. "One room," I said to the clerk. "Two beds," I added. I wanted to keep an eye on Eli, but I needed to keep some distance so I could fucking think. Yesterday, I'd been so sure about my plan to leave Seattle for good, but between Jonas's words about not telling fate to fuck off and Eli calling me out on my cowardice, the seeds of doubt had been planted.

Eli was on auto-pilot from the moment I parked the car in front of our room. He placed his things on one side of the long dresser, toed off his shoes and then went to the bed and crawled between the covers, putting his back to me. I spent a few minutes sending texts to Ronan and Mace to let them know everything was done and that we'd be flying out the next day, but I didn't say anything about whether or not I would be joining Eli on the flight back. I set my phone on silent and then put it down on the nightstand. I stared at Eli's back. I needed to leave him alone. But just like the night before, my body had a mind of its own and I went to his bed and sat down on the edge of the mattress so that my hip was pressed up against his backside.

"Eli," I said softly. "Would you please look at me?"

Eli took several long seconds to finally roll over onto his back. I braced my hand on the bed next to his hip. "Tell me how to not hurt you anymore," I whispered as I reached up to brush his hair from his forehead.

His dark eyes held mine for a long time and I was glad to see a little bit of light come back into them. "Promise me you'll go back to Seattle. Even if it's not tomorrow or if you have to wait till I've left, promise you'll go back and give them a chance." When I didn't respond, Eli sat up and cupped my face. "They won't turn their backs on you, Mav," Eli whispered and then he kissed me gently. "Trust me, okay?"

I nodded, because my throat felt too tight for words. Eli swiped his thumb back and forth over my jaw a couple times before he released me and lay back down. I didn't stop him when he turned back on his side. Anxiety rolled through me as I realized what I'd just agreed to and the jumble of emotions had me stumbling to my feet and searching out my bag. I'd take a shower to clear my head and then get some sleep. Then maybe I could figure everything out.

But as I reached for my bag which was sitting on the dresser near Eli's, I saw the picture I'd discovered in my mother's purse the night before when I'd gone through her personal possessions that the cops had given me. I hadn't looked at the picture for more than a few seconds, despite the surprise of finding it in her purse. From the condition of the photograph, I could tell it had been handled numerous times. Without thinking about it too much, I grabbed the picture and took it with me as I headed for the bathroom. I turned on the water for the shower and while I waited for it to heat up, I sat down on the closed toilet and stared at the image of the woman who'd been the first one to teach me that I would never quite be enough.

Chapter Twenty-Two

Eli

As tired as I was, I couldn't sleep. Because every time I closed my eyes, I could feel Mav's lips against mine. It would be our last kiss. I knew it without a shadow of a doubt. This morning I'd been willing to give him any part of me he wanted or needed up until the moment he walked away from me. But seeing the hurt in his eyes as he asked me to tell him how to stop him from hurting me anymore had been proof that I couldn't let it happen again. Maybe if I was better at hiding my emotions when he made love to me, or if I could keep from telling him that I loved him, it would be possible to have one more night with him. But the fact that I'd gone so far off the deep end after he'd admitted that he wasn't even going back to Seattle to get his Harley, had been proof enough that I couldn't separate my heart from the physical act of loving Mav.

I lay there for at least half an hour before I realized that Mav hadn't come out of the bathroom yet. I'd heard the shower come on shortly after he'd gone in there and from what I could tell, it was still running. I waited another fifteen minutes before the concern began to gnaw at me and I slowly got out of bed. When another five minutes passed and the shower stayed on, I got up and went to the bathroom door and knocked.

"Mav?" I called, but there was no answer. I knew there was a likelihood that he couldn't hear me in the shower, but that wasn't enough to stop me from testing the knob. I was relieved to discover the door unlocked and as I pushed it open, I continued to knock and call his name. I saw him instantly because he wasn't in the shower. No, he was sitting on the closed toilet still fully dressed, the picture of his mother in his hand.

"Mav? You okay?" I asked as I entered the room and came to a stop in front of him. The agony in his eyes was nearly unbearable.

"She's really gone," he whispered as tears started sliding down his face.

"I know, Mav. I'm sorry," I said softly as I pushed his hair off his face.

"I told you she only called me when she needed money, but that wasn't true. She used to call me on my birthdays too. Every year without fail. No matter how stoned or drunk she was, she always made that call. And not once when she did it did she ask for money." Mav's eyes dropped back down to the picture. "I fucking hated her for what she did, but God, I couldn't wait to get that damn phone call."

Mav let out a harsh sob and then covered his eyes with his hand. I pulled him against my belly and held on to him as his arms wrapped around my waist. I pressed kisses against the top of his head as his tears soaked through my shirt. When he finally quieted and lifted his head, I shifted until I was sitting astride his legs. I used my sleeve to wipe his wet face.

"They should have done better by you, Mav," I said softly as I straightened his loose hair so it wasn't stuck to his damp face. "They're the ones who lost out by not knowing you…by not watching you grow up to be such an amazing man."

Mav wrapped his arms around me again and settled his face against my neck. "As awful as that place was, I would have stayed if they'd shown me even an ounce of kindness," he admitted.

"I know you would have. But I'm so glad you got out of there," I added. I pulled back so I could look him in the eye. "I know it must have been terrible for you, being so young…" I said with a shake of my head. "But to think of you being condemned to that life." I couldn't even continue the thought because it was so disturbing. Mav was so vibrant and strong and those men had all looked like they'd died a thousand deaths and were just waiting for the one that would stick.

"I almost didn't," Mav said as he settled his hands on my hips. "My friend Travis and I made plans to get out together. We'd been saving every penny we could make from selling scrap metal. This guy on the reservation paid us a couple bucks a week to collect as much as we could and then he'd drive it to the city and sell it for cash. Between us, Travis and I saved up a couple hundred bucks – enough for bus tickets to the city where we figured we'd get jobs, find an apartment."

"What happened?" I asked.

261

"I came home one night after I'd been out looking for one of my uncles who'd wandered off drunk. I used to sleep on this porch behind the house – it was old and falling down, but no one wanted to share it with me so it was all mine. Anyway, I found this envelope under my pillow. There was a hundred dollars in it and a note from Travis telling me he was sorry."

Mav dashed at his eyes as his voice became husky. "Travis was gay too, but he had it worse than me 'cause his family used to beat him up all the time. But they'd also fucked with his head a lot and he was scared to leave them. When I saw that note, I knew…" Mav sucked in a breath before continuing. "I ran to his house…it was almost a mile away. I found him in the tent he used to sleep in behind the house. He'd shot himself with his father's hunting rifle."

I shook my head as I struggled to find the right words. But there just weren't any so I leaned forward and kissed his temple. "I'm so sorry."

Mav nodded against me. "I left that night. I wasn't sure I could do it without him – I was so fucking scared – but I was more scared for what would happen if I didn't go."

"Where'd you end up?"

"I hitched a ride with this trucker going East for a while, but had to bail when he insisted I blow him as payment for the ride. I decided it would be safer to take the bus after that. I ended up in Minneapolis and stayed there for a couple years working odd jobs. I lived on the streets when I had to, but sometimes I had enough money to get an apartment or a motel room for an extended period of time. Then I want to Chicago, Indianapolis…I basically just kept heading East whenever I got the urge to keep moving. But things changed for me in Philadelphia."

"How so?"

"I got a job working for this guy who fixed up Harleys," Mav said. "That's where I met my girl," he added with a light chuckle that made my insides light up with warmth.

"Your girl?" I asked with a smile.

"A custom Harley Davidson Night Train," he said. "My boss let me work nights and weekends to pay for it and after that I used every extra penny I made to fix her up."

"How long did you work there?"

"Until I was about 24 or so. I liked working on bikes, but it wasn't what I'd been dreaming of doing my whole life."

I smiled. "I just realized I don't even know how old you are."

"I'm 32."

I gasped in mock horror. "You're an old man."

Mav laughed and slapped me on the ass. I was glad to see some of the anguish had left his face. "So what was it that you wanted to do?"

Mav became serious as he said, "I wanted to be a cop."

"Really?"

He nodded. "Joined the force when I was 26. A year later it was over."

"What happened?" I asked in surprise.

"Found out the cop I was assigned to work with was taking bribes. Did my duty and reported him. I actually thought my fellow cops would back me up," he added with a harsh laugh.

"They didn't?"

"No, not since most of them were on the take too," Mav murmured. "My little report ended up taking down almost a dozen veteran cops. And let's just say it didn't make me any new friends, but I did manage to get a lot of enemies out of the deal."

I froze at that. "Did they come after you?"

"Since most of them were looking at life in prison with some of the same guys a lot of them had put there, yeah, they came after me. In a big way. Because without my testimony…"

Even though Mav was right in front of me, I was still unreasonably terrified for him. "What happened?" I managed to ask.

"Mace."

"What?"

"Mace happened."

"Mace was a cop?"

Mav nodded. "He used to be on the same force a couple years before I signed up. He'd quit when he lost his son. But he still had connections with the force so he knew what some of the guys were planning. He literally saved my life because some guys jumped me one night outside the garage I used to work at – I still went there to do work on my bike every once in a while. The guys were kicking the shit out of me and planned to make it look like I'd been killed during a robbery. Would have worked too if Mace hadn't shown up."

"What happened to the men?" I stammered as I tried to fathom how close to losing his life Mav had truly come.

"Three of them had to show up for their trials in wheelchairs," Mav murmured. "I testified and every single one of them went to prison. Mace knew there was no way of me going back to my job or even joining any police force after all that so he introduced me to Ronan."

I felt some of the tension ease from my system, but I finally began to understand why Mav was so unwilling to accept the idea that he was a part of anything bigger than himself. Because he'd tried that before. Despite the horror of his childhood and the cruelty of his family, he'd given himself over to another family. The Brothers in Blue. Only he'd once again been the outcast, simply because he'd chosen to do the right thing.

"Those guys…they can't still get to you, right?" I asked.

Mav shook his head. "Ronan and Mace helped me disappear, so to speak. Maverick is my real first name but James is actually my middle name. And since I never talked about my mom or my past with any of the guys on the force, they had no way of linking me to anything so I just quietly disappeared."

I was toying with Mav's hair when I asked, "Did your mom have a crush on Tom Cruise or something?"

"What?"

"You know, Maverick from Top Gun?"

265

Mav laughed heartily. "God, I wish. That would be a whole lot cooler." Mav's fingers began stroking up and down my spine and I tried not to shiver at the contact. "No, there weren't a lot of things to watch on TV on the reservation and with lots of people all wanting to watch at the same time, they had to agree on certain shows. There was an old TV show from the late fifties called Maverick that they all liked – some type of black and white comedy western show starring James Garner."

"Really?"

"I can't really complain because the lead guys were named Bret and Bart Maverick so I lucked out that she picked Maverick instead of Bret or Bart."

I couldn't stop the bubble of laughter that started deep in my chest. Maybe it was the stress of the last two days or maybe it was just the idea of trying to call Mav by either of those names, but I just completely lost it and began laughing so hard, my entire body was shaking. I didn't really expect Mav to be angry or anything, but I wasn't expecting him to join in either. So when his laughter filled the steamed up room right along with mine, I felt like some kind of valve inside of me had been opened and all the pressure released. I wrapped my arms around Mav's neck and just held on to him as I laughed, and he didn't hesitate to do the same thing. A good ten minutes passed before we'd both quieted and just held on to each other. I knew I needed to let go of him and let him finish his shower, but despite my earlier promise to myself not to be intimate again with him, that was exactly the urge I was battling. And I knew he was in the same boat because he whispered, "Take a shower with me?" in my ear.

I tried to say no, but not very hard because only a couple of seconds passed before I was nodding against his neck. Mav held me for a while longer before pushing me back to begin working my shirt buttons loose. When he pushed the shirt off my shoulders, his hands skimmed over my skin as he slid the shirt down my arms. I wanted him to kiss me, but at the same time I also didn't.

He didn't.

He just kept up the sensual torture as he undressed me bit by bit and I was reminded of the night before when I'd done the same to him. At his urging, I climbed off his lap so he could stand and then I helped him get undressed. As turned on as we both were, there wasn't anything sexual in the way we touched each other…at least not to the extent that we were both desperate for the next level. No, it was more like we were exploring each other…soothing each other.

I expected the water to be cool or lukewarm after having been on so long, but it turned out to still be hot when we stepped under the spray. We took turns washing each other and when Mav turned me around so he could work some shampoo into my hair, I relaxed against him and enjoyed the sensation of his fingers massaging my scalp. He made quick work of his own hair, but instead of turning off the shower, he pulled me back against him so that my back was pressed up against his front and held me there under the spray of water, his forearm wrapped around my shoulders.

I could feel his erection pressed up against my ass, but he never once upped the heat level of his touches.

We stood there like that for a good thirty minutes before Mav finally turned off the water and dried us both off. I wasn't sure what he was planning next and while I told myself I couldn't make love to him again and expect to walk away in one piece, I didn't hesitate when he led me to my bed and pulled back the covers and crawled in after me. We ended up in the same position as in the shower, my back to his front, but instead of just one arm around me, they both were and his lips were resting against the back of my neck. It wasn't even four o' clock in the afternoon, but that didn't stop me from reaching up to turn the light above the bed off. My eyes grew heavy very quickly and I knew I was going to finally be able to give in to my need to sleep. But just seconds before all sense of reality escaped me, I heard Mav whisper, "Thank you, Eli."

They weren't the three little words I wanted more than anything to hear from him, but they still warmed me from the inside out. Maybe they'd be enough to tide me over when I started the next chapter in my life.

Maybe.

Chapter Twenty-Three

Mav

It was late when I finally heard my phone vibrating on the nightstand next to the other bed in the room. The last thing I wanted to do was get up and answer it, but mostly because of the warm body that was pressed up against mine. At some point after we'd fallen asleep, Eli had rolled over and turned into me so that his face was pressed against my throat and his arm was wrapped around my waist. One of his legs was thrown over me, putting his dick precariously close to mine. But even though I was turned on, I was content to just lie there and feel his heart beating against mine and his slow, even breathing that meant he was finally finding some peace.

Unfortunately, I couldn't ignore the phone, especially when it began vibrating again within a minute. It was well past midnight and although Eli and I had managed to get a good eight hours of rest, I knew we both needed more. But clearly the rest of the world didn't give a shit.

I carefully untangled myself from Eli's body and climbed out of bed, but not before I brushed a soft kiss over his temple. I left the lights off as I walked naked to the phone which started ringing again for the third time and my heart sped up when I saw Jace's name come up on the Caller ID. There could be only one reason the man was calling me.

Eli's stepdad.

"Hello?" I said softly as I began heading towards the bathroom so I wouldn't wake Eli.

"It's me. We have a problem."

"Eli's stepfather?" I asked as I searched out my pants on the bathroom floor and began pulling them on.

"No, Caleb."

I stilled and said, "Did something happen to him in the hospital?"

Jace was quiet a moment before saying, "I got him out of there."

"What?" I asked as I pulled up my pants and then sat down on the toilet.

"After I checked on him a couple days ago, I couldn't get past the feeling that something was off. So I went back this morning to see him again. He was more lucid this time around and he begged me to help him. They had him tied down, Mav," Jace said, the anger clear in his voice. "Ronan says you're in South Dakota and you're with his brother."

"I am."

"The kid's pretty messed up. Can you get down here as soon as possible? There's something you need to see."

270

My body tensed up at that, but before I could ask Jace for details, I looked up to see Eli watching me from the doorway. "Where are you?" I asked.

"West Virginia. I'll text you the information."

"We're on our way."

I hung up the phone and stood up and flipped on the bathroom light.

"What is it?" Eli asked nervously and I couldn't really blame him since the last time I'd taken a call like this, I'd ripped him to shreds with my cruel words.

"It's Caleb."

Eli stiffened even more and asked, "Is he okay?"

"Yeah, he's with Jace. But Jace needs us to come down there. Can you get dressed and I'll tell you what Jace told me on the way to the airport?"

Eli nodded and began scooping up our clothes. He handed me pieces of mine as I called the pilot to have the plane readied. I also called Ronan and told him the plan. I suspected he already knew what Jace wanted to show me, but with Eli in the room, I wasn't prepared to ask him about it. We were on the road within ten minutes and stopped only long enough to grab some food from a 24-hour fast food place. I explained to Eli what little I knew about Jace getting Caleb out of the psychiatric hospital, but he didn't say much.

The pilot and co-pilot were as professional as ever when we arrived at the airport and while it took a little longer to get through the security process since it was a major airport, we were airborne within a couple of hours of Jace's call and dawn was just breaking over the horizon when we landed in West Virginia. Ronan had already gotten a car for us so we were on the road within minutes of touching down and I asked Eli to navigate to the motel using the GPS on my phone. I did it more to give him something to do because his anxiety seemed to be increasing the closer we got to our destination.

The place Jace had selected was deep in the Appalachian Mountains and the fact that it was so secluded had me even more worried. I remembered Ronan's comment about how many of Jack Cortano's former army buddies had hired themselves out as paid guns. I had my knife on me, but when we arrived at the motel, I grabbed my Glock from my bag and quickly reloaded the gun and stuck it in the waistband of my pants at my back. The motel was quiet and there was only one car parked in the lot. I knew it was Jace's since it was right in front of the room number he'd texted us, but I still kept my eyes open as we approached it. The door opened even before we reached it and I quickly ushered Eli inside.

"Hey," Jace said as he reached out to shake my hand. I had worked with Jace quite a bit in the few years he'd been on the team, but like most of the men that found their way to Ronan, I knew little about his background. He was about my height, but with a slightly leaner build and his brown hair, while still on the long side, was nowhere near as long as mine and had considerably more curl to it than mine did, making it almost pretty. But nothing else about Jace was "pretty." With his ripped body, trimmed beard, dark, penetrating eyes and bronzed skin, he was stunningly gorgeous and I'd often wondered which team he played for early on when we'd first met. I'd eventually gotten the answer to my question, but by that time we'd built a professional relationship that neither of us had been willing to mess with just to slake our physical curiosities.

"Eli, this is Jace Christianson. Jace, this is Eli."

Jace nodded. I looked around the room, but didn't see anyone else. But before I could ask, a young man rounded the corner from the bathroom. I knew from my research that Caleb was only seventeen, but he looked younger to me and he'd clearly had it rough because everything about the way he held himself screamed "hands off!" He was a good looking, all-American boy next door type with light blond hair and startlingly blue eyes. He was on the slimmer side, but I suspected he would fill out as he got older.

His eyes stayed on me only for a moment before shifting to Eli, but he didn't say anything and the young men just stared at each other. It was Jace who broke the tension when he stepped past us and went to Caleb's side. He murmured something in Caleb's ear that seemed to relax him and then led him to one of the beds and had him sit down. Eli finally moved and sat down opposite him.

"Are you okay?" Eli asked.

Caleb nodded, but didn't say anything. He fidgeted nervously and couldn't seem to stop running his hands over his legs like he was trying to wipe something off of them and onto the gray sweat pants he was wearing.

"What happened?" Eli asked.

The question seemed to drive Caleb's anxiety higher, but surprisingly, he calmed when Jace sat down next to him and covered one of Caleb's hands with his own. Even though they'd been together for only 24 hours, they'd clearly formed some kind of bond.

"I don't know where to start," Caleb whispered, his voice sounding ragged. His statement was directed at Jace.

"Start wherever you feel comfortable," Jace murmured.

I went and sat next to Eli, but didn't reach for his hand even though I was tempted to. I made sure our bodies were touching though.

Caleb's pain-filled eyes shifted back to Eli and he shook his head. "We didn't know, Eli," he said softly, his voice barely audible. "Nick and me…we thought...we thought you wanted it. That you liked what he was doing to you."

I felt Eli stiffen next to me and he sucked in a deep breath.

"What is he talking about?" I asked Eli as my insides knotted up. Eli looked at me, his eyes wide and his mouth open, but nothing came out and he'd gone deathly pale. He climbed to his feet and took several steps away from me. Fear gripped me as I looked at Caleb. "Liked what?" I asked more angrily than I'd intended and Caleb automatically shifted closer to Jace.

"Caleb, don't!" Eli whispered, his voice cracking.

Caleb looked confused as his eyes shifted back and forth between me and Eli. "Eli, I'm sorry." He fell silent after that and I knew he wouldn't be giving me the answers I needed. I stood and went to Eli who immediately began backing away from me.

"Eli," I said gently as I reached for him, but he whirled away and tore out the door.

I ran after him, but with the few seconds head start he had, he made it to the woods before I finally caught up to him. I grabbed him, this time expecting him to lash out at me, but he didn't. He just began screaming the word "no" over and over again. Deep down I already knew what Caleb had meant, but I hadn't wanted to believe it. But now that Eli was shaking and crying against my chest as his fingers twisted in my shirt, I knew it was true. I held him as tight as I could and murmured inconsequential things in his ear at first, but when that didn't work, I whispered the Lakota prayer that had helped soothe him once before. I repeated it over and over until he settled in my hold. It had to be at least ten minutes before he quieted enough to hear me.

"Nothing you tell me changes anything, Eli," I murmured against his head. "Do you understand me?"

Eli disengaged himself from my arms and took several steps back. He wiped the tears from his face with his sleeve. "I was the one who started it," he whispered.

I didn't believe that for a second so I said, "Eli-" but he cut me off.

"It was a few days after my sixteenth birthday. My mom had flown to Mexico to visit relatives and Jack…Jack and I were celebrating the fact that I'd gotten my driver's license with an action movie marathon." Eli took in several deep breaths before continuing. "He let me have a beer. I liked it so I asked for another one and he gave it to me." Eli's voice cracked when he said, "It was so much fun hanging out with him like that. But the second beer was too much for me. When I woke up the next morning…"

Eli shook his head and wiped at the tears that had started to fall again. "I was still on the couch in the den and there was a blanket over me. I knew right away that…that I'd had sex. I was really confused and when Jack came in to check on me, I started crying and asked him why he'd done that to me."

Eli began sobbing, but when I reached for him, he pulled away. "Please…please just don't touch me right now, okay?" he begged.

"Okay," I said softly, though touching him was all I wanted to do. Except for finding Jack Cortano and ripping his fucking head off.

"Jack was really upset and told me it was a mistake. He said…he said I'd gotten drunk and had started touching him inappropriately and that he'd tried to stop it, but that he hadn't wanted to hurt me. He said I seduced him."

"Bullshit," I snarled.

"He showed me proof."

Fury was rolling through my blood so my voice was louder than I'd meant for it to be when I asked, "What proof?"

"There were security cameras throughout the house. They were always on, including in the den. He showed me the video of what we'd done."

Disbelief tore through me and I started shaking my head.

"It's true," Eli whispered. "I saw myself performing oral sex on him…I wasn't fighting him and there was a point when he tried to stop me, but I didn't. I didn't struggle when he was fucking me either."

I grabbed Eli, even though he'd asked me not to. "Even if I believed that shit, it wouldn't fucking matter! He was the adult and he had no right to touch you. He raped you, Eli. Pure and simple!"

Eli flinched and tried to escape my hold. His despair quickly turned to anger. "Don't you get it, Mav? I let him do it! That time and all the others! I never told him no! I whored myself out just like when I was a kid!"

"Others?" I bit out. "How long did it go on for?"

"Until I left for college and a few times after."

Nausea rolled through my belly. Eli must have taken my silence as proof that I believed what he was saying, because he yanked his arm free and said, "I told you, I deserve whatever I get."

"Just because you never told him no doesn't mean you wanted it and it sure as hell doesn't mean you consented!" I snapped. I stepped forward and grabbed Eli by both his arms and forced him backwards until his back hit a tree. "He raped you, Eli! And when I find him, I'm going to make sure he never hurts you again, do you hear me?"

Eli refused to look at me and my anger intensified.

"Tell me the truth. Did you want him to do that to you?" I asked. "The truth," I said firmly. "Forget the guilt about what you think happened that first time, forget what you think you deserve."

"No," Eli answered without hesitation. "I didn't want it."

"Then why-"

"He never let up!" Eli cried out.

"What do you mean?"

"After that night, he kept telling me I'd done something to him. I'd changed him. He still loved my mother, but he loved me too…that I could give him something that no one else could. I told him that it couldn't ever happen again. That I didn't want it to happen again, but he wore me down until one night I finally stopped saying no. I didn't let him fuck me again, but I…I…"

"You performed oral sex on him," I finished for him.

Eli nodded. "And then that stopped being enough and he wanted more. The guilt of what I was doing was killing me. My own mother's husband," Eli whispered. "I told him I couldn't do it anymore…that it was wrong and I wanted to stop. He started making threats after that…subtle ones. He talked about leaving my mom because he couldn't live with being around me and not being able to touch me. He…he made her so happy. I couldn't let that happen."

"So you gave in," I ventured, easing my hold on his arms so I could run my hands up and down his chilled skin.

"I hated it," Eli whispered. "I threw up every time he did it to me. Every single time. I told him it was making me sick, but he didn't care."

I reached up to wipe at the tears that were still slipping down his face.

278

"About a year after it started, I finally told him I wouldn't do it anymore. I told him if he ever touched me again, I'd tell my mom and Dom the truth. He laughed at me and told me to go ahead. He said no one would believe me after they saw the video. Then he…he threatened to pull his support for Dom's contracts with the army."

I stilled my movements at that as things finally started to click into place.

"He told me how much money Dom and his brothers would lose. He said he could ruin their business. I knew he would do it so I stopped saying no after that."

"Why didn't you tell Dom?" I asked. "He would have helped you. He wouldn't have cared about the money."

Eli shook his head. "I couldn't let him find out what I'd done," he said quietly. His eyes lifted to meet mine and he whispered, "I fucked my own mother's husband. He's one of Dom's closest friends."

"Eli-"

"You saw me in that parking garage, Mav. You saw what I was capable of."

I knew he was talking about the day he'd tried to trade a blowjob for the self-defense lessons he'd wanted. He'd been on autopilot in that moment and if I hadn't seen how empty and dead his eyes had been, I would have let him suck me off and from the seemingly eager, expert way he'd handled me, I would have thought he was completely into it. But none of that negated what had been done to him…what that fucker who'd claimed to be the father he wanted had done to him.

"I don't care if you stripped all your clothes off and begged him to fuck you, Eli! You were a kid and you were in no position to consent! He raped you!"

Eli closed his eyes and shook his head and I bit back my frustration. Nothing I said was going to convince him otherwise. "When did it stop?"

"It stopped for a while when I left for college. It was why I picked a school on the east coast. Then Jack got the job at the Department of Defense. The first time I went to see their new house in Virginia, he did it again. My mother was in the house," Eli whispered on a broken sob. "I stopped going there after that unless I absolutely had to and I avoided being alone with him. It happened a few more times, but he finally stopped pursuing me my sophomore year. But I didn't trust him not to want to start things up again so I decided to go back to Seattle for school."

Eli slumped against the tree. "I thought things would be better if I was around Dom and his family, but every time I'm with them, all I can think about is what I did. They'll hate me if they ever find out," Eli whispered just before looking up at me.

"No they won't," I said softly and then I leaned down to kiss him. "You didn't do anything wrong, Eli. I know it. Dom will see that."

"No," Eli cried out as he shook his head violently. "Dom can't know. My mom…it would kill her if she knew. Please,

Mav…please promise me you won't tell anyone. Please, I'm begging you," Eli said desperately as he grabbed my arms.

"He needs to pay for what he did to you."

"Mav, please. I just want to start over somewhere else. Please, please, please," he repeated over and over until I dragged him into my arms. I could feel his breathing ticking up and I knew he was seconds away from a panic attack.

"Okay," I said softly against his ear. "I won't tell anyone," I reassured him.

Eli's relief was palpable as he sagged against me. I held on to him for several moments until he completely relaxed in my arms. "We need to go back and talk to Caleb," I said quietly.

Eli nodded.

I took his hand in mine and led him back across the parking lot. I gave the door a light knock and waited for Jace to open it, then tucked Eli against my side as I sat him down on the bed. Caleb was still in the same position and his worried eyes stayed on Eli before finally shifting to Jace who went to his side and nodded his head.

Caleb took a deep breath and then started talking.

Chapter Twenty-Four

Eli

Focusing on Caleb's voice was impossibly difficult since I was still reeling from everything that had just happened. When I'd first walked into the motel room, I'd been stunned by how broken and small Caleb looked. He'd always been quieter than Nick, but he'd always had a smile on his face and he was the type of guy who naturally drew people to him. And while he hadn't exactly been kind to me when we were younger, he hadn't seemed as resentful as Nick always had.

I hadn't had any idea of what Caleb would tell us about what had happened to him from the time he'd left me that message, but I certainly wasn't expecting him to expose my biggest secret in front of both a virtual stranger and the man I'd hoped would never find out what I'd done. Even now, the knowledge that Mav knew I'd fucked a man I considered a father – my own mother's husband – was making me violently ill, and I wished more than anything that Mav would stop touching me because my skin felt like there were a million ants crawling beneath it.

"Caleb, what happened after you called Eli?" I heard Mav ask, and I forced myself to focus.

"My dad overheard me leaving that message," Caleb began. "He took my phone from me and hit me. He said I'd be sorry if I tried it again. I told him I knew the truth about what had happened to Nick and that he wasn't going to get away with it. I also told him that I had proof of what he'd been doing to me and Nick and Eli and that if he ever touched me again, I'd give it to the cops and the press."

"What?" I whispered in disbelief as his words sank in. "No," I said as I shook my head. "No," I repeated and I looked at Mav in the hopes that he would tell me I'd heard Caleb wrong.

"Caleb, did your father…did he touch you and Nick?"

Caleb's gaze shifted to Jace who nodded his head and then reached up to tenderly brush Caleb's hair from his forehead. My stepbrother turned his attention back to Mav and sucked in a deep breath before saying, "I don't know exactly how old Nick was when it started for him, but I was thirteen the first time my father touched me."

"Oh my God," I said as I got to my feet. "No," I repeated dumbly before looking at Caleb. I did the math in my head and felt the bile rise up my throat. When Caleb had been thirteen, I'd been eighteen.

"I left for college," I whispered and I closed my eyes.

"It started before that, Eli," Caleb said softly. "It had nothing to do with you leaving."

I opened my eyes to look at him and shook my head.

"It's true," Caleb said. "He started doing it to Nick long before he married your mom."

"Baby, come sit back down," Mav said gently as he held out his hand. I took it and let him settle me in next to him again, but my mind was racing. My stepfather had told me I'd been the cause of his obsession to be with another man. Except I hadn't been a man. Not really. And I hadn't been his first. The sick fuck had gone after his own kids.

"I'm sorry, Caleb, I didn't know," I said as tears flooded my eyes. "I would have tried to stop it, I swear."

Caleb dashed at his own eyes and nodded. "I know," he said. "He was good at keeping secrets. We all were."

"Caleb, you said something about what happened to Nick," Mav said.

"Um, yeah, he was going to college, but still living at home. One of his classes got canceled so he came home early. Eli's mom was at lunch with friends. Nick...he walked in on me and my father..."

Caleb's words trailed off and I saw Jace give his hand a little squeeze. The move seemed to settle the younger man. "Nick pulled him off of me and called him a liar and said he was going to send the proof to the media. I didn't know what he meant, but he and my father started fighting. My father pushed Nick hard and he fell backwards and hit his head on the edge of the coffee table. He didn't move after that," Caleb said, his voice sounding dull and lifeless. I knew he was going someplace else in his head to escape the memories.

Just like I always had when I'd been a kid. With my customers. With my stepfather.

"My dad started flipping out. He grabbed me and told me that it was an accident. I was crying and told him that we needed to get Nick help, but he wouldn't let me call 911. He told me that he'd go to jail if anyone found out what had happened."

Caleb's eyes shifted from me to Mav and then to Jace. "I know the stuff he did to me was fucked up, but he was still my dad," Caleb whispered in earnest.

Jace nodded in understanding. "It's okay," he reassured Caleb.

Caleb nodded shakily and then dropped his eyes to his hands. He focused on the one Jace was holding. Jace's thumb was rubbing over Caleb's and as Caleb continued to talk, his own finger began to stroke the other man's.

"My father left me alone with Nick for a couple of minutes and I sat down next to him. I went to hold his hand when he suddenly opened his eyes. I began screaming for my dad saying that Nick was still alive. I told Nick to hold on, that help was coming, but he kept talking about the proof...said it would keep me safe. He...he told me to call Eli for help and to tell him he was sorry."

My chest hurt at hearing that and I realized how little I'd really known my stepbrothers...both of them.

"Nick closed his eyes again just before my father came back into the room and I started telling him that Nick was still alive. I told him we needed to call for help, and he knelt down next to Nick and put his fingers against his neck to check for a pulse. He finally told me to go call 911. I did, but when I got back, Dad was leaning over Nick and checking his pulse again. And then he looked at me and said Nick was gone. I was so messed up, I didn't really pay attention to what happened next. This cop started asking me all sorts of questions, but I couldn't make sense of anything he was saying."

"You were in shock," Jace murmured.

"Yeah," Caleb said. "I didn't even realize until the funeral that my dad had told the cops I'd been the one to find Nick's body. That was when I started hearing people say the Coroner had found heroin in Nick's system and that was what had caused him to pass out and hit his head on the table."

Caleb used his free hand to wipe at his puffy eyes. "That was when I knew the truth," he said quietly.

"What truth?" I asked.

"I think my dad injected heroin into Nick while I was calling 911."

Terror swamped me at that. Being a kiddie rapist was one thing, but a murderer too?

"Why do you think that?" Mav asked. "Your brother had a drug problem, didn't he?"

Caleb nodded. "He did, but he was getting help. Part of the treatment program was daily drug screens. He'd had one that

286

morning. I found the test results on his desk in his room when I was looking for pictures to have enlarged for the service. If he'd shot up between then and when he got home, I would have been able to tell that he was high."

"Where would your father have gotten the drugs?" Mav asked.

"Nick wasn't the only one with a problem," was all Caleb said.

"Tell them the rest," Jace urged.

Caleb nodded.

"The day I called Eli, a friend of Nick's stopped by to bring me an envelope. Nick had asked him to give it to me if anything ever happened to him."

"What was in it?" I asked.

"A piece of paper with a location on it. Fisherville Quarry. Nick and I used to freshwater dive there all the time and after we were done, we'd explore these caverns."

"You think Nick hid whatever proof he was talking about there?" Mav asked.

"He did," Jace said as he pulled a flash drive from his pocket and held it up. He handed it to Mav.

"Did you check it yet?"

Jace nodded. His eyes shifted to me briefly before he said, "It's full of videos."

My chest constricted painfully and I actually reached up my hand as if I could stem the pain that way. "Of all of us?" I asked, unable to lift my eyes from where they were staring at the ugly brown carpet beneath our feet.

Jace was silent for a moment. "Yes."

I couldn't stop the tears that fell because I knew what would happen next. I turned to look at Mav and whispered, "Please don't watch it."

"Eli," Jace said gently and I looked up at him. "Caleb told me that Nick saw you and your stepfather the night you got your driver's license. Apparently Nick asked his mom to bring him over that night to spend the night and your stepdad either forgot or never got the message. When he saw what you and your stepfather were doing, he left and caught up to his mom before she left. He told her he'd changed his mind and didn't want to spend the night anymore. He told Caleb you were into what was happening to you."

Humiliation tore through me at that and I gladly leaned into Mav when he pulled me against his chest.

"Eli, listen to me," Jace implored and then he was leaning across the distance between the two beds so that he could put his hand on my knee. "I found the video of that night and I watched it...all of it."

Fuck, would this never end? "Mav, please, I can't do this," I bit out as the shame sent heat flooding through my entire system. Mav's arms tightened around me.

"I've got you, Eli," he murmured against my ear. "I've got you."

I wished Jace would stop talking, but he continued. "Eli, he drugged you."

It took me several long seconds to process what Jace had said. I turned my head on Mav's chest so I could see the other man. "What?"

"There was a small bar in the den. It had a refrigerator in it, do you remember?" Jace asked.

I nodded. "That's where he got the beers from."

"The security camera captured him putting something in one of the bottles after he opened it and before he handed it to you. He did it to the second beer too."

I straightened and wiped at my face. "I saw the video…he tried to stop me from…"

Jace shook his head. "My guess is the video he showed you was one he edited to make it look like you instigated the whole thing. Did the video you saw have sound?"

"No."

Jace pointed to the flash drive in Mav's hand. "The real video has sound. And you are clearly saying no from the moment *he* first touches *you*."

Logically, I understood what Jace was telling me, but I couldn't process it. Because along with this new reality came a worse one. I'd made so many decisions based on that one video…on those few seconds of seeing myself seduce my mother's husband and the friend of the one man I admired above all others.

This time when the bile crawled up my throat, I knew there was no stopping it and I ran to the bathroom. I heaved into the toilet over and over again until my stomach was empty. My throat ached as tears streamed down my face. A washcloth was passed over my face and then a plastic cup of water was handed to me. I rinsed and spit the water out in the toilet, but I couldn't find the strength to stand. Mav was kneeling in front of me, his eyes heavy with concern.

"He raped me," I finally whispered, the words making my throat burn. "He fucking raped me," I said again in disbelief and then I just let go.

Completely and terribly. I couldn't hold back the anguished sobs that tore from my throat as I absorbed the truth about what had really happened that night and the path of destruction through my life that had followed. Every time I'd let Jack touch me after that had been because I'd believed his lies…

"Oh God, what did I do?" I cried in disbelief as everything came crashing down around me. And when I no longer had the strength to keep myself upright, Mav was right there waiting to catch me.

Chapter Twenty-Five

Mav

"Do you think I should watch it?" Eli asked quietly, his voice rough. We'd been lying on the bed for more than an hour with me leaning against the headboard and Eli resting his head on my chest. Jace and Caleb had moved to the room next door to give Eli some space to process what had happened to him, but Jace had left his laptop on the nightstand for me so I wouldn't have to search out mine.

Eli had let everything out in that bathroom and I'd been completely helpless to do anything but hold him. When he'd finally calmed down, I'd helped him to his feet and we'd gotten into bed fully dressed and with just the small light next to the bed turned on. My hope had been that Eli would fall asleep so that I could watch the videos on my own using the ear buds I had stashed in my bag, but I suspected the stress was keeping him too wound up to get the rest he so badly needed.

"I honestly don't know," I admitted. The idea of Eli having to witness what had been done to him was unbearable to me, but I was also worried that a part of him would never truly believe what Jace had told him. His stepfather's doctored video had had a profound impact on him and his brain might not be able to rid itself of those images without proof that they were all lies. I let my fingers trail down Eli's spine as I tried to deal with everything that had happened in the past 48 hours. A few hours ago, I'd been contemplating if I could really have the life I'd been too afraid to hope for in the years since I'd left my life on the reservation behind me.

But now?

Now I knew.

And I was fucking terrified.

"I lied to you," I whispered.

Eli tensed, but didn't move away from me like I'd expected him to.

"When?" he asked softly.

"On the plane. You asked me if I wouldn't even try to love you," I said, my voice catching in my throat. "I lied when I said no because I already knew then that I was in love with you." I swallowed hard. "I love you, Eli. More than you'll ever know."

The fingers Eli had been using to draw circles on my chest stilled, but when he didn't respond otherwise, all my old fears came rushing back. But I forced them down and said, "I know the timing's not great and that the pain I've caused you is unforgivable, but I can't lose you. If there's even a chance that you want to be with me-"

That was as far as I got because Eli leaned up at the same time that his hand snagged the back of my neck. His mouth closed over mine and when I let out the pent up air I'd been holding on to, his tongue slipped past my lips. The kiss was over too soon, but when Eli whispered, "I love you, Mav. So much," against my lips, I felt the relief in every cell in my body. I rolled Eli until he was flat on his back and he instantly wound his arms around my neck.

"You refused to leave me," I murmured.

Eli tucked my hair behind my ear before trailing his finger over my jaw. "You make me a little less broken."

I kissed him long and deep before saying, "I'm going to make you whole again, Eli. I'm going to show you how perfect you are and I'm going to love you for the rest of my life."

Tears slipped down Eli's face even as he smiled tremulously and said, "You're never going to be alone again, Mav. I'm never going to let anyone hurt you ever again and I'm going to love you for the rest of my life."

I couldn't help but feel a rush of joy go through me at Eli's last words...in a crazy way it felt like we'd just said our own private version of vows to one another.

I kissed Eli again and then sat up, pulling him with me. I teased his mouth with mine as I dried his tears. "We'll go wherever you want when this is all over. We'll be each other's family."

Eli nodded and then pressed his head against my chest. "I can't keep running from this," he said softly. "I...I know now I didn't do anything wrong," he said and my heart swelled with pride. But my stomach bottomed out when he said, "I need to watch the video, Mav."

I understood his need, but I wished there was a way I could give him what he needed without putting him through more pain. "You sure?" I asked even as I reached for the laptop since I already knew what his answer would be.

"I want to put it behind me."

I booted up the laptop, but Eli didn't stiffen against me until I put the flash drive in. There were at least a dozen files that appeared on the drive. It took only seconds to realize how they'd been named and I sorted them alphabetically so all the ones that started with the letter "E" were together. There were seven files in total so I knew either Nick hadn't managed to copy them all, or Eli's stepfather hadn't saved all the recordings. My guess was that it was the former, because the fact that he'd saved even any evidence that could put him in prison for the rest of his life was proof of how confident the man was that he would get away with everything he'd done to all three boys. As I selected the earliest file based on the date, I wondered if the man had more victims somewhere.

I didn't ask Eli if he was ready because I knew there was no way he truly could be. The video started with the image of Eli and Jack sitting on the couch in front of a flat screen TV, a big bowl of popcorn between them. They laughed and joked about whatever was happening on the screen, but when Jack asked Eli if he wanted a beer, I felt Eli tense up against my chest. Just like Jace had said, the security camera got a clear shot of Jack spiking one of the beers and I felt my chest nearly implode when I saw a very young looking Eli take the drugged drink. By the time the first beer had started to make

Eli groggy, Jack's frequent touches had started to linger and grow longer. And when Eli asked for another beer, Jack had smiled widely, ruffled his hair and gotten up to get the drink. He again put something in it and then sat back and waited as Eli drank it and began to look like he was about to fall asleep. What followed was a series of inappropriate touches that were meant to test how heavily drugged Eli was and even though Eli tried to push Jack's roaming hands away, he was completely helpless to do anything but say no as Jack began taking his shirt off.

I felt Eli's fingers dig into my chest as Jack began unbuttoning his pants, but that was as far as he went before he grabbed Eli's arm and forced him to his knees on the floor in front of him. Eli was clearly confused and began telling Jack he didn't feel good. Jack's response was to tell Eli that he knew how to make him feel good, and then he was forcing Eli's head to his crotch. Eli's hands came up to steady himself on Jack's thighs and at that exact moment, Jack lifted his arms in the air and began shaking his head. But even as he made it look like he was trying to resist, he was commanding Eli to take him out.

"That's the part he showed you, isn't it?" I asked.

Eli nodded against my chest.

Jack pulled out his cock and forced Eli's head down and then put his hands on Eli's shoulders. He again wore an expression of shock, but his words belied his countenance because he was telling Eli to suck him. When Eli tried to pull away, Jack forced his mouth open with his fingers and then shoved his dick between Eli's lips.

It took every ounce of control I had not to throw the laptop across the room and go hunt Jack Cortano down. Eli remained quiet on my chest and I tried to angle my head so I could see his face. One tear after another welled up in his eyes and fell down his cheeks, but he didn't make a sound and he didn't look away from the screen.

There were a few seconds here and there where Eli actually did seem to suck on Jack's dick, but he consistently pulled off and tried to get away. I had no doubt Jack had edited those parts out when he'd shown Eli the doctored version. When I watched Jack pull Eli to his feet and bend him over the arm rest of the couch, I reached out to stop the video, but Eli grabbed my hand. He didn't speak, but threaded his fingers with mine. I felt my own tears begin to fall as Eli began begging Jack to stop because he was hurting him, but without the sound, it would have just looked like a drunk Eli was getting fucked hard. And just as Eli had said, he didn't physically struggle, but only because he was clearly too far gone to fight back. But when Jack began calling him his little whore and asking him if he liked being fucked by a real man, I reached out and slammed the laptop closed. Rage was vibrating through every part of me and I wanted nothing more than to get up and put my fist through a wall.

Eli didn't react right away when I shoved the offending laptop away, but then he turned so that he was facing me, his head still pressed against my chest. He reached up to run his fingers through the tears that were still falling down my face and then he pulled me down for a kiss. He continued to cry silently as we kissed, but when he pulled me down farther so that our cheeks were pressed together he whispered, "I'm okay."

I nodded against him because I couldn't find my voice. When I finally regained the power of speech I breathed, "I love you," against his ear. The words were repeated back to me and then we just held on to each other and cried for the little boy on the screen who'd just started his journey through hell and back.

* * *

Eli hadn't let go of me for more than a couple of minutes at a time as we'd made our way back to Seattle. After watching the video earlier in the day, I'd texted Jace to tell him Eli and I needed some time to rest. In actuality, we'd ended up falling asleep and we hadn't woken up until Jace had knocked on the door to bring us some food he'd gotten from a fast food place a few miles away. Caleb had been with him, but hadn't said much and as we'd eaten, we'd talked briefly about what to do next. It was clear that Caleb would be coming back to Seattle with us, but when Caleb had asked Jace if he was coming too and Jace had said no, Caleb had lost it. Eli had tried to talk to Caleb, but he'd jerked away from Eli's attempt to comfort him. At that point Jace had taken Caleb outside to talk to him. They'd returned within a few minutes and Jace had announced that he would be traveling with us. Caleb had still looked like he was at his breaking point, but he never once left Jace's side and the older man hadn't seemed to have an issue with it.

After Caleb and Jace had returned to their room, I'd waited until Eli had fallen back asleep before calling Ronan to let him know that we would be leaving the following morning. He'd told me he would let the pilot know and that he'd pick us up from the airport. The flight home had been quiet, but unlike when we'd left Seattle, I'd sat next to Eli on one of the small loveseat style seats that faced the interior of the plane rather than the front of it. Caleb and Jace had ended up on the other one and about an hour after takeoff, Caleb had fallen asleep against Jace. I hadn't missed how often Jace touched Caleb and how he seemed to know exactly when the younger man needed it. I'd already started to feel protective of the teenager since he would have no one but Eli and Eli's mother after Jack was held accountable for his crimes, and I couldn't help but wonder if the bond that Caleb and Jace had formed would end up causing Caleb more harm than good. Because I knew Jace and not only was he too old for Caleb, he was also very much the *love 'em and leave 'em type*.

It wasn't until the plane was in the process of descending that Eli finally began talking beyond providing simple yes and no answers when presented with a question.

"I'm worried about my mom," he said softly and I suspected it was because he didn't want to wake Caleb up. "She's still in Germany, but I don't know when she's planning on flying back. And if Caleb's right about what Jack did to Nick…"

I used my hand to massage the back of Eli's neck as I said, "I talked to Ronan about your mom last night after you fell back asleep.

He's got someone watching her until you have a chance to talk to her. Ronan's guy will escort her home when the time comes."

"This is going to kill her," Eli said sadly.

"If she's anything like you, she'll find the strength to deal with it."

"She really loves him," Eli murmured. "I guess I did too," he added. "Even after everything he did to me, there'd be these moments where he acted like a real dad. That's fucked up, isn't it?"

"No," I said. "I think we compartmentalize the people who hurt us the most so that they become two different people."

"I wanted him to be Dom," Eli admitted. "I wanted what Dom had with his real kids."

"You don't think Dom thinks of you as one of his own?"

Eli shook his head. "I know he loves me, but I think he's only ever seen me as the kid he saved. He's never going to forgive me for this."

"Eli, none of this was your fault."

"I let Jack fool me with that video, Mav. But it doesn't change the fact that I still let him do all those things to me afterwards. I had a choice. Even if I didn't want it, I still had a choice."

I sighed as I realized that as much progress as Eli had made in accepting what had happened, he still had a long way to go before he forgave himself for what he perceived as his decisions – his choices. When things settled down, I'd talk to him about getting some professional help since I had no idea how to convince him that he'd never had a choice…not since the day that monster had stepped into his life. And I knew that Eli's mother and Dom Barretti were going to be just as challenged to forgive themselves for the involuntary roles they'd played in what had happened. My hope was that they were both strong enough to put Eli's needs above their own.

Eli fell silent and didn't speak even once we were in Ronan's SUV headed north towards the city. Caleb and Jace were in the last row in the SUV and while I'd had the option to sit up front in the passenger seat, I'd chosen to sit in back with Eli since his anxiety had ratcheted up when he'd overheard Ronan telling me that he suspected Jack Cortano was on his way to Seattle, if he wasn't already here. Luckily, Caleb hadn't heard that news.

"Breathe, baby," I whispered as I could hear Eli struggling to draw in air.

Eli nodded as he tried to calm himself. The plan was to go to the hotel we'd been using as home base during Matty's cancer treatments, but the more Eli began to shake next to me, the more I knew he needed all the help he could get.

"Ronan," I called and Ronan looked in the rearview mirror at me. "We need to go get the dog."

Ronan's eyes shifted to Eli and then he nodded. He took the next exit that would take us to the University campus. My plan had been to get Baby later after we'd gotten settled at the hotel, but my hope was that the big dog could help ease some of Eli's fears about Jack possibly being in the same city. There was an open spot right in front of Eli's apartment building and as soon as he put the SUV in park, Ronan handed me Eli's house keys.

I gave Eli a quick kiss and said, "Stay here with Ronan. I'll go get Baby, okay?"

Eli nodded numbly and smiled. "Thank you, Mav."

I kissed his forehead and then got out of the car. I glanced over my shoulder at Eli who was sitting in the open doorway of the SUV trying to draw in enough air to keep himself from going over the edge. Since my eyes were on him, I didn't notice anything off right away. But when I glanced up towards Eli's apartment, I stopped suddenly at the sight of the wide open door. A spray of bright red blood was spattered across the doorframe.

"Ronan!" I shouted as I pulled my gun from my waistband. I didn't look to see if Ronan heard me or not as I ran up the stairs, but I saw him racing across the small yard towards me, gun drawn. And right behind him was Eli. I didn't bother to see where Jace and Caleb were because I needed to focus so I raised my gun and scanned the inside of the apartment. Ronan reached me just as I started to enter the apartment and the first thing I saw was a body face down on the floor, a pool of blood beneath it. There was another body on the far side of the loveseat and I could see the man had been shot in the head. I ignored the sight and scanned the apartment and then saw what I was looking for. Baby was lying on the ground next to someone who was hunched over. Ronan and I held our guns on him as Ronan yelled at him to raise his hands.

"Ronan!" the guy shouted. "He can't breathe."

I knew the gravelly voice before the man cast a glance over his shoulder at us.

Memphis Wheland.

The relief at seeing our team leader was short lived as I realized Memphis was leaning over another body. Ronan was already moving past me and kneeling beside the young man. Terror flooded my system as I recognized the young man's face and I managed to grab Eli the second he came rushing into the apartment.

"What happened?" he yelled as he looked around and then saw the dead bodies on the floor. "Baby!" he said frantically as he searched the apartment before finally seeing the dog. I felt Eli's relief at the sight of his pet. The animal was covered in blood and had what looked like several long cuts on his side but seemed to be okay despite the injuries. Baby didn't get up when he saw Eli. Instead, he stayed exactly where he was lying next to the two men who were frantically trying to help the third man.

"Who-" Eli started to say when he spotted the man on the floor, but then he went silent for a second when he recognized who it was.

"Brennan?" he whispered. "Brennan!" I held Eli back as he tried to get to his friend.

Jace came running into the apartment, gun drawn and Caleb behind him. "Clear the apartment," I said and Jace quickly scanned what was going on and then grabbed Caleb's hand in his and dragged him back towards Eli's bedroom.

"Brennan!" Eli screamed again and when Ronan shifted, I saw blood covered the young man's stomach.

"Ronan," I called, needing more information. If Brennan was already gone, I needed to get Eli the hell out of there.

"He's alive," Ronan said as he leaned down to listen to Brennan's chest. Memphis was holding the young man's hand tightly in his and I could see that Brennan's eyes were open, but he was struggling to breathe.

Eli had stilled at Ronan's announcement that his friend was alive, but he was holding on to me with painful intensity.

"Why can't he breathe?" Memphis asked, his usual cool and detached demeanor completely obliterated.

"Tension Pneumothorax," Ronan said as he sat back on his heels and looked around the apartment.

"What is that?" Memphis asked.

"His lung's collapsed," Ronan responded.

"I called 911. They should be here in a few minutes."

"He doesn't have that long," Ronan replied, his voice calm and steady. His gaze settled on Eli. "Eli, do you have any kind of tubing?"

Eli didn't respond at all and I had to grab his chin to force his eyes to mine. "Baby, listen to me. Do you have any tubing?"

"What?" he asked numbly.

"Tubing," I repeated.

Eli looked around the apartment, but I could tell he was struggling to keep it together. "Eli, Brennan needs your help. Now think, do you have any kind of tubing in the apartment?"

I sensed Jace and Caleb behind me, but I didn't look at them as I willed Eli to calm down. His eyes latched onto mine and he slowed his breathing. A few seconds passed before he said, "Yes," and pulled free of my hold. He ran to the cabinet beneath the kitchen sink and began pulling things out of it. "The super was going to put an ice maker in the freezer. He left the kit here."

"Mav, your knife," Ronan called as he kept his finger on Brennan's pulse.

I grabbed the knife from my ankle holster and searched out Jace. "Check the bathroom for any kind of antiseptic. Caleb, can you check the kitchen for alcohol?"

Caleb nodded, though his eyes were wide with shock. He began rifling through the cabinets and the refrigerator as Eli finally found the box he was looking for. He rushed to the table and began tearing the cardboard open. He let out a cry of relief when he found the clear plastic tubing.

"Will this work?" Caleb asked as he handed me a bottle of tequila.

I nodded and doused my knife with it. I grabbed the tubing and the alcohol and hurried to Ronan's side. Brennan was gasping desperately for air and tears were streaking down his face.

"Hold on Brennan," Memphis whispered. "You're going to feel better in a minute."

Brennan's eyes fixed on Memphis and I saw Memphis use his free hand to cup Brennan's cheek.

"Cut the tubing in half and clean it with the alcohol," Ronan said. I did as he said and the second I was done with the alcohol, he grabbed it from me and dumped a generous amount over his hands. He took my knife.

"His shirt," he said to me and I leaned over and ripped the shirt open, exposing Brennan's chest and the gaping gunshot wound in his side. "Help Memphis keep him still," Ronan ordered. I moved around Ronan's other side and put my hands on Brennan's shoulders. "Hold his arm up," he said. To Brennan he gently said, "Brennan, this is going to hurt, but I need you to stay as still as possible. It's going to feel better real soon, okay?"

Brennan managed a nod, but the second Ronan found the spot he was looking for and cut into him, he cried out in pain. I held him down as Memphis got up into his face and softly said, "Keep your eyes on me."

At some point Eli had dropped down next to Ronan. I could see his hands were wet from alcohol and he was holding the tubing in his hands. Ronan handed him the knife and took the tubing and began working it into the incision he'd made. "Okay, Brennan, it's in…just a few more seconds, okay?"

Brennan managed a nod, but he kept his eyes on Memphis. I felt the second the chest tube began working because Brennan relaxed beneath my hands as his breathing began to improve. Ronan leaned down to listen to Brennan's chest and then quickly began assessing Brennan's gunshot wound which was leaking blood at a rapid rate.

"Eli, we need to put pressure on this. Do you have any clean towels or rags?"

Eli jumped up and rushed from the room. He was back a second later with a stack of laundered hand towels. Ronan placed two towels over the wound and ordered Eli to put as much pressure on the wound as he could. I was glad when I heard sirens out front and to the paramedics' credit, they didn't react at the sight of the dead body just inside of the doorway other than one of the men checking for a pulse. They didn't bother checking the man with the gunshot wound. Eli and I both stepped back as the paramedics got to work and neither man argued as Ronan began giving them orders. I heard one of the paramedics speak into a radio that they were doing a scoop and run and I knew it was bad.

Really bad.

They worked quickly to get Brennan on the gurney, but when Brennan's eyes slid shut, Ronan snapped, "We need to go now."

"We'll meet you at the hospital!" I called as Ronan rushed out the door with the paramedics. Memphis started to follow.

"Memphis, the cops will need to question you," I said.

"Then they can fucking come find me at the hospital," he retorted and then he was following Ronan and the paramedics.

"Go," Jace said as our eyes met. "We'll stay here and wait for the cops," he said as nodded at Caleb.

I was already tugging Eli to the door when I said, "Can you take care of getting the dog help? His name is Baby. Keys are in the SUV."

Jace nodded and then I was dragging Eli down the stairs. The paramedics had just finished loading Brennan when we reached the curb. I saw that Ronan had climbed into the back of the ambulance and was frantically working on Brennan. It took me several long seconds to realize he was doing chest compressions on the young man.

Memphis was standing shell shocked behind the ambulance as the doors swung closed and I could only hope that Eli hadn't seen what was happening to his friend. "Memphis, keys!" I called. Memphis looked at me as if he'd forgotten where we were and then he was moving. He tossed me his car keys and strode to the dark blue luxury sedan that was parked in front of Ronan's SUV. Eli got in the back while I ran to the driver's side. I knew I wouldn't be able to keep up with the ambulance, but since I suspected which hospital it was going to, I wasn't worried about it.

"Eli," I said as I glanced over my shoulder at him. I had to call his name several more times before he looked up.

"We need to call Brennan's family. Can you pull up his father's or mother's phone number and give the phone to Memphis?"

Eli numbly removed his phone from his pocket. His hand was shaking as he scrolled until he found what he was looking for. He handed the phone to Memphis and said, "Zane is his older brother. He works downtown so he'll be the closest. Zane's husband, Connor, teaches at a school in Queen Anne."

Memphis grabbed the phone and dialed. He explained the situation to whoever answered and after several more seconds, he hung up and handed the phone back to Eli. "Eli, call Dom," I said.

Eli managed a nod and then dialed the phone. "Dom?" he said, his voice breaking. "Can you come to the hospital? It's Brennan…"

I missed the rest of whatever Eli said to Dom, but by the time he hung up he was crying. I forced myself to ignore his distress as I focused on the road and minutes later I was pulling in to the emergency department parking lot.

Chapter Twenty-Six

Eli

"Baby, drink this for me, okay?"

The can of soda felt cold as Mav pushed it into my hand. I wanted to tell him I wasn't thirsty, but I was too tired, so I did what he said and drank. I kept taking sips until he told me it was enough and put the can down on the table next to the chair I was sitting in.

"Is he dead?" I whispered.

Mav hesitated and I knew it was because he was trying to decide whether to tell me the truth or not.

"I don't know," he finally said. "If anyone could have gotten him here alive, it's Ronan."

"He was doing CPR," I said.

Mav sighed and put his hand on the back of my head. He rested his forehead against mine and said, "He's going to make it."

"They were after me," I said when Mav released me. "Those guys," I added as I remembered the two dead men lying in pools of blood. "They thought Brennan was me."

Mav nodded. "It looks like they were looking for something in your apartment and Brennan walked in on them when he was bringing Baby back to your place."

"The flash drive."

Another nod. I felt numb inside as I remembered the look of terror in Brennan's eyes as he'd tried to draw in breath. And the blood. So much fucking blood.

"Eli?"

I looked up when I heard my name being called and I felt my stomach drop at the sight of Zane Devereaux, Brennan's older brother. He was an older version of Brennan with his tall, fit body, black hair and green eyes. I climbed to my feet and began shaking as Zane hurried up to me.

"I got a call from someone using your phone. They said Brennan was in an accident."

I couldn't stop the sob that got caught in my throat and as tears filled my eyes, Zane's face fell.

"Zane?" Mav said as he put his hand out to steady Zane who looked like he was going to collapse.

"Where's my brother?" he asked.

"They're working on him right now," Mav said.

"What happened?" Zane asked and I could tell by the way his voice broke that he was barely keeping it together.

"He was shot," Mav said.

Zane froze and then the phone he'd been carrying in his hand hit the floor. Mav grabbed him by the arm and helped him into a chair. "Shot?" Zane whispered. "How is that possible? He was taking Baby back to Eli's apartment."

"It happened at Eli's apartment. Two men had broken in and Brennan walked in on them."

Mav didn't expand any further and Zane didn't seem particularly interested.

"Where is he? I need to see him," Zane said in a rush as he stood.

"Mav," I heard Memphis call and I saw Mav follow Memphis's gaze towards a set of double doors that had opened to reveal Ronan. He spotted us and began striding our way. I nearly threw up when I saw the blood covering his shirt. When Ronan reached us, Zane let out a gasp as he saw the blood.

"Is that…is that Brennan's blood?" he asked in horror. He didn't wait for an answer. "Brennan!" he began screaming as he started heading for the doors Ronan had just come through.

"Are you Zane?" Ronan asked as he stepped in front of Zane. Zane stilled and managed a nod.

"Brennan's alive," he quickly said. "He's in surgery. His surgeons have already managed to stop the bleeding and they're giving him blood to replace what he lost at the scene."

Zane visibly relaxed somewhat and I felt my own fear subside a little bit.

"He's going to be okay?" Zane asked, his voice sounding small.

"The bullet hit his kidney so they might end up needing to remove it, but he can live a normal life with just one. They're still assessing to see if there is any more damage, but it's looking really good."

Zane managed a nod and sank back down on the chair. He looked at me and suddenly grabbed my hand. "You're okay?" he asked.

The question unleashed something raw and powerful inside of me and I ripped my hand free of Zane's and fell to the floor in my effort to escape the chair. Zane stood. "Eli-"

"Eli-" Mav said at the exact same time. He automatically stepped forward, but I put up my hand.

"Don't. Please," I whispered as I scrambled to my feet. "I can't do this."

My need to flee was greater than anything else, but Mav stepped in my path and when I tried to pull free of him, he held on to me and snarled, "You will not do this! You will not take this on yourself too!"

I slammed my fists against Mav's chest as the helplessness and fear gave way to an uncontrollable rage. Mav didn't try to stop me as I hit him over and over again. I lost count of how many times I lashed out at him and even though in my mind I knew I was hurting him, I couldn't stop hitting him. Because at some point he'd stopped being Mav.

My arms burned as my physical strength began to wane and by the time I became aware of my surroundings, I'd stopped striking Mav and was just resting my fisted hands on his chest as he held my upper arms. His mouth was next to my ear and he just kept telling me he loved me, over and over again. When I let out the final howl of pain that was trapped deep inside of me, Mav dragged me forward into a bone-crushing hold. I had no idea how long he held me like that for, but when he finally eased his grip on me, I was terrified to let him go.

"Eli?"

The sound of Dom's worried voice felt like both a balm and a bullet and I pulled back enough from Mav to see Dom standing next to Zane, his hand on Zane's arm. But he wasn't alone.

I closed my eyes as I heard my stepfather call my name and opened them just in time to see him striding towards me.

Only he never even got close because Mav laid him out with one punch and then he was on top of Jack, his big hands wrapped around the man's skinny throat.

Chapter Twenty-Seven

Mav

Twenty seconds…twenty seconds of pure bliss before I was being pulled off the fucker. Twenty seconds of watching the man acknowledge that he'd taken his final breath. I cursed my own stupidity for not just snapping his neck. No, I'd wasted precious time because I'd wanted to see in him the same fear and pain he'd inflicted on Eli…that he was still inflicting just by breathing the same air.

It wasn't my own men who pulled me off the bastard. One set of hands belonged to Dominic Barretti, the other I didn't recognize.

"What the hell?" Dom bit out as he reached down to help Jack to his feet. I tore free of the hands holding me and went for Jack again, but this time it was Ronan who stepped in front of me.

"Don't," was all Ronan said and then he motioned to the man who'd been holding me. While the big blond guy was wearing street clothes, a police officer's badge stuck out of his shirt pocket.

"I don't give a fuck!" I snarled.

"Enough!" the cop said as he stepped in front of me and shoved me back. It was only when Ronan and Memphis each

314

grabbed one of my arms and forcibly dragged me back that I realized I was outnumbered. But when Jack made a move towards Eli again, I tore free of Ronan and Memphis.

"You fucking touch him and I will rip you apart!" I warned. It took all four men to hold me back, which left no one between Jack and Eli. But before I could even say anything when Jack reached for Eli, Eli's hand shot out, catching Jack in his already sensitive throat and he let out a gasp of air.

"You don't get to touch me ever again, you sick fuck!" Eli shouted, and then he kicked Jack hard in the nuts. Jack hit the floor, moaning in agony. I watched as Dom released his hold on me and shifted his gaze back and forth between Eli and Jack and then he was moving to put himself between the two men. I could see him putting the pieces together in his head as he studied Eli who was still standing defensively like I'd taught him, fists at the ready.

"Dom," Jack groaned as he held out his hand, but Dom didn't do anything to help the man to his feet.

"Eli, talk to me," Dom said as he turned enough so that he could see Eli, but not take his eyes completely off of Jack who'd managed to stagger to his feet.

"Brennan got shot because his men" – Eli pointed at Jack – "thought he was me!" Eli took a deep breath to calm himself and said, "They were looking for a flash drive."

"Dom, this is what I was talking about," Jack said, injecting a hint of sadness into his voice. "He's been acting erratically which is why I came up here to check on him."

"You said you came up here to look for Caleb," Dom said coldly.

"Yes, C-Caleb too…" Jack stammered.

"What's on the flash drive, Eli?" Dom asked.

I saw Eli hesitate and then his gaze met Dom's and he shook his head. Tears filled his eyes and I started to step forward, but Dom reached out his hand to gently cup Eli's face. "It's okay, Eli. You can tell me anything."

The tears fell and Eli dashed angrily at them. "I'm sorry, Dom," he whispered. "I wanted…" Eli shook his head and fell silent.

"Dom-" Jack implored.

"Shut the fuck up!" Dom ground out. As harsh as his voice was, his hold on Eli was gentle and his hand moved to the back of Eli's neck so he could force Eli to look at him. "What's on the flash drive?"

"Proof," Eli finally whispered.

"Proof of what?"

Eli looked at Dom almost pleadingly and I knew he didn't want to voice the words. I wanted like hell to tell him he didn't have to, but in my heart I knew he needed to do this.

"Proof that he raped me," Eli finally admitted, his voice low. "Caleb and Nick too," Eli added.

Dom held Eli's gaze for a long moment even as Jack yelled, "He's lying!"

The man didn't get anything else out because Dom's big fist slammed into his jaw in the same exact place I'd hit him. Jack hit the

316

floor again, but Dom remained standing above him, fists clenched. "You raped my kid?" he asked, his voice deadly.

"He's lying!"

Dom bent down and punched him again, this time breaking the man's nose. Blood sprayed all over Jack's face and the floor, but Dom didn't even pause when he loomed over him and snarled, "I trusted you to watch out for him!"

Jack put his hand up to ward off the blow he sensed coming. "He...he seduced me, Dom!" Jack stammered and I felt Ronan grab me as I strode forward.

"What the fuck did you just say?" Dom whispered.

"You know what he was, Dom! He used his body to-"

The man didn't get even another syllable out because Dom slammed his fist into Jack's face yet again and this time he didn't stop. Eli finally turned away when more blood slicked Dom's fists and the floor, but it wasn't until Jack stopped moving that the cop stepped in to stop Dom from killing the man. As big as the police officer was, he was no match for an enraged Dom and it took Memphis's help to push Dom back.

"All right, Declan!" Dom bit out and then he pushed away from the two men and turned his attention to Eli, whose shoulders were shuddering as sobs tore through him. I barely noticed as Ronan checked Jack's pulse and seemingly satisfied that he was still alive, stepped away from him. The police officer, who I now realized was Declan Barretti, one of Eli's uncles and also a Captain in the Seattle Police Department, knelt down and unceremoniously turned Jack over and yanked his arms behind him and slapped cuffs on him. A small crowd of doctors and nurses had surrounded us, but none made a move to help Jack. Several more men I could only assume were Barrettis arrived and began talking to Zane and Declan, but I ignored them and focused on Eli.

When Dom carefully put his hand on Eli's shoulder, Eli let out a ragged sob and turned into the man. Dom's arms went around him and he whispered, "It's okay," in his ear. "You're home now," he added and Eli nodded.

Long after the crowd started to disperse and Declan yanked a groggy Jack to his feet and dragged him to a room to be treated for the damage to his face, I stayed and watched Eli cling to the man who'd been his father all along. He just hadn't known it.

* * *

It was like some surreal game show.

Me, Ronan and Memphis on one side, Dom, Declan and a big dark haired guy named Cade who turned out to be yet another Barretti, but by marriage, on the other side. I hadn't understood the reasoning for his attendance in the small hospital conference room Declan had commandeered, but I had figured out that he was there because of a special connection he seemed to share with Eli. Because the second he'd strode into the room, he'd gathered Eli into his arms and had held him for a long time. If the man hadn't been happily married, I would have been struggling with the green-eyed monster.

Fuck, I'd struggled with it anyway, but my jealousy had dissolved when Eli had chosen to sit next to me rather than on his family's side.

It had been nearly an hour since the showdown with Jack in the ER waiting room, and while I'd been able to get Eli back in my arms after Dom had held him and murmured softly to him for a while, he'd been pulled away from me time and time again as Barrettis had started showing up one right after the other. And while I'd lost track of who was who after a while, I'd watched some of the tension ease out of Eli as each person had held him. But it hadn't completely dissipated until we'd gotten the news that Brennan had survived the surgery and was expected to make a full recovery. Eli was itching to go see his friend for himself, but Declan had insisted on this meeting first so that he could get all the facts he needed to deal with the two dead bodies in Eli's apartment. He'd already had a patrol car take Jack down to the precinct to be booked for sexual assault. At some point, Declan would need to talk to Caleb, but he'd already agreed to hold off until the following day to give Caleb some time to recover from the events of the afternoon. I knew it would be difficult for the young man since he would not only need to recount the details of his own sexual abuse, but he'd also have to share the details of his brother's death and their father's role in it.

"Mr. Wheland," Declan said as he glanced at his note pad. "I understand you were the first one to arrive at Eli's apartment?"

Memphis nodded, but didn't say anything. I had to hide a smile when Ronan kicked him under the table. Memphis sent him a dark look, but then turned his attention back to Declan. "Yes, I was the first one to arrive at Eli's apartment."

When he didn't say anything else, Declan said, "Would you care to expand on that?"

"No-"

"Yes," Ronan interrupted. "Yes, he would."

Memphis leaned back in his seat like he didn't have a care in the world and that he hadn't just been involved in a double killing.

"When Ronan told me Jack Cortano was possibly on his way to Seattle, I decided to sit on Eli's place to see if he showed up there."

"What were you planning to do if he did?"

"Have a chat with him," Memphis said, though it sounded more like a question than a statement.

"Cut the shit, asshole," Cade snapped, but he fell quiet when Dom put his hand out.

"What happened when you got to the apartment?" Declan asked.

"I got to the apartment about a minute before Brennan arrived with the dog. I watched him take it into the apartment and a few seconds later, I heard a gunshot."

Eli stiffened next to me. I wasn't sure if Ronan had already talked to Memphis about all of this, but it was our first time hearing Memphis's version of events.

"When I got into the apartment, Brennan was lying on the floor and the dog had one of the guys by the arm. His gun was on the ground, but he had a knife and was stabbing at the dog. The other guy took a shot at me when he saw me. He missed, I didn't."

"And the guy that Baby had a hold of?" Dom asked.

"I couldn't risk hitting the dog, but it wouldn't let the guy go when I tried to call it off. I went to check on Brennan when I heard the guy scream as he fell. The dog got him by the throat and that was it."

Eli let out a startled gasp at that and I sat back in my chair. I'd seen the blood beneath the guy, but he'd somehow ended up on his front when he'd died so I hadn't seen his throat. My respect for the Rottweiler jumped several notches. Damn dog would get steak dinners for the rest of his life if I had anything to say about it.

"What happened next?"

"Brennan was still conscious, but he was having trouble breathing. I called 911 and tried to keep him calm and talking."

I felt Eli reach for my hand under the table and I gave it a gentle squeeze.

"Ronan and Mav arrived a couple minutes later."

Declan's eyes shifted to Ronan. "I understand you're a trauma surgeon, Dr. Grisham," Declan said.

"I was," Ronan said. "But I'm not anymore. And it's just Ronan."

"So what is it that you do now, Ronan?" Declan asked as he glanced at all three of us one by one. "That necessitates you carrying a gun."

"Protection," Ronan said simply and then he looked at Dom pointedly. "Seems we're in the same business."

Dom didn't respond so I wasn't sure if that was a good or bad thing.

"You saved Brennan's life, Ronan," Dom murmured and then he glanced at Eli. "But I suspect you did a lot more than that." He sent Eli a quick smile and then his eyes settled on me.

"What about you, Mr. James?"

"Dom," Eli began, but Dom put up his hand and Eli fell silent.

"What about me?" I asked casually, though my insides were tight with worry. I could not afford to piss this man off. He was way too important to Eli.

"When did you know Jack was a threat to Eli?"

"The day you came to his apartment and found us arguing."

"What did you do about it?" Dom asked.

"He followed me," Eli interjected. "And when he couldn't have eyes on me, he asked his friends to do it. He also taught me how to defend myself. From the moment he knew I was in trouble, he refused to walk away from me."

Dom studied me for a moment and then glanced at Declan. "You think you have enough for now?"

Declan nodded. "Mr. Wheland, I'll need to collect your firearm for ballistics testing, but it's just standard operating procedure."

"He'll provide it to you, Captain," Ronan said before Memphis could spout what I could only assume were some very crude words, if the look on his face was anything to go by.

Everyone began to stand when Declan did, but Dom pinned me with his gaze and said, "Mr. James, I'd like a word with you."

"Dom…"

"It's okay, Eli," was all he said.

"Come on squirt," Cade said as he threw his arm around Eli and began to lead him from the room. Eli forced him to stop and turned to face me. I got up and went to him and not caring who was watching, I leaned down and kissed him.

"I'm not going anywhere."

Eli visibly relaxed and I realized my guess that he thought I would let Dom run me off was right. "I'll see you in a few."

Eli nodded and followed Cade. Cade's dark eyes settled on me for a moment before he left the room with Eli, and I swore I saw something akin to respect.

I sat back down and watched with interest as Dom came around the table to sit down next to me. I turned my chair so I was facing him.

"Tell me what he needs," Dom said.

I was expecting an interrogation, but when I saw the pain flood Dom's eyes, I knew he was letting the reality of what had happened to Eli sink in.

"He needs to forgive himself," I said. "Cortano fucked with his head…made him believe he brought it all on himself and that it was his choice."

Dom ran his hand over his bald head and shook his head. I wasn't surprised to see tears flooding his eyes. He wiped them away and said, "Why didn't he come to me?"

"I think Eli saw Cortano as a substitute for you – the father he didn't think he had."

"I've loved that kid from the moment I met him," Dom croaked. "I thought he knew that I considered him my son."

"I think if he'd had more time before his stepfather got to him, he would have eventually figured that out. But the second Cortano had him believing he was still that same kid you saved from the streets, he started to pull away from you. When he did finally threaten to tell the truth if Cortano didn't stop, the fucker used your contracts with the army as leverage."

Dom stiffened at that. "Our contracts? That piece of shit had nothing to do with us getting awarded those contracts. Yeah, he had the connections, which was exactly why I never told him we were putting in bids. Once we got the first couple of contracts, we earned the rest by proving we were the best."

"Eli wouldn't have had any way of knowing that, would he?" I asked gently.

Dom's face drew up in anger and he rose to his feet. I watched him walk to the window and grip the small ledge in front of it hard. "I trusted that bastard. I encouraged him to pursue Eli's mother even when she initially resisted."

"Dom," I interjected. "Blaming yourself won't serve any purpose. Eli already carries enough guilt; don't add to it."

Dom nodded in understanding. "Did he tell you about my brother, Rafe?"

"No," I said. "But I know what happened to him."

Dom turned to face me and leaned back against the window, his expression questioning. "Let's just call it research and leave it at that."

Dom chuckled and nodded. "I thought after what happened to Rafe, I'd know a monster the next time I saw one."

"I've been dealing with monsters for the past five years and I'm here to tell you that not one of them looks the same as another. You couldn't have known. Eli's mother couldn't have known. Your big ass family couldn't have known," I added with a laugh. I sobered and said, "I wouldn't have known if he'd let me walk away from him like I'd intended."

Dom eyed me for a moment. "And what are you intending now?" he asked.

I laughed heartily. "Really? The w*hat are your intentions?* speech?" I asked.

Dom shrugged. "He's my son," he said simply.

I nodded. "I intend to spend the rest of my life with him," I said simply.

Dom came around the table, his expression unreadable. I stood as he neared me. He held out his hand to shake mine and when I took it, he said, "Welcome to the family. Family dinners are Saturday nights and we rotate holidays and birthdays so you'll need to get on the schedule once you get a place together. And I'll expect you to play the host because my kid's going to be busy with medical school."

I chuckled until I realized the man wasn't joking. "Uh, yeah, sure," I murmured as I wondered why I felt so hot all of a sudden.

"Oh, and I'd like you guys to stop by for dinner tonight. My husband would like to meet you. Hope you like kids because our daughter is having a sleepover tonight and Tanner – that's Eli's little brother – has a day camp recital tomorrow that he's going to be singing in so he'll want to do a dress rehearsal for us," Dom said as he walked towards the conference room door. "Actually, I'll talk to Logan about getting you and Eli tickets for the recital," he said with a smile as he opened the door.

I wasn't surprised to see Eli standing worriedly at the door. His gaze flicked to me before going back to Dom. "He'll do," Dom murmured before he pulled Eli into his arms for a bear hug. "I love you, my boy," Dom whispered and I saw Eli nod against his chest.

"I love you too."

Dom dropped a kiss on his head and left the room. Eli twisted his fingers together as he walked towards me.

"Everything okay?" he asked.

I nodded and then I pulled him into my arms and kissed him. "It's perfect," I whispered before kissing him again. "It's fucking perfect."

Epilogue

Mav

"Shit, we're going to be late," I murmured as I slapped Eli on the ass and said, "Get a move on."

"Please tell me you're not actually afraid of Dom," he said with a laugh as he lagged behind me on the narrow trail.

"Of course not," I said. "It's just common courtesy to be on time."

"Family dinners never start on time," Eli said.

"Well, we can be late to the next one, not this one."

"Because it's your first one," Eli suggested.

"Why the hell didn't they just cancel it since Brennan won't be there, which means Zane and Connor won't either?" I grumbled. I felt Eli snag my hand to pull me to a stop.

"Look at you learning everyone's names."

"What? I'm good with names and faces."

"So it had nothing to do with Matty quizzing you with the flashcards Seth made for you?" Eli asked, a broad grin on his face.

"Damn kid," I muttered. "He swore he wouldn't tell."

"I think it's cute that you asked a five-year-old to help you with your homework."

"Fuck you," I growled. Eli chuckled and pulled me down for a kiss.

"He may or may not have given me a certain doll to help you with your nervousness. I put it in your saddlebag."

I smiled at that and resumed the short walk back to my Harley which was parked near the end of the trail. I hadn't yet had the honor of borrowing the coveted Spiderman doll. Apparently, I couldn't even hide how nervous I was at the prospect of meeting Eli's entire family from the little boy who still refused to let me win at Tic Tac Toe. I'd also been more than a little in awe of Matty who'd somehow managed to memorize all the different people from the flashcards Seth had created since the kid wasn't old enough to read all the names. "Just wait till he has to face all those people when he gets out of the hospital in a week," I grumbled, though I knew Matty would do just fine with Eli's family.

Matty's third round of chemo had come to an end and while he still needed to wait for his white blood cell count to normalize, he was already happily talking to Eli about all the animals the Barretti family members had. If everything went as planned, Hawke, Tate, Seth and Ronan would be bringing Matty to the very next Barretti family dinner. I hadn't expected Ronan to accept the invite when Eli had extended it, but he hadn't hesitated for even a second when Eli had brought it up. The idea of my badass, assassin family members meeting what I knew would one day be my massive family of in-laws was daunting to say the least. With my luck, Hawke who had more kills on his list than several of us combined, would end up sitting next to the straight-laced Captain Declan Barretti.

"And by the way, they were going to cancel, but Brennan asked them not to."

"What?" I asked as I stopped and turned around.

"He thought you might appreciate your first time out to be with a smaller group," Eli said, the humor in his voice on full display.

"You're enjoying this just a little too much," I murmured.

Eli wrapped his arms around my neck. "It's kind of my first time too," Eli said before he brushed a kiss over my lips. I didn't need to ask Eli to explain because I knew what he was talking about. Admitting the truth about what Jack had done to him had finally set Eli free, and while he had a ways to go before he could relinquish the bits of self-doubt that still had him wondering if he hadn't done something or said something to bring what had happened on himself, he was making great strides in accepting that his family had never seen him as an outsider. It had only been a few days since Jack had been arrested, but Eli had been through the wringer more than once.

His mother, Mariana, had arrived in Seattle the following day and hadn't had any clue what was going on until Dom had brought her to mine and Eli's hotel room to break the news to her. It had been brutal. There was just no other word for it. And I'd been there to bear witness to it all. The tears, the guilt, the regret, the anger, the rage, the denial...the emotions had been endless for all three of them. But the best thing that had come from the ordeal, was the

330

decision that Dom, Eli and his mother would seek professional help, both together and individually, to try to deal with the trauma. Mariana had filed for divorce that same day and she'd made arrangements to have hers and Caleb's things sent up from D.C. rather than traveling back there to collect them. When asked what should be done with the house, she'd told her lawyer to find someone to burn the fucker down.

Caleb had been a different story. He'd met with Declan the day after Declan had met with us and he'd shared the same information with him that he had with me, Jace and Eli. When Eli's mother had arrived, she'd told Caleb that they would still be a family and that he would be staying with her in Seattle, but the young man had seemed disinterested. And I suspected the reason why.

Because Jace had left.

I had no idea if Jace had told Caleb if he was going or not, but one day the man had been there and the next day he wasn't. It seemed he'd only been waiting long enough for Eli's mother to arrive to look after Caleb before he'd taken off. Caleb had shut down after that and while there were plans to get him some professional help as well, my gut was telling me it wouldn't be so easy. He'd also be tasked with testifying against his father at some point when Declan worked with the D.A. to add murder charges to the many counts of felony rape the man had already been charged with.

"We need lots of these," I whispered against Eli's mouth.

"Lots of what?"

"Firsts together," I said.

Eli smiled and took my hand in his. "That gives me an idea," he said coyly as he led me across the small stream that was one of many that carried runoff from Mount Rainier. We'd decided on taking the spur of the moment day trip this morning after we'd dropped a still healing Baby off with Eli's mother and Caleb who were staying at the same hotel as us. Fortunately, the dog's injuries hadn't been life threatening, and the first thing I'd done when we'd gotten the Rottweiler back to our hotel room the day after the attack, had been to order him the best cut of steak the hotel restaurant offered.

I had a lot of firsts planned with Eli, one of them being getting a place together. For me, it also meant having a place to call home for the first time in my life. And one day there would be a wedding – a huge first for both of us. I wasn't so sure about kids, but I wasn't ruling them out. I'd ended up enjoying myself at Logan and Dom's during their daughter's sleepover, despite the fact that all the little girls had taken turns brushing and playing with my hair before Eli had come to rescue me from their clutches. And last night I'd had another first when I'd told Eli the truth about what I did for a living. I'd been worried that he would struggle with the fact that Ronan's group worked outside the same law that his own family so strongly believed in, but he'd surprised me when he'd told me he'd already figured as much, considering all the resources that had been used to protect him. There'd been no requests for me to quit the business, which I was grateful for. Would there be a day when it was time for me to get out? Probably. But my work had been one of the few things in my life I'd been proud of, and I suspected it was something only Eli could ever understand about me.

Once we reached my motorcycle which I'd parked in a grove of trees at the trail's head, Eli said, "Climb on." I did as he said and started to grab the helmet for him when he grabbed my hand to stop me. Instead of climbing up behind me, he straddled the bike in front of me so that he was facing me. I was intrigued until he pulled me down for a searing kiss.

After that, I was just crazy with need. I glanced around the trail as Eli tugged his T-shirt off. While we were secluded from the main road, if any hikers came along the trail, they'd end up getting quite the show. But as Eli dropped his shirt to the ground and ran his hands over his chest, I found that I didn't give a fuck and I dragged my own shirt off. Eli pulled me down for a kiss as his hands roamed my back. My man definitely had a thing for my tats, but the snakes were a clear favorite because he played with them every chance he got.

And I'd made sure he had plenty of chances.

Eli's nimble fingers left my back long enough to start working my pants loose and then he pulled my cock out and began stroking me with heavy drags. His thumb kept tracing the ridge beneath the head and just when I was about to demand he get the rest of his clothes off, he released me and climbed off the bike. He took his time getting undressed, despite the chance of discovery. I kept my eyes on him as I pulled a packet of lube from my wallet and lubed myself up.

"I wasn't done playing," Eli said. "Are you still worried about being late?"

"Late for what?" I asked as I grabbed him by the waist and dragged him forward and up onto the bike. I settled him on my lap and kissed him long and hard as I let my lubed fingers push through his crease to search out his hole. Eli gasped against my mouth as I pushed one finger inside of him. With the second finger, he was squirming desperately against me.

"Lie back," I urged as pulled my fingers free from his body and wiped the excess lube on my pants. It took Eli a second to get situated so that his head was resting in the middle of the handlebars. I doubted that the position was very comfortable, but Eli didn't seem to notice because he was wrapping his legs around my waist and trying to work my cock into his crease. I slapped him on the ass in warning and waited until he stilled.

"Grab the handlebars," I said. Once he had a hold of them, I let my hands explore his beautiful chest and tight abdomen. I teased his leaking cock with touches that would do nothing to get him off. When he began bucking his ass against my dick again, I used my hand on his hip to hold him still.

"Please, Mav," he whispered.

"Please what?"

"Fuck me," he said harshly.

When I didn't respond, he picked up on his mistake and said, "Please fuck me, Mav."

I leaned forward to reward him with a kiss and then grabbed my cock and guided it to his opening. He moaned as I began to work my dick inside of him with little, teasing thrusts. I held on to his hips as I kept my feet flat on the ground so I could keep the bike upright. As more of my length sank into him, Eli closed his eyes and bit down on his lip. He twisted his hips trying to draw more of me inside of him.

"Please," Eli ground out and I finally gave him what he wanted and slammed my hips forward, burying myself in one sharp move.

"Yes!" Eli shouted and then he began rolling his hips so that he was the one doing all the fucking. I let him have control for a few minutes as I basked in the pleasure of all his delicious heat. Then I took over.

Eli let out a sharp wail when I rammed into him the first time and I quickly covered his mouth with my hand to muffle his cries of delight. I used my other hand to drag his hips towards mine every time I pushed into him, but after a dozen hard lunges, I found it wasn't quite enough and I leaned down to pull Eli up so that he was sitting astride me. I covered his mouth with mine in time to catch his loud groan as my cock shoved even deeper in side of him. Eli took control of the kiss while I took control of the fucking. He didn't stop even as I fisted his dick in my hand and began jerking him off to match my thrusts. I held off for as long as I could in the hopes that I could watch Eli come first. But he was determined to hold off his own orgasm and when mine crested and crashed in one glorious instance, Eli told me he loved me and went over with me.

There was no doubt in my mind that he'd resisted going over before me because he was keeping his promise to never leave me, even for a moment.

Never again would I have to be the one to leave first just so I wouldn't be left behind.

It was another first Eli had given me and I knew it would be one of many.

The End

Continue to the next page for a sneak peek of Memphis's story

*** Sneak Peek ***

Vengeance (The Protectors, Book 5) (M/M/M)

Sloane Kennedy

Prologue

Memphis

I hadn't expected to find him alone, especially considering the seemingly enormous family he had. But the late hour and the fact that his doctors had assured his older brother and the man's husband that the young man would make a complete recovery had probably played a role in the fact that no one lingered around his hospital bed or was trying to awkwardly sleep in one of the small guest chairs in the room. The floor was also quiet and the two nurses sitting at the nurse's station only paused briefly in their conversation to give me a polite nod. Even though it was well after visiting hours, I had no doubt that the young man's powerful family meant that not all the rules necessarily applied to him or to the family of men he was a part of. And the nurses likely thought I was a part of that family.

I wasn't.

Family was a luxury I'd lost a long time ago. And I had no desire to get it back.

The room was dim, but there was a little bit of light above the bed, presumably so the nurses could do their work without having to turn on the overhead lights and wake their patient.

As I moved closer to the bed, I felt the knot of anxiety in my belly ease as I watched his relaxed breathing.

So different than what it had been less than twenty-four hours ago.

I'd seen the young man before I'd met him yesterday, but I'd been limited to marveling over his beautiful features with just a couple of photographs as I'd done my recon on the Barretti family. And even though the young man wasn't technically a Barretti, he'd been included in my research because of his close association with the subject of our case, Eli Galvez.

Eli had become the lover of one of my team members and I and the rest of the team had been charged with trying to figure out if

Eli was in danger after he'd been physically assaulted by his stepfather as well as experiencing a random break-in attempt at his apartment a few days later that we hadn't been sure was all that random. And while I'd only come to Seattle to meet with our vigilante group's founder, Ronan Grisham, about taking over the day to day duties of running the team so he could focus on returning to a career in medicine, I'd had no issue with helping to figure out if Eli was truly in danger or not.

Which was how I'd crossed paths with the young man in the hospital bed.

Brennan.

His name was Brennan.

Even though I'd been mesmerized by Brennan's stark beauty from the moment I'd laid eyes on his picture, I hadn't made any plans to interact with him, despite my intense longing to hear what his voice sounded like, to feel his touch, to tease his perfect lips and drink down his sweet taste. No, I had more self-control than that. There were plenty of hot guys around for the quick fuck I occasionally needed…some were even worth a second one. But I had no need to seek them out. They came to me.

Perhaps that made me an arrogant son of a bitch, but facts were facts. I never lacked for male company if I wanted it.

I just rarely wanted it.

Until now.

I'd just pulled my car to a stop outside Eli's apartment the day before when I'd seen the young man who'd literally haunted my dreams the previous night getting out of a vintage Mustang that I'd suspected was in the process of being restored. Brennan had been behind the wheel of the sleek car and when he'd climbed out, I'd nearly swallowed my tongue at how even more stunning in real life he was than on film. He'd pulled a huge Rottweiler from the back seat of the car and I'd instantly suspected the animal belonged to Eli.

Brennan hadn't noticed me sitting in my car as he'd crossed the street and walked to Eli's apartment which was near the back of a converted house and was accessed via a set of stairs alongside the house. The way Brennan had moved with easy grace and the slight smile on his face as he'd talked to the big dog had done something to me. I had no idea what, but whatever *it* was, I hadn't been able to take my eyes off of him until he'd disappeared inside the apartment.

And then all hell had broken loose.

I'd been out of my car and running within a second of hearing the gunshot ring out and instead of feeling cool and calm like I usually did when I was headed directly into danger, all I'd felt was a stark fear that I'd be too late. The scene inside of the apartment when I'd gotten up the stairs had been chaotic and I'd registered several things all at once.

The Rottweiler in a death match with one gunman who was trying to stab the dog to get him to loosen his hold on his arm.

A second shooter with his gun pointed right at me.

And Brennan...

Brennan's still, bloody body lying motionless on the floor.

Taking out the guy aiming at me had been easy. His bullet had flown past my head while mine had gone straight through his. After realizing I couldn't shoot the second guy without risking hitting the dog, I'd gone to check on Brennan. And all I'd felt was relief when I'd seen his wide, glassy eyes staring up at me as he'd drawn in breath after heavy breath.

"It's you."

I was startled back to the present both by Brennan's voice and his touch and right after I looked up to see him watching me with his insanely bright green eyes, I dropped my gaze to see that at some point I'd rested my fingers near his hand on the bed and he was now stroking a couple of his fingers against mine.

I shifted my eyes back to his and could tell that he wasn't one hundred percent aware of where he was and what was going on. With the almost dreamy way he was looking at me, I suspected he was both still half-asleep and on some heavy duty pain killers.

I didn't respond to him and told myself to move my hand so I wouldn't feel the sparks of electricity shooting up my arm from the spot on my hand where he was touching me.

I didn't.

"The 1970 AAR Cuda," he whispered.

I hid the smile that threatened and nodded. I'd told him about the sports car the day before when he'd started to slide his eyes shut as the blood had continued to seep through my fingers where I'd had my hand pressed over his gunshot wound.

Brennan's eyes slid shut and then slowly opened again. "You promised to let me drive it."

"I did," I finally said, keeping my voice low in the hopes that he'd drift off again. I'd come here to check on him, not to interact with him.

I couldn't interact with him.

I couldn't want him more than I already did.

"I thought you were a dream," Brennan whispered quietly and then his eyes closed as he fell back asleep. His fingers stopped rubbing against mine, but they didn't fall away and the heat continued to spread throughout my entire body.

I needed to remove my hand to stop the sensation.

Because while I'd managed to keep Brennan talking until help had arrived, I'd ended up hearing the one thing that would keep me from pursuing the young man no matter what. He'd said it just before he'd started to struggle to breathe and right after he'd asked me if he was going to die.

Tell Tristan...tell him I love him...tell him I'm sorry I never told him.

That message, which fortunately I would never have to deliver, had been the deciding factor for me. Because while I could have overlooked all the other things about Brennan that broke all my rules including his young age, his obvious innocence and his inherent goodness, I couldn't overlook that he wanted someone else. Even if he wasn't in a relationship with whoever Tristan was, it didn't matter in the least. Because when I set my eyes on someone,

342

even if it was just for a few good fucks, there was one rule I never broke.

I didn't share.

Ever.

Even if it was a no-strings, quick fuck.

I didn't do guys dealing with boyfriend drama or unrequited love or any of that shit. They were either focused on me one hundred percent for whatever amount of time we used each other to slake our needs, or they weren't even in my orbit.

I forced myself to pull my hand away from Brennan's and allowed myself one more quick look at the peaceful expression on his face and then I turned away and left the room. Time to go back to what I did best and leave Brennan and his Tristan to whatever cute little white picket fence life they would dream of having together.

They'd figure out soon enough that there was no such thing.

Connect with Sloane Kennedy

Thank you for reading Forsaken!

Dear Reader,

I hope you enjoyed Mav and Eli's story. They will be back in the next book in the series, Vengeance, which will be M/M/M and feature Memphis, Brennan and Tristan's story.

You met Memphis and Brennan in Mav and Eli's story, but I would highly recommend you read my entire Barretti Security series as well as Logan's Need to learn more about all the characters who will appear in this next book as well as future Protectors books. Start with Logan's Need (if you read m/f you can also check out the first two books in the Escort series. If not, you can skip them and you won't miss anything). After Logan's Need check out Redeeming Rafe, Saving Ren and Freeing Zane (if you read m/f you can also check out Loving Vin which should be read after Logan's Need). Brennan and Tristan are introduced in the last book in the Barretti Security series, Freeing Zane.

As a new author, I am always grateful for feedback so if you have the time and desire, please leave a review, good or bad, so I can continue to find out what my readers like and don't like. You can also send me feedback via email at sloane@sloanekennedy.com

Friend   me   on   Facebook:
https://www.facebook.com/profile.php?id=100009132831061
Follow me on Twitter: @sloane_kennedy
Visit my website: www.sloanekennedy.com
Facebook Group (Sloane's Soulful Sinners):
https://www.facebook.com/groups/982204491818765/

Other books by Sloane Kennedy

(Note: Not all titles will be available on all retail sites)

The Protectors Series

Absolution (Book 1, The Protectors) (M/M/M)

After four years abroad, artist Jonas Davenport has come home to start building his dream of owning his own art studio and gallery. But just as he's ready to put the darkness of his past behind him forever, it comes roaring back with a vengeance.

The only thing keeping ex-cop Mace Calhoun from eating his own gun after an unthinkable loss is his role in an underground syndicate that seeks to get justice for the innocent by taking the lives of the guilty. Ending the life of the young artist who committed unspeakable crimes against the most vulnerable of victims should have been the easiest thing in the world. So why can't he bring himself to pull the trigger?

After years of fighting in an endless, soul-sucking war, Navy SEAL Cole Bridgerton has come home to fight another battle – dealing with the discovery that the younger sister who ran away from home eight years earlier is lost to him forever. He needs answers and the only person who can give them to him is a young man struggling to put his life back together. But he never expected to feel something more for the haunted artist.

Cole and Mace. One lives by the rules, the other makes his own. One seeks justice through the law while the other seeks it with his gun. Two men, one light, one dark, will find themselves and each other when they're forced to stand side by side to protect Jonas from an unseen evil that will stop at nothing to silence the young artist forever.

But each man's scars run deep and even the strength of three may not be enough to save them...

Salvation (Book 2, The Protectors) (M/M)

Trauma surgeon Ronan Grisham lost everything the day the man he loved was stolen from him in a brutal attack. Driven by a thirst for vengeance, he turns his hatred into building an underground group that can do what he couldn't that fateful day...take the lives of the guilty to save the lives of the innocent. But years later, he's forced to confront the one link to his past that he can't sever.

Seven years after the loss of his parents in a violent home invasion that left him permanently scarred both inside and out, 21-year-old Seth Nichols is trying to put his life back together so he can take over the reins of his father's global shipping empire. But the last person he expects to come back into his life is the man he drove away with one innocent, stolen kiss.

With one brush of his lips, Seth managed to do to Ronan what no other had since the day Ronan watched the light in his fiancé's eyes go out forever. He made him need again. But Ronan can't need anyone, least of all his dead fiancé's younger brother. Because even one touch from Seth could shatter Ronan's carefully constructed world and Ronan knows there's no coming back from that a second time.

But when a series of escalating attacks against Seth forces Ronan back into his life, Seth knows it's his last chance to show Ronan he can be the man the broken surgeon needs. Only the Ronan who returns isn't the Ronan Seth fell in love with so long ago...

Can Seth be Ronan's salvation or will he end up destroying them both?

Retribution (Book 3, The Protectors) (M/M)

Ex Special Forces soldier Michael "Hawke" Hawkins has spent every day of the last ten years waiting for the moment he would get to watch the life fade from the eyes of the men who brutally murdered his wife, but when he finally gets the break he's been waiting for, the trail leads him to someone he wasn't expecting.

After nearly two years of running, 24-year-old Tate Travers has become an expert at hiding...until the day a dangerous stranger shows up looking for vengeance and threatens to destroy the fragile life Tate has managed to build for himself and his five-year-old son. Except the life Tate has been struggling to hold on to started unraveling long before Hawke showed up looking for the same men Tate has been running from...his own father and older brother.

Retribution – it's all Hawke has wanted since the day he held his wife's hand as she took her last breath. And he won't give that up for anything or anyone...not even the tormented young man trying to give his little boy a better life. Because Tate is the only one who can lead Hawke to the men he's been searching for. And if it means forcing the young man to confront the past that nearly destroyed him, then so be it.

Only the last thing Hawke expects to feel is something besides the hatred that has driven him. And he definitely never expected to feel it for a man.

But when it comes down to choosing between the unwanted feelings Tate stirs in him and the revenge he's finally close enough to taste, will Hawke be able to give up the one thing that has kept him going for a second chance at a future he gave up on ever having?

The Escort Series

Gabriel's Rule (Book 1, The Escort Series) (M/F)

After nearly ten years of moonlighting as a professional escort, Gabriel Maddox is good at giving women the forbidden pleasures they crave. They don't need to know that something inside of him dies a little each time he does it or that his desperate need for cash is the only reason he can't walk away. They just need to know that to get what they want, they have to play by his rules.

Riley Sinclair is starting over. She's left dry, dusty Texas and her ultra conservative, fanatically religious parents and cheating, mean-spirited fiancé behind for a new life in Seattle. But one look at her stunningly gorgeous new neighbor Gabe brings back all the insecurities she's trying to escape.

Gabe can only offer Riley pleasure, but when she discovers that his perfect outside hides something terribly broken on the inside, will she risk her heart to give him what he needs?

Shane's Fall (Book 2, The Escort Series) (M/F)

Shane Matthews loves women, sex and money and as a professional escort, he gets to have all three whenever he wants. So what if he's not the same, naive person he was when he started – it's what he's good at. But life is catching up with Shane and he's losing the battle against an addiction that has haunted him for years. He's managed to keep the truth from his friends and family, but the pressure of pretending to be perfect may just be too much.

Savannah Bradshaw needs to get her life back under control before the fear and pain consume her. A brutal assault from someone she trusted has left her fearing sex and men and the dangerous method she uses to cope is stealing her life. She needs Shane to show her how to escape the pain, but as his best friend's little sister, he's keeping her at arm's length.

Savannah's desperate plan to bring them together for one night has Shane agreeing to show her the pleasure her body can experience, but she has to agree to his terms. Giving her what she needs should be easy, as long as he doesn't do something stupid like fall in love with her...

Logan's Need (Book 3, The Escort Series) (M/M)

After Logan Bradshaw's dreams go up in smoke, he's left broken and haunted by a cruel betrayal from his former business partner, a man he once thought of as a friend. His life as a professional escort helped pay for his future once, so maybe a few more jobs can give him back what he's lost. And if that means being a third for one night for a wealthy couple living out a ménage fantasy, then so be it. It might just be the final payout he needs to get his life back on track.

Dominic Barretti has everything money can buy, but it can't save his beautiful young wife as cancer steals her away from him. He also can't deny her one last request - a ménage encounter with another man. It's the perfect excuse to meet the man who's been haunting his dreams. On paper, Logan is the perfect choice to give his wife what she needs, but he doesn't expect his own fierce desires to flare up when the young man enters their lives.

Dom and Logan don't know it, but Sylvie Barretti has decided to play matchmaker from beyond the grave. Unfortunately, getting two broken men to find each other makes dying seem like the easy part.

Logan can't deny his attraction to Dom, but the surprise desire for another man has left him reeling and questioning everything he's ever

351

known about himself. But when a threat from the past surfaces, will Logan be able to let go of the life he knew and embrace the one he needs?

Barretti Security Series

Loving Vin (Book 1, Barretti Security Series) (M/F)

She was the daughter of a serial killer and she was living in his house...

After years of searching war torn Afghanistan for his MIA brother, Vincenzo Barretti has finally come home and now he's ready to settle back into life as co-founder of Barretti Security Group. But his home is no longer cold and empty the way he likes it.

Mia Hamilton needs a quiet place to hide from the press to try to rebuild her life. Being the daughter of a notorious serial killer is bad enough, but being the one who killed him has made her a target for every news agency in the world. She wants nothing more than to be left alone, but the reporters are relentless and will stop at nothing to get their story. With no place to go, she accepts an offer from Dominic Barretti to stay at his older brother's home until she can figure out what to do next. But she didn't expect the homeowner to return so soon or to feel something she's never felt when he's around.

Vin doesn't need or want a woman in his life and certainly not one that comes with so much baggage. So what if Mia evokes feelings in him he thought were long dead? She's a liability and he wants her gone. But forcing the quiet, strong-willed young woman from his life turns out to be a lot harder than he thought...

Redeeming Rafe (Book 2, Barretti Security Series) (M/M)

He wants revenge against the brothers who betrayed him but first he has to get past the one man he can't resist...

At the tender age of eight, Rafe Barretti lost everything. His parents, his childhood, his innocence. And the brothers who were supposed to protect him let him go instead. Twenty years later and he's finally ready to exact his revenge by taking away everything they hold dear - their company, their reputations, their futures. But even that isn't enough - their loved ones will have to pay too and all their precious secrets are fair game.

Former mercenary Cade Gamble's only job is to take down the hacker stealing sensitive, private information from Barretti Security Group and Cade is damn good at his job. But there's more at stake because the co-founders of BSG, Dom and Vin Barretti, are like family and no one touches Cade's family. The fact that the vengeful young man turns out to be the youngest of the Barretti clan doesn't matter. But when their tumultuous encounters turn into something more, Cade will have to decide between protecting the only family he has and giving in to his need to save Rafe from himself.

Can Cade help Rafe find redemption so he can forgive the sins of the past or will Rafe's quest for vengeance destroy them both?

Saving Ren (Book 3, Barretti Security Series) (M/M/M)

Three men brought together by circumstance who found something none of them knew they needed...

Ren Barretti has finally come home after a year of being held captive by the terrorists who slaughtered his entire Special Forces team. But he can't escape the nightmares that torment him or the guilt that he was the only one to walk away. The life his older brothers have brought him home to doesn't exist for him anymore and to keep them and their loved ones safe from the rage and pain that consume him, Ren needs to disappear.

Police Detective Declan Hale has felt an undeniable pull towards the very straight Ren Barretti since the day Ren's brother married Declan's younger sister almost a dozen years earlier. But even though the Ren who has come home isn't the one who left, all of Declan's feelings come rushing back to the surface and he steps in to help the only man he's ever truly wanted. And even though there's no future for them, keeping Ren safe is all that matters and Declan will risk anything to make that happen.

Tough as nails former soldier and mercenary Jagger Varos has returned to Seattle after years of running from his past and he's hoping that joining Barretti Security Group will help him finally call the city he left behind home. But within weeks, his new beginning is tested after multiple run-ins with the gruff, infuriating Detective Hale. When he inadvertently discovers that Declan is hiding Ren from the very brothers offering Jagger a new start, Jagger finds himself torn between his newfound loyalty to Vin and Dom Barretti and the need to protect the young man he himself helped rescue from his captors.

For Declan and Jagger, it's hate at first sight but they soon realize that they will need each other if they have any hope of saving Ren from himself. And neither of them expects their mutual distrust in one another to grow into something else entirely or that Ren himself will find in both of them what he needs to rebuild his life and come to terms with who he really is.

Can the fierce attraction between three men become something more or will the demands of the real world tear them apart?

Freeing Zane (Book 4, Barretti Security Series) (M/M)

Zane doesn't do relationships and Connor is definitely the kind of guy who does...

Criminal defense attorney Zane Devereaux is on the verge of having everything he's worked his entire life for. He's on track to become his firm's youngest managing partner and he has enough money in the bank to ensure he'll never have to be at the mercy of anyone ever again. He's left his past exactly where it belongs and refuses to look back. And he sure as hell isn't going to risk a repeat of his former mistakes by letting someone as sweet, sexy and endearingly vulnerable as Connor Talbot into his life. His bed maybe, but not his life.

Connor Talbot has no regrets about serving his country, even if it did cost him more then he'd imagined. Two years after an IED took his leg and left him with permanent brain damage, Connor is still struggling to put his life back together, but he's managed to find a makeshift family in Seattle that helps ease the pain of losing his own at a young age. Unfortunately, a string of bad relationships and an abusive ex have taken their toll on Connor and he's given up on finding the lifelong partner he'd always envisioned he'd have. But a chance encounter with a man he has absolutely nothing in common with except for an intense, white-hot chemistry has him thinking that maybe a no strings, physical relationship is exactly what's called for.

What begins as two men meeting each other's needs between the sheets turns into something neither one was prepared for but the wounds of the past run deep and both men will have to decide if a future together will cost them too much or if what they could have together is worth fighting for.

Finding Series

Finding Home (Finding Series, Book 1) (M/M/M)

Vengeance. It's the one thing on ex-cop Rhys Tellar's mind and he's spent every day of his two year prison sentence planning how he'll bring down the former lover and partner who sold him out and cost four people their lives. A six month parole stint working at the CB Bar Ranch in Southwestern Montana should be the easiest thing he's ever done. But the last thing he expects is to feel something for both the charismatic ranch hand who befriends him and the enigmatic foreman who's pretending to be something he's not.

A future. That's what Finn Stewart wants, but to have it he must leave behind the man he wants above all others, his very straight boss and best friend, Callan Bale. As the only openly gay man in a small, homophobic community, Finn has to fight every day to be who he is and walking away is starting to seem like the easier path. Until Rhys Tellar shows up and changes everything.

A Lie. Callan Bale's entire life has been about hiding the man he really is and it's about to cost him the one person who's managed to worm his way past the walls he's spent years putting up. But choosing Finn would mean giving up everything he's worked for and breaking the promises he's made. At least losing the younger man to Rhys means Finn can have the life he deserves.

Three men. Three choices. One chance at finding home.

Finding Trust (Finding Series, Book 2) (M/M)

He wanted a new beginning. What he got was a glimpse of a life he could never have...

Widower Dane Winters just wanted a new beginning for himself and his six month old daughter after his estranged husband's cold-blooded murder and moving to a small town in Southwest Montana seemed like a good place to start. But he never expected a favor for a friend to turn into a deadly encounter that puts him on a collision course with a mysterious stranger passing through town.

Former FBI agent Jaxon Reid stopped in Dare, Montana to right a wrong, not get caught up in the life of an uptight, country vet with a holier-than-thou attitude. But he soon finds himself drawn to the quiet, insecure single father who's trying to leave behind a life of pain and heartbreak.

Dane can't deny his attraction to Jax, but he knows that pursuing a relationship with the gorgeous, younger man will only end in heartbreak and turn him into someone he swore he would never be again. But when danger looms, he's forced to accept Jax into his life and home, along with the emotional vulnerability that being around Jax brings to the surface.

As their connection deepens, can Dane find the trust Jax needs from him in order to build a life together or will he let his past destroy his one chance at a real future?

Finding Peace (Finding Series, Book 3) (M/M)

Author Gray Hawthorne has it all and he's on the verge of having even more. His bestselling detective novels are being turned into a movie series that will make him a household name and he's rubbing a lot more than just elbows with Hollywood's elite. Money, fame and good looks mean an endless supply of men, both groupies and celebrities alike, which suits Gray just fine. He's smart enough to know that his 5 minutes in the spotlight will be just that and he plans to enjoy every moment. Until he gets the devastating news that threatens to steal everything away...

Army Ranger Luke Monroe lives and breathes the military. They're the family he never had and a life without his brothers-in-arms is unfathomable. But the ultimate betrayal has Luke on the run and a twist of fate leads him to the small town of Dare, Montana to seek help from the foster brother who saved him once before. Only the brother he's searching for isn't the man he finds and he has no choice but to keep running. Until an encounter on the side of the road with a stranger changes everything.

The last thing Gray wants when he seeks refuge at his cabin in the secluded Montana mountains is company but a run-in with the mysterious and very straight Luke has Gray offering the damaged soldier a place to regroup. And since a physical relationship isn't even on the table, Gray finds himself enjoying something he hasn't had in a long time...a real friend.

But what happens when friendship just isn't enough? When a man who's only been with women begins to crave more?

Finding Forgiveness (Finding Series, Book 4)
(M/M)

He was only there for a business deal...

A couple of days...that was all it was supposed to take for property developer Roman Blackwell to decide if the strip of land just south of Dare, Montana would be the perfect spot for his next luxury resort. He wasn't interested in repairing his frayed relationship with his half-brother who'd moved to the small town a few months earlier and he definitely wasn't interested in doing anything more than scratching an itch when he checked out the gay club near his hotel. But when his plans for a quick hook-up are waylaid after he steps in to save a young man being brutalized, Roman finds himself building an emotional connection he never saw coming.

One bad decision changed everything...

College student Hunter Greene has spent 18 months trying to forget the one night he gave in to temptation and made a decision to hide one lie by telling another. But the guilt of knowing he shattered another young man's life to protect his own secret shame is slowly destroying him and he knows that soon even his spiral into a dangerous pattern of self-destructive behavior won't be enough to keep his entire world from imploding. But the last thing he's looking for is someone to save him.

But fate works in mysterious ways...

Forced to return to the town he grew up in, the last person Hunter expects to run into is the mysterious savior who changed everything with one soul shattering kiss. While he can't deny his attraction to Roman, Hunter knows that he'll never be free to act on it and once Roman discovers the terrible secret he's hiding, it won't matter anyway.

Because some things just can't be forgiven...

Non-Series Books

Letting Go (M/F)

After years of running from her brutal past Casey Wilkes has finally managed to carve out a quiet life running an animal shelter with her best friend in a small Northern Wisconsin town. And even though her menagerie of unwanted animals can't keep the nightmares at bay she can at least finally breathe again. But everything changes when a mysterious stranger walks into the shelter with news of her sister's death and a plan to get custody of the niece Casey never knew she had.

Multi-millionaire Devlin Prescott made a promise to protect the child of the woman who saved his son's life and if keeping that promise means dragging Casey back into her past kicking and screaming then so be it. After all, it's just another business deal.

But what he finds is a damaged woman struggling to put the pieces of her life back together and her quiet strength, steely determination and gentle heart have him questioning his methods and his feelings.

Can he find a way to keep his promise to a little girl and still prevent Casey from slipping back into a life that may end up destroying her for good?

42353364R00204

Made in the USA
San Bernardino, CA
01 December 2016